Beyond the Windswept Sea

Carole Gift Page & Doris Elaine Fell

HARVEST HOUSE PUBLISHERS
Eugene, Oregon 97402

BEYOND THE WINDSWEPT SEA

Copyright © 1987 by Carole Gift Page and
    Doris Elaine Fell
Published by Harvest House Publishers
Eugene, Oregon 97402

ISBN 0-89081-608-5

Printed in the United States of America.

To the officers and staff
of the S.S. Rotterdam
and the M.V. Stardancer
for sharing their knowledge and experience

And to Doris Carter
for her steadfast prayer support
throughout our writing of
the MIST OVER MORRO BAY Series

Cast of Characters

MICHELLE MERRILL BALLARD: A modern, tawny-haired Sherlock who walks into a mystery when she accepts a college honor.

DAVID BALLARD: Michelle's husband, a successful business-man, whose anniversary present to his wife threatens their lives on the windswept seas of Alaska.

DR. JASON THATCHER: A world-renowned thoracic sur-geon—a secretive, silver-haired man whose deep-set eyes mirror a troubled soul.

NOREEN THATCHER: The physician's young wife—a well-bred, genteel lady, proud and protective of her husband.

SETH MUELLER: A tennis pro turned missionary—an ego-tistical, self-made man bent on feeding the world's hungry at any cost.

ABIGAIL CHADWICK: Michelle's sensitive, brilliant college professor who harbors unrequited love for the dashing Seth Mueller.

BRETT SEATON: A rough-hewn Marine colonel—one of the elite breed of NASA astronauts grounded after the Challenger disaster.

CANDY SEATON: Brett's strikingly beautiful wife who wants her husband grounded—permanently.

CAMERON "CAM" ELLIS: A ruggedly attractive man—the stormy, bearded hunter caught in a web of bitterness and revenge.

STEPHANIE ELLIS: A wistful, melancholy woman whose hid-den grief threatens to destroy her.

PAM MERRILL: Michelle's restless kid sister who is torn between the man she loves and a dangerous mission.

SILAS WINTERS: The love of Pam's life—the handsome, Argus-eyed DEA agent whose unexpected appearance on board ship may cost him his life.

JACKIE TURMAN MARSHALL: Michelle's best friend—a flawless beauty who risks her own life to be with David and Michelle.

HORACE STODDARD: The Lincolnesque president of Hopewell College.

STEVIE TURMAN MARSHALL, JR.: Jackie Marshall's five-year-olld son.

ROB THORNTON: David's buddy—hero of Michelle's best-seller.

CHAPTER ONE

I was lying contentedly in David's arms, savoring the lime-fresh scent of his after-shave, when he popped the question that made me sit bolt upright in bed. "How would you like to have a baby, Michelle?"

I stared incredulously at him, then melted a little as the bedside lamp caught the twinkle in his eyes and cast a golden, coppery glow over his sturdy, tanned features. His dark hair, damp from the humid June heat, was mussed like a little boy's. I loved it that way. It reminded me that David wasn't simply the impeccable Southern California computer magnate and business mogul his public image portrayed—a role he wore as comfortably as his old sneakers. He was just my David, who sometimes forgot to change his socks, draped wet towels over my nylons, and ate Snickers bars before breakfast.

"Well?" he said, lifting up on one elbow. "What do you think?"

"A—a baby?" I squeaked. Like a timid schoolgirl, I pulled the sheet up over my sheer nightgown. "This is theoretical, right, David—as in someday we want to have kids, right?"

With a jaunty little laugh David pulled me over against him and pressed his lips against my ear. "No, Michelle, I'm not talking theory." His breath was a warm, pungent mixture of wintergreen and coffee. "In fact, talking isn't what I have in mind at all."

I felt myself stiffen against the solid warmth of his bare chest and muscular six-foot frame. "You're not playing fair, David."

"I'm not *playing*, Michelle. I'm serious. We've been married 11 months tomorrow. I think it's time we had a baby."

I inched away from his embrace. "That's easy for you to say. You're not the one who has to go around with morning sickness and a watermelon tummy for nine months."

David's tone lowered to a subtle reprimand. "You're exaggerating, Michelle."

"No, I'm not. It's all that and more. Much more." My voice rose shrilly. "It's not something you decide on the spur of the moment, like whether or not to have scrambled eggs for breakfast."

"We've talked before—"

"Sure, like someday we'll live in a big house, have kids, grow old . . . but I wasn't planning to do any of those things tomorrow. Honest, David, there's still lots of time."

Frown lines creased David's brow. "Time? I suppose. But, remember, I've got ten years on you, Michelle. I'd like to play kickball with my son while I'm still young enough to beat him."

"Son?"

"Okay. Daughter. Whatever." His voice grew animated. "It's just that we've got so much to offer a kid, Michelle. I don't see any sense in waiting. . . ."

"It's not that simple, David, and you know it. You can have a child and still have your career. But me . . ."

David eyed me quizzically. "Is that the problem—your writing career?"

"It's just now taking off, David," I reminded him, emotion filling my voice. "Look, my biography, *Rob Thornton: A Vietnam Legacy*, is actually on the bestseller list. Who would have thought such a thing could happen? And my Caribbean novel about Solidad is ready to come off the press."

"I'm aware of all that, Michelle."

"And you know I've signed a contract for my third book. I'm committed to a deadline, David. And there's the promotion tour. It's all set up. I can't cancel now."

"I'm not asking you to."

"But I can't make bookstore appearances waddling around like Tweedledee and Tweedledum."

"Who on earth are they?"

"Didn't you ever read Lewis Carroll? They're characters from *Alice in Wonderland*. With balloon-shaped bellies!"

David lay back against his pillow, looking irritated. "Come on, Michelle. Don't pull literary rank on me."

"I'm not trying to pull any kind of rank on you, David. I'm just trying to let you know how I feel."

"I get the picture." David lay down, yanked the sheet up to his bronzed shoulders, and turned his back to me.

"Are you angry?" I ventured.

"No. Frustrated."

I lay back down beside him, keeping my distance. "Don't you want to talk it out, clear the air?"

"Let's just sleep on it," he said in the low, controlled business voice he assumed whenever we were at a stalemate. "Besides," he added, the words muffled against his pillow, "neither of us is in the mood to make babies tonight anyway."

* * *

The next morning as I roused myself from a troubled sleep, I found the other side of the bed empty, David's pajama bottoms tossed on the chair. Even on Saturdays he was a stickler for schedules—a precise, efficient man who kept appointments on time and resented waiting for others. But efficiency did not include hanging up his pajamas or picking up his dirty laundry.

David's mornings were predictable. He always muffled the alarm clock before it really had time to ring. Usually he'd give me a quick kiss before swinging his lanky legs out of bed and grabbing his jogging togs. But not this morning. I was certain he hadn't kissed me this morning. Inside, I felt a gnawing aggravation, a rare sense of neglect. Was David still miffed over last night's squabble?

I climbed wearily out of bed, showered, dressed, and headed for the kitchen. As usual, I'd have breakfast ready when David got home from running. Juice and fresh fruit. Sausage, two eggs, and toast with a tablespoon of peanut butter.

I halved a grapefruit, poured orange juice, and popped some bread in the toaster. There wasn't anything else I could do until David got home. I wandered into the living room and gazed out the bay window, wondering what was keeping him so long. Absently I picked up several travel brochures from the end table. For weeks now I'd been after David to plan a trip to celebrate our first wedding anniversary. But he stood firm, adamant. No trip.

I looked again down the rugged, grassy hillside for some sign of David. Our Laguna Beach condominium sat high on a bluff overlooking the Pacific Ocean. The endless expanse of water stretched as far as I could see—calm and blue in the hazy morning sun. Even now, the ocean rolled into the cove at Crescent Bay Point, not in pounding fury like it sometimes did, but in riplets of foamy waves.

David and I loved Laguna Beach—the quaint art galleries, wood-carving stores, specialty shops, and our favorite French restaurant near the Black Iris Florist. Would David take time to hike that far today? Had he ordered flowers for our 11-month anniversary? Would they be *baby* roses to remind me of his heart's desire?

It seemed an eternity before I spotted David jogging up the winding roadway, a long white box under one arm. He hadn't forgotten. I ducked back from the window, peered in the hall mirror, and fluffed my long tawny hair. I was already smiling, my heart quickening when David opened the door.

"David, I was worried about you. You've been gone so long."

"Didn't you get my note?" he asked as he opened the linen-white box with a flourish.

"Your note?" I echoed, gazing down at my 11 red roses. "Oh, David, they're—"

"I tucked a love note under your pillow," he said, following me to the dining room. "Didn't you get it?"

"I . . . I didn't make the bed yet this morning."

His brows arched with interest. "Oh? You changed your mind about last night . . . about the baby?" He spoke in jest, but I knew he was serious.

"Not that again, David, please." I took a crystal vase from the china closet. "We talked about that already."

"We didn't really talk about it," he said defensively.

I picked up a rose and trimmed the stem. "I thought we decided to wait to start a family. You know I'm just getting somewhere with my writing. Maybe after my third or fourth book, I'll be well-established."

"I told you, I'll be an old man by then."

"That's cruel, David. You know the publisher has already asked for the synopsis on my third book."

"I know." David stood on the other side of the table, his eyes more on the roses than on me.

"Ouch," I said, pricking my finger on a thorn.

"Be careful, Michelle."

I grinned impishly. "I'm trying to be. That's why I want to wait until after the third or fourth book."

"Then maybe we can sandwich a baby and diapers between books five and six?" he said, a hint of sarcasm in his voice.

I glanced across the crystal vase at his handsome face. His eyes said it all as they met mine. His gaze was suddenly tender. It frightened me. I had no resistance when he looked at me that way. I really did want David's child, but I also wanted to wait awhile. "David, you know how much I want to pursue my writing career."

"I know. I've done everything to support it—an office as well-equipped as I know how to make it, plenty of time . . ."

"Yes, as long as dinner is on the table by six and the weekend is free." I rolled the green tissue from the flower box into a ball and tossed it playfully at David.

He tightened his fingers around the wrapper. "I'm not trying to stop your career, Michelle. I'm proud of you. It's just . . ."

"Just what?"

The Vietnam battle scar across his cleft chin pulsated. "I just hoped you'd be happy, content with marriage as a career."

"You thought a book or two would get it out of my system?"

"Something like that."

I blew him a kiss but his smile was slow in coming.

"I just thought babies came before books," he said.

"They do alphabetically, David. I just want to reverse the order for a little while."

"I don't want to lose you to a career, Michelle."

"You're not losing me, David. I—I love you more every day."

"Then why—?"

"Why the delay?" I centered the vase of flowers on the table. Their fragrance filled the room, yet this time there wasn't the joy we usually shared during these special celebrations. "David, I do want children, but not right away. Please understand." My words turned sour in my mouth. Had I told David the whole truth? Without warning I was barraged with guilt; past doubts hurled themselves at me.

David stared, perplexed. "Is something wrong, Michelle?"

"No, it's just—oh, it's too silly even to mention, but someone once told me I wouldn't make a good mother. . . ."

"Who? Scott? Your old college sweetheart?"

"Yes—Scott. He didn't want children—didn't think we'd make good parents."

"Hon, I'm not Scott. I'm David—the man who really loves you."

"But, David, I never even baby-sat. My sister Pam's the one who cuddles babies and swings kids in the park. Not me."

"But you love little Stevie Turman, your best friend's son."

My voice was barely a whisper as I answered, "It's easy to love Jackie's boy. But, except for Stevie, I've never allowed myself to get close to any child. David, I think I'm scared. It's easier for me to write a book than have a baby."

"It's not like you have to do it all alone, Michelle. I'll be with you all the way. We can even do the Lamaze bit with the lollipops and panting exercises."

He looked so earnest I relented just a little. Reaching across the table, I patted his smooth cheek. "I know you'll make a terrific daddy—I've seen you with Stevie—but I'm just not ready to be a mother yet."

I love you, Michelle," he said simply. "I don't mean to push you. You wouldn't be happy if I did." He walked around the table and drew me toward him.

"Don't, David." I felt his chin nestling against my head, his muscular body pressing against mine. "David, we can't settle anything this way." My words were muffled against his broad chest. "It's just—I believe God wants me to write. It's my *commitment*."

He drew back and stared down into my eyes. "Am I losing you to a commitment then?"

"David, you're not losing me at all."

He crushed me to him again, his voice husky. "I'm sorry, Michelle. It's my own battleground. Not yours. I didn't realize how complex everything would be—babies, books. Your career. I thought having a baby would be a solution. . . ."

"Oh, David, a baby isn't a solution to anything—it's a whole new commitment."

"Maybe I'm riding an ego trip, Michelle. My whole life is you and computers. I hoped my career would be ample for both of us. I don't know. Maybe your career threatens the balance of power in our lives."

"David, are you saying you're jealous of my books?"

He cupped my chin gently. "For so many years I thought I might never marry or have children, Michelle. Then when I wasn't even looking, you were there. Handpicked by God Himself just for me." David leaned down and kissed my forehead. "I've spent so much of my life not sharing my plans and decisions, just making them. I'm really trying to do better, but if writing is your commitment before the Lord, then I'm not just fighting your dreams, I'm fighting God. And, Michelle, God knows I never want to run against His will."

"I know, my darling," I whispered back. For a long moment we remained locked in a silent embrace.

David was breathing hard when he released me. "I'm going into my study to think awhile." As he reached the door he turned back, smiling. He seemed his old self caring, confident.

"David, have you given any more thought to an anniversary trip—Hawaii, for instance? I think it would do us both good."

He shrugged slyly. "We gave our Hawaii tickets to your folks last year. Remember?"

"Then how about the Canadian Rockies, or Europe, or Niagara Falls? Anyplace. I've got brochures on them all."

"I can't risk it," he protested. "I don't want another disastrous incident in Paradise or another wild-goose chase in Morro Bay."

"But we've got to do something special," I insisted. "We've just got to celebrate."

"We will. Right here. At home. I'll take the day off from work. We'll lock the door, take the phone off the hook . . . and we'll really celebrate."

"David, wait. I started breakfast—but what about a stroll on the beach and brunch out on the point?"

"Dutch treat?" he teased.

"No. My treat." I blew him a kiss. "I'll use my book royalties."

He grinned slowly. "It's a date."

"And, David . . . what did your love note say—the one you tucked under my pillow?"

"It said, 'I love you and I'll be home with 11 red roses to prove it.' "

"Thanks—they're beautiful."

"You're beautiful, too, Michelle. Thanks for the best 11 months of my life. And, sweetheart, even if it's always just you and me . . . I'll still love you."

As the study door closed behind him, I sat down at the dining room table, stared blindly at the 11 red roses, and began to weep. *Was there room in my study for a baby crib?* I wondered. *Could I juggle diapers and books? Careers and commitments?* "Oh, God," I whispered, "am I being unreasonable? Have I got my priorities out of whack?"

I touched one rosebud, so tiny and delicate, marveling at its complexity. Marveling at its Creator. The silence felt peaceful, comforting. It was as though God were saying, "One step at a time, Michelle. One step at a time."

Step? I thought. "Sometimes, God, I just inch along while David leaps to Your side. I grope, stagger, trying to do Your will while he delights in it." I nodded toward David's closed study, as if pointing the room out to God. "You know that my beloved David is probably in there deep in prayer, searching his own soul, juggling his own pressing commitments."

I touched the red bud again. In another month—July—there would be 12 roses on the table for our first wedding anniversary. Reluctantly I stood up and walked to the kitchen, then on into our living room, slowly gathering up the travel brochures that I had planted in every nook and cranny. It wasn't fair for me to keep pressuring David for a trip he didn't want to take. Perhaps he was right. We'd just stay home, set our careers aside, take the phone off the hook . . . and celebrate.

* * *

An hour later I brought in the morning mail and stacked it on the table beside the vase of roses. "More travel brochures," I noted with a wistful sigh. "Face it, Michelle. Staying home just isn't enough. I want to do something special. Take a real trip and get David away from his work."

I was wading through the junk mail when I spotted my college paper, *The Hopewell Alumni News*. I flipped through the pages, absently scanning the headlines. Then I saw it—the large photo of a passenger ship, the S.S. *Mendenhall*, cruising the Alaskan waters. COME AND GO WITH US! the headline read. "Celebrate Hopewell College's 50th anniversary as we honor some of our favorite sons and daughters." Four names stood out in bold print:

Dr. Jason Thatcher, Thoracic Surgeon
Brett Seaton, Astronaut
Seth Mueller, Missionary
Michelle Merrill Ballard, Author

"What? My name? How can they do this?" I said aloud. "They already have me on board and I haven't even been invited." I ran to David's study and burst through the door uninvited. He was stretched out on the floor doing his push-ups. "David," I cried, waving the alumni paper like a flag. "Hopewell's going to Alaska!"

"Yeah," he groaned.

"And I'm supposed to go!"

"Huh?" There was a momentary break in his concentration.

I knelt down on the floor beside him and spread out the pamphlet. "Look, I'm one of Hopewell's honored sons and daughters."

David turned his face toward me. "Daughter, yes," he grunted. "Son, no."

"Can we go, David?"

"Go where?"

"To Alaska. David, we can celebrate our anniversary on board."

"On board what?"

"The ship, silly. The S.S. *Mendenhall*."

"I thought we were going to celebrate at home."

"It's so bizarre, David," I babbled on. "I don't understand. How could they list me in their newsletter without asking me?"

David rolled onto his back and chuckled. He reached for me and drew me down against his chest. "I knew it," he said merrily. "I knew we couldn't keep a secret from you."

"You knew?" I demanded. "You knew about this trip—had it planned all this time? And I've been force-feeding you brochures on Europe and Hawaii?"

He brushed the hair from my face, flashing a wry twinkle. "I've been working on it for weeks now. I thought it would make a great anniversary present."

"David, you sly old fox."

"No, sweetheart, you're the fox," he murmured. "I goofed. Your sis Pam warned me to intercept this Hopewell paper, but I forgot."

"You've already bought tickets?" I asked, amazed.

"Just one ticket."

"One ticket? You're not going, David?"

He kissed the nape of my neck. "Oh, I'm going."

"But—"

"You're one of the honored sons and daughters, remember? That means you go free."

I thumped his chest playfully. "Then all that stuff about being afraid of another incident in Paradise was just a put-off?"

"Oh, I'm concerned, all right," he said, his lips close to mine. "You have a way of walking into trouble, Michelle."

"Oh, David, what trouble could I get into at a Hopewell College reunion? I've told you, they're strict. They'll all be good people. No mobsters, no cocaine rings . . ."

"Yeah, we'll risk it. Besides, I'm proud of you. The little rebel of Hopewell returning as a famous author."

"Oh, David, I was such a rebel," I said, stifling a laugh. "After the pranks I pulled, I'm amazed they'd even want to honor me."

"Like I said, you're a famous author now."

"But I'm not famous yet, David."

"You're getting there. Rob's story in its third printing isn't bad, you know." He touched my face gently and pulled me closer. "What will it be this time, Michelle?"

"What do you mean?"

"Maybe you could do your third book on Alaska."

"Oh," I said, brightening at once. "I bet I could do a fabulous frontier mystery with an old gold mine and craggy miners—"

My creative musings were cut short as David's lips sought mine, tenderly at first . . . and then with a lusty, compelling ardor.

CHAPTER
TWO

I spent the next four weeks planning and packing, buying and dreaming . . . and avoiding the topic of babies. I wanted a new, fashionable wardrobe for our Alaskan cruise, not a maternity outfit.

Realizing that a whole new wardrobe was impractical, I settled instead on a few classic pants and blouses and one trendy sports outfit with enough pizzazz to make David sit up and take notice. To prove to David that my sense of economy was still intact, I had his tuxedo and my dusky rose evening gown with the chiffon cape dry-cleaned for the captain's reception on shipboard.

Then, on one final impulsive shopping spree, I tossed my frugality to the wind and bought a splashy designer swimsuit, matching windbreakers for David and me, and two evening dresses from the fabulous Giorgio Armani collection.

On Friday, the day before we were scheduled to fly to Seattle, David called from the office and said, "Michelle, don't forget to pack our ski sweaters and your wool duffle coat."

"That'll take another suitcase," I protested.

"Can't be helped," he answered. "Alaska's weather reports are a bit gloomy. When we feel those winds off the glaciers cutting through us, we'll be glad for something warm to wear."

"When will you be home, David?"

"I have the Wilson appointment at two. Then I'll be on my way."

"Good. I'll be waiting."

"Love you."

Early Saturday morning, Rob Thornton—David's best friend and the hero of my Vietnam bestseller—arrived at the house just as the sun cast a pink glow over the ocean. He stopped short in the doorway and feigned shock at the mountain of luggage. "Hey, I thought you were going for only two weeks, Michelle. Not two years."

"And I thought you were going with us," I countered amiably.

"Can't. I didn't graduate from Hopewell."

"It wasn't one of the requirements, Rob."

He grinned slowly, his wide saucer-blue eyes too large for his narrow face. "I'm not looking for limelight, Michelle. This is your big chance. You wrote the book."

"But it's your story."

"Yeah," he said. "I know. I lived it."

I wasn't sure how he really felt. Rob, thirtyish, still had a boyish charm and vulnerability, a certain shyness that endeared him to me. He was a Purdue graduate, a loner—a man who had come a long way from the listless, forlorn young Navy lieutenant salvaged from years in a prisoner-of-war camp. He had wanted his story written—the Vietnam legacy that almost destroyed him. But he hadn't counted on the book's success. He was still a very private, guarded man.

Rob bent his lanky form and gripped two of the heavy cases, then made his way out the front door, his limp barely noticeable. He was back with quick strides. "David ready yet?" he asked.

"You know him. He's making a last-minute call to Eva at the office."

"Checking up on his business partner?" Rob grinned. "David doesn't have to worry. He knows my mom's indispensable. She'll keep things buzzing while he's gone." Rob scooped up the last suitcase and groaned. "What'cha got in this one, Michelle? Rocks?"

"Books."

"Mine?"

"How'd you guess?"

"I suppose you'll have a fancy autograph party on board, eh?"

"Maybe . . . but it would be better if you were there."

"Nope." He banged out the door, moving with a relaxed confidence I hadn't seen before. He had come a long way in the past 18 months. Vietnam was still there, buried in his soul but no longer tearing at his gut.

Moments later, David, Rob, and I were on our way in Rob's sleek new Jaguar. He patted the leather-wrapped steering wheel with his long, scarred fingers. "How do you like this slick baby?" he asked proudly. Rob was still a strange mixture of boy and man, given to moodiness and impulsiveness. He drove carelessly at times, like he was doing this morning, as if he thrived on risks.

"I'd like it better if you stayed within the speed limit," I cautioned lightly.

He continued to weave through downtown Laguna, past the Crescent Bay Lookout, then sped along Coast Highway, making a sharp right on MacArthur Boulevard.

I leaned forward, gripping the front seat. "You know, Rob, it doesn't seem right for me to be honored at Hopewell's reunion for your story without you being there."

He gazed at me through the rearview mirror, his deep, azure-blue eyes intense, probing. He had brooding good looks— thick, dark lashes, finely carved lips, high cheek bones, too narrow a nose. But his expression was fragile, gentle like Eva's with a certain secrecy and childlikeness to it.

"I can't go to the reunion, Michelle. I'm flying to D.C. next week."

"Washington again?" I asked, surprised.

David perked up. "Something new come up, Rob?"

"Yeah, Dave. I contacted another senator—from the South this time. He's a Viet vet and the reports I read on him are good. If anyone can help me find Liana . . ."

"Then you have an appointment with him?" David asked.

"Not exactly. In fact, the senator doesn't want to see me. After our initial phone call, he's been conveniently out of his office when I telephone. He thinks it's a waste of time trying to track down one unknown Laotian in a camp of 50,000 refugees. I told him Liana befriended me when I escaped from Vietnam. I didn't tell him I love her, need her. I still call the senator and leave messages, but . . ."

"Then why go to Washington?" I asked. "Why set yourself up for another disappointment?"

Rob ran a yellow light and took the left lane that curved toward John Wayne Airport. We could see silvery jets coming in and taking off. Rob kept his eyes straight ahead, ignoring my question.

I tried again. "We worry about you, Rob. You've knocked on so many doors."

He shifted lanes, passing too closely to the Buick beside us. "For over a year I've done everything but go back to Indochina to find Liana myself."

David twisted around uneasily. "You're not planning on that, are you, Rob? You might not get out this time. You know that would kill Eva—break your mother's heart."

"Mom's the only reason I haven't gone long ago. Besides, Dave, the problem isn't getting out of Indochina any longer; it's getting in. But if I ever get a lead—if I could get past these political barricades—a government that doesn't want me to rattle the cage of foreign diplomats . . ." He pulled to a stop in front of the terminal and pocketed his ignition key.

As he helped me out of the car, he grinned. "Have a good trip, you two. And stay out of trouble!"

"You, too. And good luck on senators' row."

I waited on the curb as David and Rob unloaded the luggage. "I still think the cruise would do you good, Rob."

"That's what Pam told me last night. But I explained I have business in Washington."

"My sister? You talked to her?"

He nodded as he handed me my overnight case. "Pam called from the Empress Hotel in Victoria. Said she's glad she went on ahead to sightsee a couple of days before the cruise. She begged me to try for a last-minute cancellation on the ship. She's crazy, you know."

"At least impulsive. But she's right. We both wish you were going with us, Rob."

"So I can forget Liana?" he asked with a hint of defensiveness.

"Pam and I just want you to be happy."

He leaned down and kissed me good-bye. "Give Pam my love when you see her."

Your love? I reflected. It was a bitter irony. Pam and Rob shared such a special camaraderie. Yet Pam couldn't forget Silas Winters, the handsome, shrewd DEA agent she had met in the Caribbean—the arrogant young man who didn't have God on his priority list. And Rob would never forget Liana, the lovely, fawnlike Hmong girl he met in Laos and lost in a refugee camp in Thailand.

Rob gave David a playful punch on the arm. "Take care of our girl, man." He gave me a wink. "Don't let her go tumbling over the ship's railing." He eased into his Jaguar, gunned the engine, and roared away from the curb, his tires squealing as he disappeared around the corner.

David nudged me. He had already checked our luggage. "Come on, hon. Our flight's waiting. Let's head for Hopewell's reunion."

Fifteen minutes later we were settled in the velvety cushioned seats in the first-class section of a Boeing 727. I closed my eyes as the plane taxied down the runway.

As we lifted off, I watched the landscape recede into a miniature city below us. Gradually the earth was swallowed up in billowing clouds. Slowly I drifted off, lulled by the steady drone of the engines. I dozed off and on until I felt the jet brake over the runway again, lurch, jolt, and shudder to a stop. "Are we there, David?" I asked.

"No, sleepyhead. We're just picking up passengers in Portland." He folded his *Wall Street Journal* and tucked it in the seat beside him. "We'll be on our way again in 20 minutes."

"Will we make it on time?" David overplayed scrutinizing his watch, one brow arched mischievously. "Looks like we have four, maybe six hours before the *Mendenhall* sails."

But David's 20 minutes stretched to 30. He began flexing his watchband, eyeing the time impatiently.

Finally, a last-minute passenger barreled on board—a solid, athletic man balancing two carry-on bags, a tennis racket,
and camera case in his muscular arms, his plane ticket clenched between his teeth.

Immediately the plane door closed and a voice boomed over the intercom. "Ladies and gentlemen, this is your captain speaking. We're sorry for the delay. We'll be cleared for takeoff in a few minutes."

The late passenger winked at the stewardess as she took his boarding pass. He was an attractive man in his late forties, with thinning gray-brown hair and a full hangdog mustache. Even as she urged him toward his seat, he hesitated, his gaze darting around, settling finally on me. He flashed me a quizzical smile, but his eyes held a troubled perplexity. He swayed in the aisle as the plane lurched, then with an almost egotistical strut he moved past us out of first class into the economy section.

I was still wondering about him as the plane inched toward the runway. When we were airborne, a petite stewardess came by with beverages. "I didn't know you would delay departure for just one passenger," I ventured.

The stewardess eyed me curiously. "It was coincidental."

"Really?" I mused. "The man acts as though he's used to planes waiting for him."

She popped open a can of Pepsi. "He's stopped planes and bombs and everything else in his lifetime."

"Then he is somebody? I mean somebody important?"

She poured the cola over the ice cubes. "He was in his day. That's Seth Mueller."

The name didn't mean anything to me, but David's interest sparked immediately. "So that's who he is! No wonder he looked familiar."

"So who's Seth Mueller?" I asked. "A senator or an ambassador?"

David's face grew animated. "He's a tennis pro, Michelle— great like Jimmy Connors. He was the Connors of ten or 15 years ago."

"You could call him an ambassador of sorts, too," the stewardess offered. "Of goodwill, at least." She reached down and picked up a news magazine from the bottom of her serving cart. She leaned forward, her dark eyes dancing conspiratorially. "Here, I'll lend you this, but I want it back. I want to get his autograph."

I flipped open the magazine to a picture of Seth Mueller in shirt-sleeves and tennis shorts, a scrawny, potbellied African child balanced in one arm. FROM RACKETS TO BASKETS, the caption read.

> Seth Mueller, 48, who amassed a fortune at Wimbledon and the U.S. Pros in the 1970s, *and spent it*, is still making a name for himself. In the last few years, Mueller has all but given up the tennis game for a new racket: collecting tax-free funds for impoverished Third World countries. His supporters view him as a philanthropist in his own right, moving all too freely among the stricken, war-torn nations and refugee camps of the world, catching undernourished smiles for his reward. But for a man who never entered a competition without a price, there are those who question whether he is politically motivated or pocketing some of the vast funds that come his way.
>
> Mueller's travels are not without risk. Only recently, he narrowly escaped with his life when an attempt to cross the Cambodian border with food supplements failed. Nevertheless, his opponents find it difficult to believe that the pro who wielded a skillful, yet ruthless racket on the tennis courts has really done a turnaround, going from racket serves to an impassioned serving of food baskets to feed the hungry of the world.
>
> Mueller himself claims that God has led him in this new career. But the man, who even in tennis had difficulty with popularity polls, brushes off interviews with the press with the same brassy indifference that characterized his attitude when he was fined for poor sportsmanship in the 1976 Wimbledon games. But there's no getting away from it—Seth Mueller can still play a mean game of tennis as long as the price is right.

For a second, before David closed the magazine, I stared at the photo of Seth Mueller and the malnourished child. The tender, careworn expression in Mueller's eyes and the pathetic face of the child stirred a responsive chord deep in my heart. But Seth's name roused something else, goaded my memory.

Seth Mueller now sounded vaguely familiar. Somewhere I had heard or seen that name before.

When I handed the magazine back to the stewardess, she said, misty-eyed, "The last time Mr. Mueller flew with us, the flight crew took up a collection for his African famine project."

"African project?" echoed David.

"Oh, yes. Mr. Mueller doesn't just talk about feeding the hungry. He does something about it. We wanted to have a part."

As she made her way back to economy class with the magazine in hand, David rubbed his square jawline thoughtfully. Almost mechanically, his fingers traced the scar that cut across his cleft chin—that familiar gesture that always accompanied his annoyance.

"David, why do you look so perturbed?" I asked. "Is it that man, Mueller? A few minutes ago you were bragging about him being such a great tennis player."

"Maybe I'm a little miffed that he held up the plane."

"The stewardess said . . ."

"I know what the stewardess *said*."

While we were wrangling about him, Seth Mueller charged back down the aisle toward the cockpit. He stopped short of the door, turned, partially facing us, and spoke earnestly with the stewardess. I heard him say, "The pilot's got to get a message through for me."

She shook her head and shifted quickly, blocking the door. "That's impossible, sir. The cockpit's off-limits to passengers—"

Her response obviously irritated Seth. The charming smile he had flashed when he approached froze on his face. He argued with her, his words muffled now by the noise of the aircraft.

Again she shook her head firmly. He stormed past us, brushing at his wide mustache, muttering, "Then I'll have to do it myself." He caught my eye as he went by, his expression anything but amused.

Moments later, after winging over majestic, cloud-shrouded Mount Rainier, we landed at rain-drenched SeaTac Airport and deplaned from the rear of the aircraft.

I craned my neck, trying to catch sight of Seth Mueller, but he was already lost in the crowd. By the time David and I reached the luggage turnstile, Seth had shoved through the glass doorway and was standing at the curb, vigorously hailing a taxi, his tennis racket and camera case slung over one shoulder.

As I watched him dart into a Yellow Cab, I had an uncanny feeling I hadn't seen the last of Seth Mueller.

CHAPTER THREE

David and I followed the lanky porter out of the airline terminal along a sheltered walkway where we could see the sun breaking through the gray, misty clouds. We made our way through the throng until we spotted a crowd by the curb waving a Hopewell banner. "David, there's our group," I said.

We were only yards from the banner when I slowed my pace and clutched David's arm. "Oh, David, suddenly I've got cold feet. With all my book's publicity, I have such an image to live up to. What if people remember what I was like at Hopewell? I wasn't exactly a model student, you know."

David stopped abruptly and tilted my chin; the laugh lines around his dark eyes deepened. "Come on, sweetheart. No one's going to recall your popcorn escapade in the laundry room."

"That was nothing, David. Just an accident. I still laugh when I think of it—my roommate Jackie filling the automatic popper too full, a sea of popcorn kernels flooding the laundry room, shooting in the air like bullets."

"I wish I'd been there," mused David. "I love popcorn."

"I did too, but after that fiasco I didn't touch popcorn for a month." I drew in a breath. "But you know my dastardly deeds didn't end with popcorn. I got demerits for writing poems after bed check and skipping chapel a few times. And, worst of all, I was campused one whole semester. Jill Monroe, my hall monitor, had to play watchdog and escort me all over campus. It was humiliating."

David chuckled wryly. "Yes, darling, I think you mentioned your unsavory past when we first met. In fact, I made a mental note not to get involved with a free spirit like you."

"Oh, really? So what happened to your resolve?"

David was laughing now. "What's a guy to do? I fell in love."

"Go ahead and laugh, David," I chided. "Getting campused wasn't funny. The only thing I did wrong was kiss my college sweetheart."

"In front of the dorm monitor," he reminded me. "And then didn't your boyfriend Scott kiss the monitor too?"

"Only on the back of the hand, but I think that's what really got me campused. The poor girl was so flabbergasted. I can still see the shocked expression on her face. Poor Erma."

"Erma?"

"Yes. Her name was Erma Moosenbocker. And, oh David, no one argued with Erma. She had the figure of a linebacker."

The porter was back, edging into our conversation. "Your luggage is by the curb, sir."

"Thanks," David said, tipping him generously.

David slipped his arm around my waist. "Are you ready to join your Hopewell colleagues, Michelle?"

I held back. "I still feel like Hopewell's little rebel."

David leaned over and gave me a quick kiss. "You must have done something right, Michelle. You made the honor roll and now you're one of Hopewell's honored alumni. Come on, sweetheart. Take a deep breath and we'll break in on the crowd with a flourish."

I glanced around. "I still don't see anyone I know."

"Well, I see someone familiar—yes, I'm sure of it—Dr. Jason Thatcher. Come with me, Michelle. I'll introduce you to him."

My gaze followed David's, settling on an attractive, dignified man. "Jason Thatcher?" I repeated. "How do you know him?"

"I don't. But the last *Hopewell Alumni News* did a splashy pictorial article on Thatcher. He's a world-renowned thoracic surgeon. Ambitious. Prestigious. At the peak of his career."

I studied the doctor curiously. Thatcher was a tall, broad-shouldered man with silver-white hair, meticulously combed. A warm smile softened his gaunt cheekbones and angular features. Craggy, uneven brows shaded his deep-set eyes as he looked down at the slender lady beside him. She was fortyish, with classic features, an obviously well-bred woman with reddish-blonde hair fluffed stylishly around her face. Her crinkly eyes looked like tiny half-moons as she gave her husband a merry, beaming smile.

"You'll be in good company, hon," David said, urging me toward them. "Jason Thatcher is one of the four honored alumni."

Just before we reached the Thatchers, we brushed against another couple. The woman looked up startled, then exclaimed with sudden recognition, "Oh, you're—you're Michelle Ballard, the writer."

Her obvious pleasure touched me. "Yes, yes I am."

"I'm Stephanie Ellis. I write, too," she said shyly. Stephanie was modestly dressed, her dark wiry hair curled slightly around her ears. She studied me with wide, sad eyes, a fleeting, fractional smile on her thin lips.

"Do you write books?" I asked.

"Just poetry," she answered softly. "Mostly about my son." She fidgeted with her heart-shaped locket, suddenly reticent, intimidated—so out of place in this crowd, so uncomfortable with me.

"Cameron, you must meet Mrs. Ballard!" Stephanie's wistful eyes darted toward her husband—a ruggedly good-looking man in a bright red polo shirt, brown trousers, and hiking boots. "Cam, she's an author! She wrote the story about the Vietnam POW."

Cameron Ellis nodded at me as he slipped his arm protectively around his wife. "You'll have to excuse Stephanie. She's a little taken with writers." He extended a free hand to David. "The name's Cam Ellis," he said.

Ellis was well over six feet tall, lean and muscular, with jet-black hair, a high, shiny forehead, and receding hairline. A closely cropped beard, full sideburns, and a brush mustache obscured the lower part of his face. Only his unsmiling lips showed through.

The four of us chatted politely for several minutes. Then David said, "Well, if you'll excuse us, we're going over to meet the Jason Thatchers. We'll talk more later."

Cam Ellis scowled, his heavy brows knitting together. His riveting charcoal eyes bored through the crowd toward the doctor. "That tall, white-haired man over there—that's Dr. Thatcher?"

"Yes," said David. "He's a famous surgeon. Do you know him?"

Cameron and Stephanie Ellis exchanged momentary glances, then Cameron said abruptly, "No, I never met the man."

"Well, why don't you come along with us and meet him now?" David suggested amiably.

Ellis's face darkened. "I'm not much for doctors," he grunted. David took my elbow. "Then you'll pardon us if we go on? . . ."

I turned away from the Ellises . . . gladly. We walked a few steps. Then I brightened as I recognized a familiar face. There in the center of all those Hopewell alumni stood a small, graceful woman in a gold-beige suit, her London Fog raincoat draped across her shoulders. Her light-brown hair with its gold tints was curly in spite of the dampness.

"Professor Chadwick!" I called. "Prof Chadwick!"

She turned toward the sound of my voice in that slow, unhurried way of hers. Then, recognizing me, she hastened my way, her blue-gray eyes shining, her gentle smile blossoming as we met.

"Michelle, my dear, how good it is to see you again." She took my hands in hers. "Let me look at you!"

She studied me as though she were sifting through her memories, recalling my days in her classes at Hopewell. I studied her too. She seemed so out-of-place outside the classroom—no chalk in hand, no chalkboard to scrawl on, no classical novel opened on her desk. The delicate cast of her smooth, ivory complexion made her look years younger. She had an attractive face with a little pug nose tipped perpetually upward, and a firm chin that never once quivered when she handed back our heavily marked term papers.

Her thin lips broke into a smile as she glanced up at David. "And you—you, young man, must be Michelle's beloved."

"And you're Michelle's favorite English professor. She's told me a great deal about you." He lifted Abigail Chadwick's hand to his lips, charming her as if he were Sir Walter Raleigh. "I'm David Ballard . . . forever in your debt."

"Well, David," she laughed in surprise, "what's that all about?"

"If it hadn't been for you, Professor Chadwick, my wife and I never would have met."

Her dark brows arched curiously. "I don't understand."

"If you hadn't inspired Michelle to be a writer, she would have settled down and wilted in her old hometown."

"David's right, Prof. . . ."

"Abigail, please. Please just call me Abigail."

Abigail. The word had a musical lilt to it. It was the perfect name for this sensitive lady. "David was right, Abigail," I continued. "I was running when I left home and went West. Running from memories. . . ."

"Scott?" Abigail asked knowingly.

"Yes, running from Scott. And running from God. Every mile I burned between Illinois and California flamed my pioneer spirit. I was seeking my own land of opportunity, my chance to get away from everything and everyone back home—and just write."

"Fortunately for me, she had to eat too," David interjected. "That's why she took a secretarial job at my computer company."

"So that's how you two got together?"

"Not exactly. Michelle and I were really thrown together on a business venture of mine."

"More like a crash landing in David's private airplane."

"Oh, Michelle, how horrible!"

"Not at all," said David. "It was one of the best things that ever happened to me. It literally put Michelle right in my lap."

"And if I hadn't fallen in love with David, I never would have written the book about his best friend Rob Thornton. . . ."

Abigail brightened. "The Thornton legacy book. Yes, let me see. I remember. *Rob Thornton: A Vietnam Legacy*. It was well-written, Michelle. I'm so proud of you."

David slipped his arm around me. "After that, Prof Chadwick—"

"Abigail," she reminded him.

"After that, Abigail, we got married, honeymooned in the Caribbean, and we've had a wonderful, incredible year together. In fact, we just celebrated our first anniversary a few days ago."

"And we're still celebrating," I smiled, "with this cruise."

As we talked, I noticed Abigail glancing around furtively at the crowd. "Are you expecting someone?" I asked.

She blushed. "An old friend is going on the cruise. I just—"

Her words were cut short as a tour bus billowing puffs of black smoke screeched to a stop in front of us. The door squeaked open and a thin-faced driver with musty blond hair stepped to the curb. "This smoking gem," he announced brashly, "is your last chance to the S.S. *Mendenhall*." Then he whistled as he eyed the mountains of luggage lining the sidewalk. "Jumping catfish," he exclaimed as he began tossing the suitcases on board, "you're all packing for a lifetime!"

I wanted to say, *Abigail, that young man certainly didn't get refined in your literature class*, but she and David were engrossed in conversation. He was telling her about my new Caribbean novel.

Abigail's face grew animated as she turned to me. "Oh, I look forward to reading that book too, Michelle Merrill."

"*Ballard*," David corrected.

"It's still *Merrill* when I think in terms of Hopewell," Abigail smiled. "The rebel years, David. The searching years. Michelle groping for answers. Always into something." She looked away for a moment, remembering, then back at David. "Michelle *Ballard*," she said softly. "Marriage changes names, David. But God changes names too. The rebel Saul to Paul. The impulsive, floundering Simon to Peter the Rock." It was as if Abigail were back at the chalkboard, pulling nuggets from the choicest of literature. "When God permits a name change, He has a good purpose. It was after you gave her your name, David, that Michelle really broke into print."

"Abigail," I protested, "I'm not Shakespeare or Tolstoy."

"I don't expect you to be," she said as we began to board the motorcoach. "You're Michelle Merrill Ballard. I expect you to live up to *that* name. No other."

The exhaust from the bus filled the air with fumes as the passengers boarded. Jason Thatcher, the distinguished physician with the silver-white hair, was coughing as he entered the coach behind his lovely wife. Without warning, Cameron Ellis shoved into the line ahead of us, on Thatcher's heels. Cameron's wife Stephanie turned and gave Abigail a hasty, frayed smile and whispered, "Excuse us. Please excuse us."

I'm not certain Abigail even heard Stephanie. Abigail had already turned to David. "Would you mind too much, David, if I sat with your wife on the drive to Canada?"

As the bus pulled from the airport terminal and turned north on the freeway, I said, "Abigail, I hear you'll be sharing a cabin with my kid sister Pam for the next two weeks."

She answered with a twinkle. "When I picked up my travel packet and learned I'd be rooming with Pam Merrill, I almost had second thoughts. I wasn't certain I needed that much energy and perfume filling one little cabin. Pam was never one to sit quietly and read or listen to chamber music."

David leaned across the aisle. "Pam's more into aerobics, jogging, skiing, and mountain climbing."

"And dating," I added meaningfully.

Abigail chortled. "Partying—that's what I remember most about your sister. But then I decided to let the chips fall as they may and let that vibrant Pam Merrill add some life and spice to my trip."

"She'll do that, all right," David agreed with a grin.

As the bus rumbled north toward Seattle, Abigail and I caught up on old times. We were so busy chatting, I scarcely realized a half hour had passed. The motorcoach was already squealing to a stop in front of a downtown hotel. Three passengers boarded—two young women gabbing giddily and balancing more luggage than they could handle; and a lone man—Seth Mueller, the tennis pro!

I hadn't expected to see Seth Mueller so soon after our flight from Portland. I turned to point him out to Abigail, but she was already following his every move, her gaze intense, scrutinizing.

Mueller looked preoccupied. He scanned the aisle fleetingly, then slipped into a seat near the door.

"That's Seth Mueller, the tennis pro," I told Abigail. "He was just on our plane. He must be going on our cruise too. So why didn't he board this bus with the rest of us?"

"You've met Seth already?" inquired Abigail with surprise.

"No, but I'm eager to."

"Everyone is always eager to meet Seth," Abigail mused.

"Do you know him?"

"Know him?" she echoed wistfully. "For a very long time."

"Are you saying he went to Hopewell?"

"Yes, we were classmates. In fact, Seth's one of Hopewell's four honored alumni . . . like you."

"That's it! I should have remembered. His name is on the Hopewell brochure."

"That's right," said Abigail softly. Her eyes moistened. As she pulled a lace hanky from her handbag, the sun caught the glow of an emerald ring on her long tapered finger.

"Prof, that ring is exquisite."

"Would you believe it was a gift from Seth Mueller? He sent it to me from the Orient long ago."

"Then you two were . . . close?"

"Yes . . . once." She dabbed at her eyes. Before Abigail snapped her purse shut, I noticed a worn snapshot of a young man on a tennis court. I wanted to ask, "Was that Seth Mueller when he was younger?" But I bit my lower lip, suddenly intimidated by our old professor-student relationship.

Abigail caught my glance and, with a little smile, handed me the photograph. "You spotted this, didn't you? It's Seth, right after he won his first game at Wimbledon. He'd probably laugh at me if he knew I still had it."

"I have a feeling he was very special to you."

"Yes. That's why I thought he would remember me when he boarded just now."

"Maybe he just didn't see you."

"Didn't he?" She looked away. "But why would I expect him to recognize me . . . after all these years?" Abigail was out of her professorial role now, away from the sanctuary of her classroom, her emotions riding the surface. "Twenty-five years makes its changes, adds its pounds, gives its maturity."

As Abigail spoke so yearningly of Seth, I felt almost sorry for her. She had evidently carried this unrequited love for many years. I was ready to defend her, protect her from the callow charms of Seth Mueller. Who was he to toy with her affections?

I thought about the article I read on the plane about Seth Mueller. Maybe he wasn't the man Abigail remembered or wanted him to be. What was he really—missionary or mercenary? I recalled the poignant photograph of Seth holding the starving African child. But hadn't the article called him ruthless, politically motivated, practically accusing him of pocketing funds earmarked for the hungry?

In spite of Abigail's obsession with him, I was already deciding that Seth Mueller, the former tennis pro turned missionary, wasn't the sort of man I would trust.

CHAPTER FOUR

Just as David, Abigail, and I boarded the immense vessel—the sleek, white S.S. *Mendenhall*—we spotted my sister Pam making her way through the clusters of passengers toward us. She looked as gorgeous as ever—her tawny upswept hair creating an elegance that contradicted her pouty innocence and direct, childlike gaze. Her apricot blouse and burnt orange skirt accented her peaches-and-cream complexion. As she swooped toward us in her three-inch heels, I noticed that she was wearing my new opal earrings she'd borrowed for her trip to Victoria.

"Michelle! Oh, Michelle! We sail in 40 minutes!" she cried, whirling me around with her usual giddy exuberance. "I was afraid you were going to miss the boat! Oh, it's so beautiful—wait'll you see—the luxury—the extravagance—I've been on every deck already. I found the gym and the swimming pools and the saunas. I think the only thing I've missed is the engine room and the bridge!"

She paused long enough to greet Abigail with an unembarrassed hug, enveloping her in a fragrant cloud of perfume. "Prof Chadwick, would you believe? We're roomies! Can you imagine them throwing the great Professor Chadwick in with a poor little nurse who never could conjugate verbs?" Pam's blue-gray eyes danced mischievously. "Don't worry though. I'm taking the top bunk so you won't have to worry about falling off the ladder."

Abigail chuckled. "I'm not quite that ancient, Pam. Actually I've been known to paint my own house, but thanks for thinking of my safety anyway."

Pam rushed on, bristling with excitement. "Would you believe there are 250 of us from Hopewell? This is going to be *some* trip! Just wait'll you see this ship, Michelle. You'll go wild!"

"Right now, Pam, we'd just like to see our room," I said patiently. "Where is it, David? The Promenade Deck?"

"Right. Stateroom 209."

"Oh, no, you can't go to your stateroom yet," Pam protested. "We've got to get up to the Sky Room. The Hopewell bon voyage party is in full swing!" She was off toward the stairway before we could reply. "Well, are you coming or not?" she called back.

"That's our Pam," said David with a grin.

"At least we know it won't be a dull cruise," I offered.

"That's what I'm afraid of." He stepped between Abigail and me and took our elbows. "May I escort you lovely ladies to the party?"

I caught my breath as we followed Pam through the wide double doors of the Sky Room—a grandiose ballroom with panoramic windows, gold-leaf decor, and crystal chandeliers. The room was resplendent with velvet wallpaper, thick carpeting, and plush royal-blue sofas and chairs. The ship's orchestra played on the center stage, filling the room with the lofty strains of "Love Is a Many Splendored Thing." A glistening ice sculpture of a mermaid graced the long, linen-draped table brimming with hors d'oeuvres, finger sandwiches, fresh fruits, and French pastries.

Pam gushed dreamily, "See, sis? Didn't I tell you? Isn't it all so utterly indescribable? I think I've died and gone to heaven!"

David nudged me. "I'm hitting the serving table. You coming?"

Pam spoke up. "I'm with you, David. I'm absolutely famished!"

"Bring Abigail and me some punch, David," I called as they headed for the refreshments. I glanced around at the milling guests, looking for a familiar face. I groaned inwardly. Stephanie Ellis was brushing through the crowd toward me.

"Mrs. Ballard—oh, Mrs. Ballard," she cried breathlessly. "I—I hope you don't mind my bothering you again—I met you at the airport, remember? I'm Stephanie Ellis. I read your book—"

"Yes, of course I remember you. You were very complimentary—"

Stephanie put a cold, nervous hand on mine. "I cried when I read your book," she said, her expression rapt with admiration. "Especially when Eva Thornton found out her son Rob was still alive." Stephanie glanced around skittishly, her hand still on mine. I had the feeling she was about to share some secret confidence as she drew closer. "I have this poetry—it's not published or anything—I don't even know if it's any good, but I wondered—I know you're a very busy person, Mrs. Ballard—but maybe you could—I mean, I—"

"Call me Michelle, please." I felt myself growing annoyed, wanting to finish Stephanie's sentences, silently coaxing her to come to the point. "Are you saying you want me to read your poetry?"

"Oh, would you? I'd be so pleased. I've never shared it with anyone except Cam. It's very personal."

I glanced helplessly at Abigail, but she gave me only a sympathetic smile. Looking back at Stephanie's crestfallen expression, I murmured, "I'm not a poet, but I'll read your poems if you wish."

A sudden light sparkled in Stephanie's melancholy eyes. "Oh, thank you, Mrs.—I mean, Michelle. You don't know how—"

Stephanie's effusiveness was severed as her husband stepped over and took her arm possessively. "Well, Stephanie dear, I see you've found Mrs. Ballard again."

Stephanie shrank back, flustered. "She's agreed to read my poems, Cam. Can you imagine—a famous author reading my work?"

Cameron's gaze met mine. "You must understand, Mrs. Ballard. My wife isn't a professional writer. Her poems— they're very private."

Suddenly my curiosity was roused. Cameron Ellis apparently didn't want me to read his wife's poetry. But why?

"Cam, please," Stephanie blurted, "I want her to read them."

Before the Ellises clashed further, Abigail stepped in and said, "Tell me, Mr. Ellis, when did you and Mrs. Ellis attend Hopewell?"

"Stephanie never went to college," he replied.

"Then *you're* the Hopewell graduate?" inquired Abigail.

"Not a graduate. I—I quit and went into business. It's been 15 years." He eyed Abigail quizzically and asked, "What's your connection with Hopewell?"

Abigail's eyes flickered with surprise. "I'm on the faculty."

"Miss Chadwick is one of Hopewell's most revered professors," I declared. "Surely you had her for freshman English. Everyone did."

"Oh, well, I—I came to Hopewell as a sophomore," said Cameron. He uttered a low, guttural sound and turned to Stephanie. "Let's mingle a little and see if we can spot some of my old classmates."

As the Ellises melded into the crowd, I looked back in relief at Abigail. But she was looking across the room, her face brightening. Seth Mueller stood casually at the periphery of a group of men.

"Come, Michelle, I want you to meet Seth."

We made our way over to the former tennis pro. Abigail tapped him gently on the shoulder. "Seth? Seth Mueller?" Her mellow words hung in midair, edged with expectancy.

Seth spun around. "Abigail!" His face glowed; his Prussian blue eyes glinted with merriment. "Abigail Chadwick." He embraced her—pushed away, grinned boyishly, and hugged her again. "I hoped you'd be on board. Counted on it."

"You haven't changed," she whispered breathlessly.

He tugged at his mustache and shot a glance upward at his tufts of thinning gray-brown hair. "Oh, a little bit," he laughed good-naturedly. "But I still remember old friends."

She winced a little. "Not *old* friends, Seth. *Good* friends."

"And I still can't write a term paper!" He gripped both of her hands in his. He couldn't take his eyes off her. "Now tell me how you are and what you've been doing—outside the classroom."

I started to move away, but Abigail called me back. "Michelle, I want you two to meet, especially since you're both

honored alumni. Seth, this is Michelle Ballard. Michelle...
Seth Mueller."

He managed to focus on me briefly. "Nice to meet you."

"Michelle writes books," said Abigail.

Seth surveyed me with sudden interest. "Oh, really?"

"She wrote the bestseller on the young Vietnam POW—"

Seth's shaggy brows knit curiously. "You've been in that area
of the world?"

"No, but I researched Vietnam and Thailand for my book."

"Seth does missionary work in refugee camps in Thailand,"
said Abigail, "around the world, as a matter of fact."

"Don't add to my credentials, Abigail," he said. "It's hard
work and I love it, but I don't quite see myself as a missionary."

"It sounds like fascinating work, Mr. Mueller," I said.

He gave me a direct, piercing gaze. "You could write a book
for me, Miss Ballard, about feeding starving nations. Some
decent publicity would help bring in the funds we need."

My interest sparked at once. "Please tell me more. I'll be
getting back to my publisher with a book proposal right after
the cruise. I was planning to do a novel, but . . ."

"Would you be free to travel? Overseas? To refugee camps?"

"Well, I—"

"Travel? To refugee camps?" echoed David skeptically, coming up behind me. "I think Michelle better stick to writing
novels. She can do that at home."

Seth gave me a half-amused smile. "Ah, it's *Mrs.* Ballard!
Then I see you're already committed."

"I'd still like to discuss your ideas for a book, Mr. Mueller," I
said staunchly as I took the goblet of punch David offered.

David eyed me with a curious grimace. "Guess I'd better
keep my eyes on you or you'll be halfway around the world
without me."

"Oh, David," I chided, "we were just making conversation."

"So was I for these past ten minutes. You'll never guess who I
ran into over by the punch bowl."

I sipped my punch. "Tell me."

He was chuckling now. "Your old dorm monitor."

I almost spilled my punch. "Not—you don't mean—Jill Monroe!"

"Wasn't she the one who escorted you around when you were—?"

I touched his lips to keep him from blurting out *campused*.

"I think she was taken with me," he teased, "until she found out I was, uh, *taken*." His dark eyes danced with mischief. "But she was even more horrified when I told her I was married to you, dear."

"Jill made a play for you? David, that's disgusting!"

"I thought it was flattering. She's very attractive, you know."

I took a gulp of punch, swallowing my sudden twinge of jealousy. David didn't notice. "And I met the linebacker she's traveling with," he added, obviously enjoying our bristling little repartee.

"Jill's married?"

"No. But her shipboard companion is another old friend of yours—Erma Moosenbocker. Remember her? They're both eager to talk with you again."

"Oh, David, you're just saying that," I scoffed. "They're not really on the cruise, are they?"

David nodded toward several women standing by the mermaid ice sculpture. "Look right over there, sweetheart. Jill and Erma, big as life. Shall we go say hello?"

I pivoted and started walking in the opposite direction. David followed and caught my elbow, stifling his laughter. "Darling, don't take this so seriously. I was just having a little fun with you."

"It's not funny, David. How will I get through two weeks on the same ship with them? Everywhere I go I'll feel them watching me!"

David slipped his arm around me. "You're not campused anymore, Michelle. You've come a long way since those days. And I bet Erma and Jill will be the first to tell you how much they admire you."

I was halfway across the room when I noticed a woman and child entering the Sky Room through the wide double doors. I gasped in astonishment. It was my best friend Jackie Turman and her little son Stevie. I gripped David's arm. "Look! It's Jackie!"

He had already spotted her and was striding in her direction. Jackie looked as stunning as ever—graceful and slender in a stylish silk pantsuit, her makeup flawless, her blonde hair piled elegantly on her head and swooping over her arched brows with a gossamer sheen.

"Jackie!" I cried as her gaze turned my way.

Her green eyes flashed with warmth and excitement. "Michelle!"

Jackie and I ran to each other and embraced like long-lost sisters. We were laughing and crying as David bent down and opened his arms wide to five-year-old Stevie. "Hey, Tiger, you rascal!"

Stevie made a beeline for David and with a flying leap was airborne into his arms. "Uncle David, Uncle David!" he shouted.

"Jackie, I can't believe it—you here on this cruise!" I cried.

She smiled through her tears. "Oh, Michelle, I wouldn't miss seeing you honored for anything in the world!"

"But aren't you taking an awful risk leaving Switzerland?" I whispered. "What if the cocaine syndicate finds out where you are?"

She glanced around anxiously. "Oh, Michelle, I'm sick of worrying about the syndicate. They've hounded us ever since Steve turned state's evidence against the mob."

"But you're still living under the government's witness protection program, aren't you?"

Jackie's voice was soft but resolute. "Yes, but Steve and I refuse to live our lives in fear any longer. Besides, I'm traveling under my assigned name, Jackie *Marshall*. And I don't plan to get off the ship and touch American soil, so who will even know I'm here?"

"You mean you're not getting off at the ports of call?"

"No, I promised Steve that much."

"Where are Steve and that new little baby daughter of yours?"

"They're still in Lucerne with my parents. But I brought all of Becky's pictures with me. I miss her already. She's such a little doll." Jackie was still smiling wistfully as she turned to David. "Stevie has been talking all day about seeing his Uncle David. Can you believe it's been nearly a year since we've seen you?"

"I'm all growed up now," Stevie announced proudly, his big, dark eyes snapping. He was still a straw-blond towhead with rosy cheeks and a turned-up nose, but he'd grown taller and lost some of his baby fat. And David was obviously as crazy about him as ever.

Just as Jackie and I were about to catch up on the past, a voice broke over the loudspeaker, calling for everyone's attention. We looked toward the center platform where Horace Stoddard, president of Hopewell College, was standing. He was a tall, Lincolnesque man with silver-gray hair, a ruddy complexion, and sharply chisled features. "Ladies and gentlemen, Hopewell alumni, and friends of Hopewell—welcome to our fiftieth anniversary celebration! We're going to have the time of our lives on this gala journey to the Alaskan frontier."

He paused, gazing out over the crowd. "We have only a few minutes before the ship sails, just enough time to meet our honored alumni—four ordinary people who have made outstanding contributions to society and who have learned to trust an extraordinary God. On this cruise we want to encourage these honorees as Jonathan encouraged David. We want to strengthen them at a time in their lives when our support will be most meaningful.

"For those of you who recognize the name *Seth Mueller*, you may think of tennis and Seth's numerous awards in that field. But for the last ten years, Seth has been consumed with a desire to feed the hungry of the world. The result has been a missionary career that has spanned the world. "Seth," said Stoddard, "we want to be available to you on this trip, to encourage you in your endeavors."

Seth waved casually, smiling.

President Stoddard turned to Jason Thatcher, standing nearby. "Dr. Thatcher was an outstanding Hopewell student and class valedictorian. Now we honor him as a world-renowned thoracic surgeon, a pioneer in the field of heart-lung surgery."

I looked over at Jason Thatcher. The crinkly laugh lines around his dark brown eyes gave him an appealing gentleness. I liked him already and made a mental note to get acquainted soon.

Horace Stoddard was still speaking. He arched his brows, sending rivulets of wrinkles across his high forehead. "We welcome you aboard, Dr. Thatcher—and your lovely wife, Noreen. We hear you're celebrating your twenty-fifth wedding anniversary on this trip. We'll respect your privacy," he added with a shrewd twinkle, "and we hope this cruise will set the course for your next 25 years together."

A wincing pain crossed Jason Thatcher's face, but he recovered quickly and managed a fleeting smile for his wife.

President Stoddard was already introducing the next honoree. "Colonel Brett Seaton, one of our country's acclaimed astronauts, attended Hopewell briefly. After graduating from the Naval Academy at Annapolis, he served as a Marine Corps combat pilot in Vietnam. During his days at Hopewell, Brett spent considerable time in my home. He filled a void that my wife and I felt for many years after our only son died."

As Stoddard's voice trailed momentarily, I looked at Brett Seaton and his wife, a strikingly handsome couple in their late thirties. Brett had a sturdy, rough-hewn attractiveness—a generous jawline; large, angular face; and a wide, smiling mouth. His wavy jet-black hair was cropped short, and heavy brows hugged his dark, dancing eyes. His wife was a statuesque blonde with platinum highlights, an ivory-smooth complexion, and impeccable makeup. Her translucent blue eyes glowed with a bittersweet wistfulness.

Horace Stoddard's voice caught my attention again. "Brett Seaton's space flight was scrubbed after the Challenger disaster, bringing his dreams to a standstill. We can encourage Brett and Candace and dream with them as he prepares for his next shuttle flight."

Finally President Stoddard's eyes sought mine. "Our fourth alumna—the only woman honoree—left quite an imprint on Hopewell."

I felt a sinking sensation inside and stifled a groan. David gripped my hand supportively as Stoddard went on. "Michelle

Merrill Ballard represents the many students who came to Hopewell searching for purpose and meaning in life. She was always creative, but sometimes her creativity got her into trouble. She thrived on tackling controversial issues. And now, most recently, she grappled with the issue of Vietnam, sensitively portraying the overwhelming struggles of one prisoner-of-war. Michelle," he said, gazing with compassion at me, "it gives me great pleasure to recognize your writing accomplishments. I admire your indomitable spirit—even the searching, questioning nature you displayed at Hopewell."

President Stoddard gazed around with a warm, caring smile. "We're going to have a fabulous time getting better acquainted. I imagine we'll all be old friends by the end of the trip." He glanced at his watch. "Well, it's time to go up on deck and watch the ship pull out of the harbor. Don't forget devotions here in the Sky Room at nine each morning. Tomorrow I have a special taped greeting from the governor of the state in honor of Hopewell's fiftieth anniversary."

As everyone began milling toward the door, Jackie and I linked arms. "I was afraid President Stoddard was going to tell about our popcorn escapade in the laundry room," she laughed.

"Me, too," I said. I turned to Abigail. She was staring ahead, looking perplexed. I followed her gaze. David was just ahead "of us walking with Cam Ellis, Brett Seaton, and several other men.

"Is something wrong, Prof?" I asked.

She nodded toward the men. "The more I think of it, the more positive I am that that fellow never attended Hopewell College. I wonder why he's posing as a former student?"

Apprehension flickered in Jackie's face. We exchanged troubled glances. I had a feeling Abigail meant Cam Ellis. Did she have reason to be suspicious? I started to ask, "Prof, do you mean—?"

But the ship's horn blared, drowning out my words.

CHAPTER
FIVE

Arm in arm David and I stood on the open deck and watched the ship set sail amid a flurry of rainbow confetti and twirling streamers. The lively sound of band music faded as we ebbed away from the gleaming skyline of Vancouver and sailed along the verdant coast of British Columbia.

Finally, we went to our stateroom where I discovered a dozen anniversary roses from David on the table. After several tender kisses to show my appreciation, I freshened up while David unpacked a few things. Then we headed for the Sea Breeze Dining Room for the evening buffet. We took our seats at a round, linen-draped table with Jackie and little Stevie, my sister Pam, Abigail Chadwick, and Seth Mueller. The Thatchers, Seatons, Ellises, and Horace Stoddard and his wife sat at the adjoining table. Large panoramic windows spanned both sides of the sprawling dining room. As we feasted on shrimp cocktail, poached salmon, prime rib, and exotic fruit salads, we caught fleeting glimpses of the rustic logging villages and picturesque fishing towns on Vancouver Island.

After dinner we hurried to the crowded Golden Sails Lounge for the gala welcome-aboard variety show—a gleeful, frenetic montage of song and dance. When it was over, David stood promptly and suggested we turn in. I—a *night* person to his *morning* person—was about to protest, but seeing the weariness in his eyes, I reluctantly agreed.

In the quiet, cozy warmth of our stateroom, David and I snuggled for a while under the covers, savoring our special moments alone. But as David drifted off to sleep, I still felt as wide-eyed as an owl with insomnia. Disappointment nudged me when I heard David snoring soundly. Even as I lay still beside him staring at the ceiling, feeling my body waft with the gentle roll of the ocean, I felt as if I were missing the party. Surely now, in these romantic, twilight hours, the ship was just beginning to come alive. I wanted to be there, see it all, hear the music, be part of the celebration.

Suddenly the telephone jangled and I sprang instinctively to answer it. It was Jackie. "Michelle, I didn't wake you, did I?"

"No. I'm too excited to sleep," I whispered.

"Me too. Feel like going to the midnight buffet?"

"You're kidding! How can you even think of food at this hour?"

"I don't want to eat, I want to mingle, see the sights, *enjoy*! How about it? Shall we be as crazy-carefree as we were in college?"

"Oh, I love it, love it! Give me ten minutes to dress and touch up my face. Right now I look like someone in a headache commercial."

"Okay. Hurry. The room steward promised to look in on Stevie."

Jackie and I met at the purser's desk. We giggled like school-girls sneaking out to a forbidden party. "I'm going to be absolutely wicked and eat a chocolate éclair," said Jackie.

I touched her arm. "Wait. The ship's library is on the way. I'd like to stop by and pick up some reading material."

Jackie laughed. "Michelle, Michelle, I should have known you couldn't stay away from books for long. You win. Let's go."

We linked arms and sashayed through the nearly empty lobby, sharing silly reminiscences of our Hopewell days. "Remember when we put spray starch in Jill Monroe's hair-spray?" said Jackie.

"Do I ever! Her hair stood at attention for a week! And remember when we hid Moosie's mountain of junk food in the dorm supervisor's closet? She thought it was trash and tossed it out."

"Moosenbocker was fit to kill. Glad she didn't know we did it."

"You kidding? She knew. She had this inner sense. Weird. And do you know—you won't believe this, Jackie, but Moosie and Jill are here—on this ship—this very cruise."

"Oh, I can't imagine it! How do they look?"

"I've avoided them so far, but David was rather impressed with Jill. And Moosie—well, you know her. The same granite expression. She never changes." Our laughter echoed in the hollow corridor.

We rounded the corner by the dimly lit jewelry and apparel shops and passed the ship's theater. When we reached the library, we groaned in disappointment. It was closed, the room already darkened.

"All this way for nothing," I sighed.

"Oh, well, you can't hold books and éclairs at the same time."

I tried the door anyway and drew back in surprise when the knob turned. "It's open. Shall we?"

"You go in first," said Jackie. "I'm not much for dark rooms."

I inched the door open and reached inside along the wall for the light switch. It wasn't there. I could barely make out the rows of shadowed bookcases interspersed with glass-partitioned writing cubicles.

"Maybe we shouldn't, Michelle."

"Why not? I just want to borrow a book." I tiptoed inside, with Jackie close on my heels. Suddenly there was a clicking sound. A chill shot up my spine. *The room wasn't empty.* I strained my eyes through the duskiness. The sallow hall light carved a strange silhouette—the torso of a man, motionless, his face hidden by a bookshelf. All I could see was the man's broad chest, his tie hanging unevenly.

A low, muffled male voice said, "I will hunt you down. I will have my revenge."

My breath caught. I could feel the hair bristle on the nape of my neck. I backed out the door immediately, pushing Jackie into the hall. She was beginning to tremble. I grabbed her hand. "Come on, Jackie!" We began to run.

"Who was it, Michelle?"

"It wasn't the ship's librarian!"

We fled to Jackie's cabin and collapsed on the sofa, panting.

"Someone's after me, Michelle. I just know it." She put her face in her hands. "Steve was right. I never should have come."

"Don't say that, Jackie. What that man said—it didn't have anything to do with you."

"You don't know that, Michelle. I'm sure it's the syndicate. They're after me. They know where I am."

Fighting my own rising anxiety, I said, "I'm sure there's a perfectly logical explanation to this—some woozy tippler or a disgruntled passenger who lost too much at the gambling table."

I could tell by Jackie's expression that she wasn't convinced.

It was after 2:00 A.M. when I finally made my way stealthily back to my own stateroom. Every sound startled me. My heart raced as I approached an early-morning straggler. I recognized Brett Seaton, the astronaut, bounding toward me in his nimble gait. He smiled and said, "Enjoy the midnight buffet?"

"Never got there," I said.

He smiled. "Me neither."

*   *   *

On Sunday morning I tried to tell David what happened in the library the night before, but in the sunny light of day my suspicions sounded foolish, so I dropped the subject. Besides, David gave me his usual *humoring Michelle* look. But even as we joined the others in the dining room, I couldn't get the voice of that strange man in the library out of my mind. Who was he? What did he mean when he said, *I will hunt you down. I will have my revenge?* Who was his intended victim? Or was it all some bizarre misunderstanding?

After breakfast David, Jackie, and I walked up to the Sky Room for the Hopewell devotions. President Stoddard, wearing a three-piece navy-blue suit and gripping a well-worn Bible in his thick-knuckled hand, greeted the alumni and guests. Then he announced that he would play the recorded congratulatory message from the governor of the state. We waited in silence as he turned on the tape recorder. There was a garbled, squawking sound followed by static. Stoddard frowned, stopped the machine, started it again, and adjusted the volume. More static. Then, after a moment, a man's deep, sinister voice intoned:

Hopewell's honored have gathered for fun,
But one will die before this cruise is done.

There was dead silence in the room followed by a rippling murmur. Cold panic stirred inside me. That voice—it was strange, and yet oddly familiar. It could be—yes!—the man in the library!

President Stoddard turned off the recorder. "Ladies, gentlemen, there's obviously been some mistake. We must have picked up the wrong tape. We'll straighten this out and get back to you with the governor's message." He paused, as if weighing his words. "It appears that one of Hopewell's pranksters is playing a practical joke."

Jackie and I exchanged startled glances. *Did he mean us?*

"I urge all of you to forget what you just heard," Stoddard continued. "We don't want anything to dampen our celebration or mar Hopewell's reputation. Be assured we'll get to the bottom of this unfortunate little incident. Now, on with our program."

I couldn't concentrate after that. I had the sickening conviction that the anonymous speaker was dead serious. Something terrible was going to happen. I could see fear written in Jackie's face too.

After devotions, David, Jackie, and I lingered while the crowd dispersed. "I'm sure that message wasn't a joke, David," I said. "It was the same voice Jackie and I heard in the library last night."

Jackie nodded. "We heard a clicking sound. We may have walked in on the man as he was making that recording."

"We have to get hold of the tape, David. Maybe there's more that we didn't hear. It could be a whole blueprint for murder."

"Hold on, sweetheart. We have no proof that anything menacing is going on. Like Stoddard said, it could simply be a prank."

"No, David," said Jackie shakily. "I think someone's after me."

"But the poem threatened one of the honored four."

"It didn't exactly say that, David. It could be a camouflage, the cocaine syndicate's smoke screen to throw us off guard."

He frowned. "All right, let's listen to that tape again." We walked back to the speaker's platform. Stoddard was standing several feet from the lectern, chatting with passing alumni. David spoke briefly with him, then walked over to the tape recorder and snapped it open. He looked up, startled, and said, "The tape's gone, sir."

We rushed over and stared at the machine. Indeed, it was empty. "But who could have stolen the tape from under our noses?" I cried.

"This is most peculiar," said Stoddard. "It was just there."

I glanced around, scanning the crowd. It had to be someone in our own Hopewell group who could walk among us without arousing suspicion. But who? There were 250 of us. One of us was crazy.

"What do you make of it, Michelle?" asked President Stoddard.

"It—it could mean we should be on guard against foul play."

"Are you suggesting we warn people—?"

"At this point there's no need to incite panic," said David, "but perhaps Michelle and I could talk privately with the other honored alumni and find out if anyone is aware of any . . . enemies."

"Keep me informed, David. I'd rather not notify the captain unless it's necessary. After all, Hopewell's reputation . . ."

"I agree, sir," said David, "for the time being."

We talked a few minutes more, then headed back to our rooms.

"I've decided something, Michelle," said Jackie as we approached her cabin. "I'm going to avoid the crowds and spend more time in my room with Stevie—at least until this message thing is cleared up."

"That may be prudent," said David.

"Oh, Jackie, this weirdo—whoever he is—is spoiling your trip!"

"Don't worry, Michelle. I'm used to these sorts of—"

Suddenly a shrill, clanging bell pierced the air. I looked up questioningly at David.

"Boat drill, hon," he said. "Let's go get our life jackets."

We returned to our stateroom and pulled on bulky, lollipop-orange vests that made us look like matching life buoys. "Now I know why they call these Mae Wests," I said, grimacing in the mirror.

"You never looked lovelier," mused David.

"We're hideous!" I laughed, patting his styrofoam-padded chest.

With the bells still clanging, we took the stairs up to our lifeboat station and joined a hundred other bulging, bright orange Tweedledums lining the deck. "We look like a pumpkin patch!" I declared. When I spotted Brett Seaton and his wife standing nearby, I nudged David. We inched our way over to them. "Well, Colonel Seaton, I bet you never had to wear an outfit like this on a space flight."

He laughed. "You're right, Mrs. Ballard. But our space suits are considerably more complicated." He introduced his wife Candy and we chatted briefly. Then he said, "What did you think of this morning's little bombshell? Some governor's message, right?"

"It was a bit unnerving," I said. "In fact, David and I—"

The ship's officer signaled for silence, so we took our places in line and listened dutifully to his instructions. After the boat drill, David turned to Brett and said, "This may sound strange, but do you know of anyone who may hold a personal grudge against you?"

"I've been asking myself that since the mysterious message this morning, but I come up with a blank. Of course, I've received my share of letters from crackpots warning me to get out of the space program so the money could be given to the poor—"

Candy's finely drawn brows arched with concern. "That message has me petrified—and I don't scare easily. I don't mind danger when I know what it is, but this—! We may be dealing with a madman!"

"Then you think it's possible Brett has enemies?" asked David.

"Sure. It could be some disgruntled pilot who's jealous of Brett's success. Astronauts are an elite breed. The competition's fierce. Only the best make it. Most are rejected."

"I could have made enemies in Vietnam too," said Brett. "I was a strict, hard-nosed fighter pilot. Not macho and hard-drinking like some, but I was outspoken and unswerving about my convictions."

"You were in Nam? Me too!" said David. The two began talking at once, closing ranks on Candy and me. We exchanged knowing smiles.

They didn't wind down until I interrupted David and told him the Thatchers were heading our way. "We should ask them about the . . ."

"Right," said David. He stepped forward, casually intercepting Dr. Thatcher. "Good morning, doctor." We made introductions and chatted briefly, then David steered the conversation around to the ominous message. "Do you take the threat seriously, Dr. Thatcher?"

"It's pure poppycock," he scoffed. "Someone's idea of a hoax."

"That's quite possible," David agreed, "but then again—"

"Please don't be offended, Dr. Thatcher," I said. "We're asking all the honored alumni. Do you know anyone who might wish you harm?"

Thatcher's eyes narrowed and his nostrils flared. "Great Scott, I'm a physician! I heal people. I make friends, not enemies!"

"I'm sure that's true," I said, "but please think carefully—"

Noreen Thatcher straightened her slender shoulders as she gazed up at her husband. "Jason, dear, what about those threatening phone calls you received some months ago after you lost that one patient?"

Thatcher's deep voice rumbled irritably. "Don't be absurd, Noreen. That matter is over and done with. How can you suggest—?"

"You received threatening calls?" I prodded gently.

"They stopped weeks ago," snapped Thatcher.

"But you were worried, Jason," said Noreen. "Admit it. You haven't been yourself since. I know how upset the calls made you."

"Do you have any idea who made the phone calls?" asked David.

"Of course I know. I lost a young patient. The family was upset over losing their child. It was a perfectly natural reaction."

Noreen's high cheekbones colored slightly. "They blamed you for his death, Jason. They called you a murderer. That's not natural."

Dr. Thatcher stepped over to the railing. "I have better things to do than to worry about prank phone calls or crank messages."

I cast David a private glance, signaling that it was time to retreat. He nodded and said lightly, "Well, Michelle, we'd better head back to our room and get out of these life jackets. It'll be time for lunch before we know it."

I smiled tolerantly. "Heaven forbid you should miss lunch!"

After an exquisite lunch of fresh fruit and seafood salad, David and I went up to the boat deck for a little fresh air and sunshine. A cool sea breeze swept over the open deck, delighting us with its tingling bite. As David and I debated over a game of shuffleboard, I spotted Abigail standing by the small tennis court watching Seth slam tennis balls against the bulkhead. They both looked our way as David and I approached. "We missed you two at lunch," I said.

Seth shrugged. "We caught a couple of hamburgers on the Lido Deck . . . talked a bit."

"About this morning's taped message, by chance?" David asked.

"Partly." Seth juggled the tennis ball on his racket.

"What did you think of it?"

"I have more important things to worry about."

"So you think it's a hoax?"

"Stupid, at least."

"Well, I think it's more than a class prankster," I said.

Seth seemed amused. "Are you defending yourself, Michelle? Abigail tells me you were quite into things at college."

"I suppose I made a few waves. And you?"

"Same thing. No pranks, but I used humor for protection."

"Really, Seth? Now, me—I just didn't like the rules."

"And I didn't want anyone to know I came up from nothing."

"I don't understand."

His hand tightened on his racket. "It's a long story."

"We have time," I said seriously. I knew Seth Mueller wasn't a man who opened up easily, but I sensed a growing rapport among the four of us. It was subtle, but I could see that Abigail felt it too.

"Why don't we sit down and have some juice?" she suggested.

"Sounds good to me," I said. The four of us found a corner table in the Sunset Lounge and ordered fancy pineapple-orange drinks. Seth still had a half-amused smile on his face, a guarded expression that dared me to pick up the threads of his past. I proceeded cautiously, asking instead, "Tell me, Seth, did you know the other two honorees before the cruise?"

Seth relaxed a little. "Not Brett Seaton. But Dr. Jason Thatcher was ahead of us at Hopewell, wasn't he, Abigail?"

"A year or two. He was an ambitious, highly principled man."

"Yeah, always striving for perfection, even in track."

"A godly young man too," Abigail added.

"That, all right. He was a spiritual leader in the men's dorm my sophomore year. Dorm rep, of some sort too. I kept my distance."

"But the years have changed Jason," said Abigail. "When I talked to him last night, he didn't seem to be the same decisive, goal-oriented man he used to be. Oh, his wife Noreen thinks he is, but something's different."

"Different? What do you mean?" I asked.

"His health, for one thing. He's just not the same robust fellow I knew. He's so pale and drawn. He's more tense, too. Seems full of self-doubt. Not the kind of surgeon who would inspire me."

"Maybe he's just overworked," I suggested.

Seth looked over at David and said, "You and I should challenge Thatcher to a game of tennis. That'll put color in his cheeks."

After a few more minutes of conversation about tennis and Seth's career, I prompted him to finish the story he'd begun out on deck. He seemed reluctant at first, but then he settled back and said, "I grew up with a father who couldn't forget the Great Depression. I spent years swallowing his poverty image. Dad was always working odd jobs, blundering hopelessly through life." He twirled his glass. "I loved that man in spite of his weaknesses, but I vowed I'd never be like him. I'd make something of myself regardless of the cost. I wanted to succeed for both of us, make enough money so he could get out of his rat race and I could live in style."

"What about your mother?" I asked.

"Mom? She's dead."

"I'm sorry, Seth."

"So am I. She didn't live long enough to see me make it in tennis. Poverty stole her youth and beauty long before her time. She worked so hard but there was never enough food. I can still remember that gnawing gut hunger as though it were yesterday. Now every time I help a woman in a refugee camp, I think of Mom. She never had anything. I mean *anything*. And she never complained."

"You've always said she had her faith," Abigail said softly.

"Yeah, she had that—it's all she had."

"Then she had everything of real value," Abigail reminded him.

He eyed her curiously, then sucked in his lower lip as though biting off bitter words that hovered there.

After a moment, David said, "So what about it, Seth? Have you made any enemies along the way angry enough to hunt you down?"

"Sure, every man I ever beat on the tennis court. And maybe a few who think I wheel and deal too much to fund my missionary projects." He drained his glass. "People like me make enemies among predator nations who see developing countries as potential conquests. But I see these poor nations as starving families—like my own—who need food in their gut and Christ in their soul."

"It's a wonderful commitment, Seth," I said. "I admire you."

"Yes, it's a great cause, but it brings me my share of enemies."

"Then you suspect the threatening message was meant for you?"

"No, David. I'm not worth chasing to Alaska. If someone wants me dead, they've had countless opportunities. They could shoot me down in an airport or a refugee camp any time they please." Seth eyed David and me with a quiet scrutiny. "What about you two? Abigail says you've had some harrowing adventures with the international cocaine syndicate. It seems you'd be more at risk than I am."

"We haven't discounted that possibility," said David.

"And what about your friend, Jacqueline Marshall? She seems so aloof, so guarded. Abigail is tight-lipped about her, but I see the lady as someone who's running. Someone vulnerable. What about her?"

"She's not one of the honored alumni," I said defensively.

"And you don't think that message is a decoy?" he scoffed. "In a way we're all honored alumni. Even Abigail. Maybe she's at risk too." He reached down, picked up his racket, and brandished it on his shoulder like a weapon. "I'm going down and shower. Coming, Abigail? I'll give you those pictures of Thailand I promised you." He stood up and pulled back Abigail's chair, then gazed down at me. "Maybe you'd like to see those pictures, too, Michelle. They'd give you some background setting for the book I want you to write."

I noticed David stiffen. He stood up and said curtly, "Some other time, Seth. Michelle and I are taking a stroll before dinner."

Minutes later, as David and I walked along the boat deck, we talked about our conversations with the honored alumni. "Think about it, David. Seth, Thatcher, and Seaton—they're all very successful, but there's a strange undercurrent. Hopewell is honoring these men for what people *think* they are. But do we really know them? Maybe they've stepped on the wrong toes all along life's way. Or maybe someone finally intends to get even with them for their success."

"And have you stopped to think that maybe one of the honored alumni has a grudge against someone else on board?" said David.

"Really, David! If you're going to make silly accusations, you might as well accuse me, or suspect Abigail. Maybe she has it in for Seth for never marrying her. You know the saying, *A woman scorned—*"

David looked down at me, his dark eyes somber. "I've thought of that, Michelle. Believe me, I've thought of that."

We lapsed into silence after that. I felt depressed. So far this cruise wasn't going the way I'd anticipated. I wanted our days to be light hearted, carefree, fun, not bogged down in suspicion and intrigue. I looked up at David. "From now on, let's try to forget that taped message and concentrate on having a good time."

David pulled me against him. "Sounds like a winner to me."

So that evening at the Captain's Gala Welcome Aboard Dinner, neither of us mentioned the word *poem* . . . until Stephanie Ellis slipped over to our table and self-consciously handed me a worn notebook. "These are my—you said you wouldn't mind reading them—my poetry, I mean. They're not polished, but they're special to me."

"Of course they're special. I'll read them soon."

"Thank you, Mrs. Bal—uh, Michelle. I can't tell you what this means to me. I'm so eager to hear what you think of them."

"Well, Stephanie, like I said, I'm not really a critic—"

"It doesn't matter—not at all. I just need your opinion."

After she had gone back to her table, David leaned over and whispered, "I hope you can find something good to say about them."

"So do I," I sighed. "So do I!"

After dinner, David and I joined Jackie and Stevie in the Golden Sails Lounge for the American Theatre Jubilee presentation of "My Fair Lady." The bright, vigorous show tunes lifted my spirits—and David's. During the intermission he leaned over and whispered, "It's sure great to see little Stevie again." Slyly, deviously, he added, "You know, a cruise wouldn't be a bad place to start a baby."

I shot him my *come off it, David* look. I was in no mood to talk about babies. All I wanted was a happy, romantic holiday together.

"What's that look mean?" David challenged.

"It means I don't want to worry about anything more serious than whether to have cherries jubilee or baked Alaska for dessert . . . or what to wear in Ketchikan tomorrow."

David pulled me close and murmured in my ear, "Give me a chance, darling. Believe me, you'll like what I'm thinking about."

After the show we drifted out to the bow of the ship and kissed in the moonlight like new lovers just discovering each other. In David's arms I could almost change my mind about a baby.

"Ready to go to our stateroom?" he asked huskily.

I turned dreamily to the door, then stopped abruptly, clutching David's arm. Look, there in the shadows! Someone was watching us!"

David swiftly strode across the deck, looked around, then returned. "I didn't see anyone, hon. Maybe you imagined it."

"No, David. I know what I saw. Someone was right there."

"Well, he's gone now. Let's go inside. You're shivering."

I slept fitfully that night. In my dreams I ran from passenger to passenger, seeking the intended victim of the ominous poem. Everyone I encountered turned the question back to me: *What about you, Michelle? Are you the one to die before this cruise is done?*

I awoke at daybreak in a cold sweat. I climbed out of bed, but my legs turned to rubber under me. When I finally found my sea legs again, a wave of nausea sent me running to the john. "Of all times to get seasick," I muttered as I swayed back to my bed.

David sat up and eyed me groggily. "What's the matter, hon?"

"Nothing. Just a little—" Suddenly I noticed the ship's daily schedule on the floor by the door. I retrieved it, only to discover a note underneath. A ripple of horror turned my skin cold as I read the neatly lettered poem:

> Leave the ship and think you're free,
> but Hopewell's best can't hide from me.

My hand shook as I handed David the message. As he scanned it, his eyes flamed. He stalked over, tore open the cabin door, and stared up and down the corridor. "No one!" he said.

I was still trembling as he stepped back inside and picked up the phone. He dialed, shook his head impatiently, then dialed again. "Hello, Thatcher? This is David Ballard." David's voice was low, controlled. "Did you get—? I see . . . yes, we did too."

After making a third call, David crossed the room and took my hands in his. "Seth wasn't in. But the Thatchers and Seatons both got the same message. Seaton is furious. He agrees with me. We're going to track this madman down."

"And Jason and Noreen? What did they say?"

"Noreen wants to get off the ship in Ketchikan and fly home."

"What about us, David?" I whispered. "I'm scared."

He hugged me reassuringly. "I don't think anyone's after us. The syndicate wouldn't play cat and mouse like this. Whoever it is, Michelle, like in Nam, I won't run from an unseen enemy."

"Then what will we do?"

David heaved a sigh. "I don't know, Michelle. I honestly don't know. But for starters, we'll go into Ketchikan for the day, like we planned."

CHAPTER
SIX

At eight A.M. the S.S. *Mendenhall* dropped anchor in the picturesque harbor at Ketchikan. Outside our window I glimpsed the gloomy overcast and heard the clamor of crewmen barking orders as they lowered the tenders. The ship no longer swayed, but my own sense of balance was still in motion. I felt mildly nauseated. Breakfast hadn't helped. I marked it off to anxiety over the latest threatening message.

David grabbed our windbreakers and urged me out of the stateroom and up the stairwell to the passenger line. Moments later, we were on a small motorized vessel cutting across Tongass Narrows, breaking a watery pathway toward the shore.

Ketchikan was a bustling community steeped in velvety green hills with Indian totems towering like bright, finely carved telephone poles. The town was squeezed against the base of dark-jade Deer Mountain, with only a wide stretch of water for a front yard. Ketchikan's fishing fleet—colorful boats of all sizes, small float planes, and helicopters—bobbed in the water. The business district edged the shoreline, with the burnished-gold Temsco building, the Air Service terminal, and a bulging logging bay to our right.

"Oh, David, it's so quaint and rustic. I love it already!"

The young seaman standing near me grinned. "She's a neat town," he said fondly. "You can see her all in a day—but you won't know her. You'll have to come back again and again for that."

At the floating dock, the seaman tossed a rope to secure our vessel. Then he reached for my hand and helped me step off the tender. "Have a good time, miss. She's a cloudy day but the folks here take pride in their rainfall. Don't let a downpour stop you."

We hurried up the slanting gangway, past the barnacle-crusted pilings to the pier of Ketchikan with its weather-beaten timber walkway and wood-framed flower boxes.

Just steps from the pier we boarded the first motorcoach and slipped into seats only two rows in front of Jill Monroe and Erma Moosenbocker. As soon as the coach was loaded, the friendly, balding driver took off, shimmying the bus to the left on a narrow, two-way street. He shot through the town's only signal light at Dock and Front Street and roared on through the crowded business district past century-old stone-edged buildings. As we rode along, I caught glimpses of picturesque curio shops, Indian art and craft stores, the Trading Post, and the pale-pink Gilmore Hotel. Bearded sourdoughs in flannel shirts and faded jeans made their way into local pubs. Steep wooden walkways zigzagged from the center of town toward quaint, colorful old homes perched precariously on the hillsides.

We drove around the waterfront, catching the pungent smells of pulp mills and salmon canneries, then wended our way past towering spruce, mountain ash with red berries, and barren cedar. Wide, fanlike roots of fallen trees edged the road. Finally we arrived at a secluded mountain lake where huge bronzed canoes bobbed at the wharf.

"We're not taking one of those, David!" I cried, distraught at the dismal prospect of paddling across the lake in a flimsy canoe.

"We sure are taking one," he teased, "unless you want to walk back and meet me in town." He raised his hand to the soft drizzling rain. "It doesn't matter if the canoe tips—we're already wet."

"I'm not worried about *wet*. I'm worried about drowning!"

A guide in slick yellow trousers and a sleeveless shirt handed us some rain gear. David chuckled as he helped me into an oversized poncho and secured my bright pumpkin-orange life jacket. As he thrust a canoe paddle into my hand, I stared down at my sloppy outfit and rubber boots. *Ugly!* I looked pregnant. In fact, I looked round as a rain barrel—just like Erma Moosenbocker, who was already galumphing toward our canoe. I gasped in dismay. Surely Erma would topple us in the water before we had time to paddle away from the wharf. The guide arched his brows, studying Erma as if tipping an imaginary scale. "Let's put you in first, miss," he told her.

The canoe dipped low in the water as Erma stepped in, balancing unsteadily then dropping with a shudder onto the bench. The young man's lips curled in half a grin. "Okay," he said. "Next."

I found myself sitting behind Erma and thinking giddily, *Moosie's so wide-bodied, maybe she'll block the rainfall.* I felt smitten at once, ashamed. Was I still holding a grudge against this poor girl for having me campused so long ago? I shot up a quick prayer for forgiveness, my heart suddenly tender.

As the canoe slipped from its berth, Erma made a strange, gurgling sound. She sat rigid with fear. I reached out and touched her shoulder. "This will be fun, Moo—I mean, Erma. Wait and see."

She shifted her bulky frame. "You kidding? I can't even swim."

"You mean you never learned?"

"No way. You think I'd appear in public in a swimsuit? In case you haven't noticed, I don't have your trim figure, Michelle."

I backed off promptly, feeling as dispirited as the bleak, murky clouds pressing in on us. The rain was pelting us now, the waves tossing our canoe like a toy boat. I looked at David's rain-drenched face and said, "If someone wanted to get rid of us, this lake is sure the spot to do it."

"You don't mean Erma?" he mouthed.

I wasn't sure if he was serious or not. Was Erma a threat?

Gradually, the choppy waves eased into a gentle roll. I stopped paddling and gazed in fascination at the hazy green rain forest surrounding the lake. As our canoe glided in a rhythmic pattern toward the opposite shore, the sun stole from behind a cloud, casting a fleeting glimmer on the rippling water.

As we reached the beach, our guide jumped out into shallow water and tugged the canoe ashore. I was stiff as I stepped onto the hard-packed sand. While our guide unloaded an ice chest, David and I watched four other canoes forge a twisting, snake-like path toward us. Finally, when everyone had settled on shore, the guides spread delicacies out on the ice chests. Erma was the first in line. She sloshed back toward us in her boots, her pudgy hands full of salmon chunks and cheese and crackers. She smiled tentatively at me, as if she weren't quite sure how the two of us should relate to each other. Our former roles of strict dorm monitor and campused student weren't relevant anymore. But how did Erma feel about me now? Did she consider me an enemy or a friend? When she offered me a chunk of her salmon, I hoped that perhaps she was calling a truce.

* * *

Later that afternoon, with the sky clearing, David and I strolled leisurely through Ketchikan, browsing among the curio shops. Then we made our way toward Creek Street—a ragged string of rustic houses teetering on spindly pilings over a raging stream. As we crossed a rickety bridge, I stared down in fascination at the salmon coursing through the rushing water and over the slippery, moss-covered rocks beneath us. We sauntered along the cramped, historic Creek Street Boardwalk, past quaint old shake-and-board buildings with warped windows and drooping porches. We stopped at the Portrait Parlor, a rusty-brown building with a sign boasting "Old-Time Photos While You Wait."

David took my hand. "Come on, Michelle. Let's get a picture for our grandchildren."

Laughing self-consciously, we posed in a gold-rush setting, David in Western garb and I in a ruffled, off-the-shoulder dress and feathery plumed hat. We were still grinning ridiculously when Stephanie Ellis poked her head in the door and exclaimed, "Oh, Cameron, look! The Ballards!"

Cam entered and greeted us politely. He looked attractively rough-hewn in his dark corduroy trousers and checkered jacket—like a rugged, native sourdough very much at home in the Alaskan frontier.

Stephanie slipped past him and said, "Michelle, would you and David like to join us as we explore the rest of Creek Street?"

Cam eyed David knowingly. "I'm heading for Dolly's House. How can a man say he's been to Ketchikan without seeing Dolly's?"

I looked questioningly at David. "Dolly's House?"

"Dolly was the infamous madam of Ketchikan. Creek Street was once a red-light district, Michelle."

"Oh, but now these houses are museums, shops, and galleries," Stephanie added hastily. "I'm finding them quite captivating—"

"We'd love to join you," I said.

We took the guided tour through Dolly's House—a charming, green two-story with red-and-white trim. The cluttered, boldly painted rooms were enchanting, irresistible. I was fascinated by the bright rose-flowered wallpaper, the abundance of doilies and knickknacks, the antique Monarch stove, and the sparkling dishes made from gold dust soap. I felt as if I had stepped back into the musty, baroque gaudiness of the 1930s. My mind whirled with story possibilities.

David nudged me. "Don't get any redecorating ideas, hon."

"Oh, David, don't be a spoilsport," I teased. "I was mentally refurbishing your office with Dolly's favorite patterns and prints!"

He grimaced. "My grandmother had a place like Dolly's."

"Oh, David, no! You're kidding!"

He gave me a scolding frown. "No, I mean *decorated* the same!"

After leaving Dolly's, we stopped at June's Cafe, where the men ordered hamburgers and I toyed with a bowl of chili I didn't want. "Are you enjoying the cruise so far?" I asked Cam conversationally.

"Today I am, but sometimes I wonder what we even came for."

"The cruise was your idea, dear," Stephanie said softly.

Sensing unexpected conflict brewing, I said brightly, "I'm looking forward to reading your poetry, Stephanie."

She looked at me, her eyes suddenly pleading. "Oh, it means so much to me, Michelle. I can't begin to tell you. . . ."

The urgency in Stephanie's voice unsettled me. I sensed that more was at stake than the literary quality of her work. But my attention was diverted back to David and Cam when Cam said, "Who can figure those weird threats to the Hopewell alumni? All I can say is, if I'd known there'd be some kook on board, we wouldn't have come."

"Well, let's not forget it could all be a prank," said David.

"Oh, no," said Stephanie, "I'm afraid it's very serious."

Cam nodded. "The astronaut said—you know, what's his name—?"

"You mean Brett Seaton?" said David.

"Yeah, that's his name. He tells me he thinks the threatening poems are from some Hopewell graduate who feels snubbed, angry that he didn't get honored for his accomplishments."

"I just hope that's all it is," said Stephanie.

"Well, President Stoddard wants us to keep this whole thing very low-key," I said. "He doesn't want to risk Hopewell's reputation."

Cam drummed his fingers on the table. "You can't kill a reputation, Michelle," he said obliquely. "You have to go further."

"I don't understand."

He gazed at me, a peculiar light in his eyes. "Nothing. I was thinking of something someone said to me in Vietnam years ago."

"You were in Nam?" said David. "What year?"

"Late sixties. I was a Marine. Still wet behind the ears. With a wife and young son at home. I went to win a war, but I grew up fast in that hellish conflict. It changed my whole life."

"Mine too," said David. "Actually, in some ways, for the better." He touched the jagged scar along his chin. "I came out physically scarred but alive spiritually."

Cam looked sullen. "It didn't do that for me. I figured God didn't have time for a bunch of Marines in a place like Vietnam."

"Really?" said David. "I'm convinced that God is interested in every aspect of our lives, no matter where we are."

"Not me," snapped Cam. "I was off in the rice paddies trying to figure what I was doing there. That war robbed me of two years of my kid's life." Cam struck at the flooring with one tan hiking boot and uttered an oath. "Maybe you had a hero's welcome home, Ballard. I didn't. When I got back from Nam, they were kicking us in the teeth for fighting a losing war. I felt old, cheated of my youth. My kid didn't even know me. If it hadn't been for Steph—"

"Oh, Cam, you more than made up for your years away from us. And you gave all you had to our son. Rodney adored you."

"Yeah, I did my best to stay close to my son," Cam said, his somber expression partially hidden behind his gray-flecked beard. "The boy and I hunt a lot—just the two of us, alone. Steph rarely joins us. She doesn't like sleeping out and fighting mosquitoes."

"Or climbing mountains," Stephanie added, touching Cam's hand.

"It was just me and my boy," Cam reminisced.

"Not the last time, Cam. Rodney had his best friend with him."

"Yeah, I remember. Kent somebody—a guy he'd gone to law school with. Worked in the same office. I didn't like his looks."

"You didn't give Kent a chance, Cam, dear."

"The fellow was an intruder." Cam's deep-set eyes became pebbles of charcoal—beady and cold. "Rodney and I planned to do some hunting in Canada this summer. We had it all worked out. . . ."

"The summer's not over," I noted. "You still have time."

Cam's voice took on a strange intonation. "You bet. All the time in the world." His fingers continued their nervous rat-a-tat on the table.

"Do you have other children, Cam?" I asked.

"No, just Rodney. He's . . . our whole life."

"Did he go to Hopewell?"

"He's a Stanford graduate. Law school. Real smart."

"Is he married?" I asked.

Cam stole a glance at Stephanie. "No, he's not married."

I realized suddenly that Stephanie hadn't said a word. Why wouldn't she talk about her child, her only son? When I met her gaze, her eyes were crying out for help. But why? What was so painful that she could express it only in a silent, wordless entreaty?

Even after the Ellises left us minutes later to do some souvenir hunting at the Trading Post, I couldn't get Stephanie's haunted expression out of my mind. I turned impulsively to David and said, "Darling, let's get back to the ship."

"Already? Why? We have plenty of time before we sail."

"Please, David. I just feel like relaxing and . . ."

"Oh, really? Relaxing, huh? That sounds good to me."

"That's not what I mean, David," I scolded. "I feel like relaxing . . . and reading Stephanie's poetry."

*   *   *

As it turned out, David and I arrived back on the ship just in time to shower and dress for dinner. Stephanie's poetry would have to wait. But all through our meal, I was constantly distracted by thoughts of Cam and Stephanie. I studied the large gulf stream shrimp that sizzled in front of me, buttered and tempting. I poked without appetite at the curry dip sauce on the crisp garden vegetables.

"What's wrong, Michelle?" David asked.

"I guess I'm not hungry. Just tired."

"We could skip dessert," he said, lightly rubbing my arm.

"I'd like that."

His eyes danced merrily. "And we could skip the dinner show—just go back to our stateroom."

"Let's," I agreed. I figured it would be good just to curl up in bed, relax, and take a look at Stephanie's poetry.

But we'd no sooner stepped into our stateroom when David put out the DO NOT DISTURB sign and clicked the double latch.

"What's that all about?" I asked.

David arched a mischievous brow. "You've been with me a year and don't know?" He was already whipping off his tie and unbuttoning his shirt. He drew near and gently unzipped the back of my dress. "You've got sunburned shoulders," he mused, kissing my bare back.

While David was in the bathroom, I slipped into my lace nightgown, pushed the pillows against the headboard, and sat propped up in bed reading. David came out smelling pleasantly of after-shave and climbed into the king-size bed beside me. He reached for the poems. "I didn't skip dessert for you to read to me, Michelle," he said in his deeply seductive voice.

I held the poems fast. "No, David. Wait. Listen. The Ellises don't seem especially religious, but it sounds here like their son Rodney knows something about God."

> You came home,
> My son, saying,
> *"God."*
> Not swearing,
> but praying.
> And I
> wondered.
> Wondered.
> Would it pass?
> Would it last?

"Strange," said David. "What's Stephanie trying to say?"
"I'm not sure, David. It's intriguing. Listen to this one."

> You strolled across the stage
> confident, with jaunty step
> in cap and gown.
> You—ready to conquer the world
> and hang your law degree.
> We, your parents—bursting with love and pride.
> Then for a moment
> you turned our way and waved.
> But something in your eyes
> was not glad.
> But sad, troubled.
> Deep inside
> my bursting pride
> shattered,

scattered.
This had been our dream,
our goal, our expectation.
Your dad's and mine.
But somewhere
along the way,
your dreams,
your music,
your lyrics
had lost
their lilting melody.

David leaned up on one elbow. "Sounds like Cam Ellis and his wife don't quite agree."

"What do you mean?"

"The way Cam talked today, his son was gung ho to be a lawyer."

"You're right, David. But Stephanie paints him so sensitive . . . musical . . . sad. It doesn't sound like he wanted to be a lawyer at all."

I turned several pages and read aloud:

My hunters,
broad-shouldered, masculine.
Two men like boys
rushing off
to favorite places
with fishing gear or rifles
or packs on their backs.
Climbing heights,
tracking deer,
scaling fish
together.
   They've memorized
   each mountain trail,
   each fishing stream
   and never seem to tire
   of chatting at the campsite,

surrounded by the smells
of the woods and smoke
and trout sizzling over an open fire.
My hunters
at home in the forest—
like chips of wood
carved from the same sturdy tree.
Two peas in a pod,
twin mountain peaks,
a double-imaged profile.
So much alike.
So different.

I paused, suddenly self-conscious. These poems were such intimate glimpses of Stephanie's family life, such personal vignettes. I felt like an intruder stepping in where I wasn't invited, where I didn't belong. It was obvious that the Ellises' son Rodney was their whole life. And apparently at times even Stephanie didn't feel as if she belonged. It was simply father and son.

"Come on," David urged. "We've got better things to do."

"Please, not now, David. I want to read."

He ran his fingers gently along the nape of my neck, then nibbled at my ear.

"Oh, David," I sighed, weakening. "Please wait. There are just a few more poems."

He drew me against him. "We're on a cruise, darling. Whatever happened to shipboard romance?"

I ran my hand teasingly over his chest. "You'll have romance, David. As soon as I finish Stephanie's poems."

David lay back and folded his arms sulkingly. "You're reading too much into them, Michelle. They're just a mother's rambling sentiments for her son. Bordering on the obsessive, if you ask me."

"Maybe you're right, David. Listen to this one."

If I could see you
but once more, my son,

and trace the strong, sturdy
Grecian outline
of your face—

If I could clasp
within my hands
your stubborn chin
and watch the laughter-ripples
slowly begin—

If I could look into your dusky eyes
dark, ginger brown,
and see the budding faith
and the secrets that deeply
troubled me—

If I could hold you close
like a child
and let you rest
your troubled, burdened soul
against my breast
   so that your heart and mine
   would beat once more as one,
   I would give anything, everything
   to do this again, my son.
If I could gently trace
each line, each angle
of your gold-tanned face—
   the shadowed beard,
   the deep-cleft chin—
   erase your angry scowl,
   coax out a dimpled grin,
   gaze into your solemn eyes
   so like your dad's,
   and rumple your tousled, unruly hair
   and whisper the mother love
   I hold within my heart.

But thoughts and dreams and love
are caught like early autumn leaves,

brown and withered before their time,
dropping, fluttering to the ground
   soundlessly,
   soundlessly.
And even before I can pick them up
they blow away like memories
tossed, twirling,
caught in soundless, chilling wind
and always, always
like winter wrens
they wing out of my reach.
   My son,
   I stand alone
   a barren tree . . .
   empty,
   empty
   and weep.

I put Stephanie's poems aside and swallowed hard over a lump in my throat. I realized I was reading a mother's deepest heart cries, and they had moved me to tears. I looked down at David. He was no longer listening. He lay in a deep, relaxed sleep, stretched out beside me, his bare, bronzed chest moving evenly up and down. "Oh, my dear David." I shifted slightly and turned back to Stephanie's poetry. I felt my throat tighten again as I read her last entry.

Dear son,
that last time together
it was just the three of us.
We wanted it that way—
to be together one more time.
I thought,
How could it be you
so thin, so wasted?
So still. Your best suit
hanging loose, ill-fitting.
Your gaunt face waxen-gray.

And I noticed
that the perpetual frown,
the scowl between your eyebrows
was gone.
Then, with hopeless finality
the door between us closed.
We could no longer see you.
Could not touch your hand.
We followed the narrow path
clinging to each other
and stopped blindly
on the manicured hillside,
alone.
No neighbors. No friends.
No business colleagues.
No curious onlookers
except the workmen
standing at a polite
distance from us,
leaning on their shovels,
shifting restlessly,
waiting to toss sand pebbles
your way.
There was no music, dear son.
No minister. No message.
Just our troubled, desperate
whispered good-bye.
I tried to remember
David's Psalm,
the one you taught me.
Phrases came back:
"My Shepherd . . . still waters,
valley of shadows . . .
house of the Lord . . ."
I mumbled the Psalm
and your dad shook,
a deep, dry sob.
But no tears.

He will not cry.
Then in a split second
the hovering clouds darkened.
Lightning pierced the sky.
Thunder roared
and you did not hear us
say good-bye.

"I don't understand," I said aloud to David's sleeping form. "Just today Cam Ellis said his son lives in San Francisco, works in a law office there. But if these poems are true, then Rodney Ellis is dead. But why would Cam Ellis lie? Or are the poems symbolic?" I closed the worn notebook and ran my hand over the title page: TO MY SON: RODNEY CAMERON ELLIS, JR.

Was there a family rift? I wondered. *A temporary separation? Or was there another child—a dead son the Ellises didn't talk about?*

Regardless of what David said, I knew that Stephanie Ellis was trying to tell me something. Was she asking for help? Warning me?

Tomorrow I'd find out. Somehow.

I dropped the notebook on the floor beside the bed, suddenly aware of the rolling sway of the ship. I sank down into the pillows and nestled against David, feeling a deep yearning for his comfort, his loving touch. "Are you asleep, David?" I whispered.

"No, just pretending," he murmured groggily.

"Come on, darling, wake up. It's early yet."

He stirred slightly. "What do you want, Michelle?"

"I want to talk."

He groaned. "About what?"

"About how much I love you."

His eyes opened lazily. "Oh, Michelle . . . not now."

My arms circled him. "Now, David," I said enticingly.

CHAPTER
SEVEN

The next morning—our first Tuesday on board ship—Jackie and I decided to don our swimsuits and catch some sun on the enclosed sun deck. We stretched out on lounge chairs in a private corner and watched Stevie Jr. splash and play in the children's pool.

Jackie and I were still both on edge over the mysterious threats, but since there was nothing we could do about them at the moment, I steered the conversation to other topics. "So tell me what it's like, Jackie, to have a new baby in the house again."

Jackie threw up her hands helplessly and laughed. "It's like starting all over. Diapers and spit-up and midnight feedings!"

"Then . . . it's not something you would recommend."

"Oh, I didn't mean that, Michelle. I adore little Becky. I wouldn't trade her for the world. Just wait. You'll know what I mean someday."

"Yeah, I—I've been thinking about that lately."

Jackie leaned forward and shouted at Stevie, "Stop splashing that little girl, young man, hear me?" Then she gazed quizzically at me. "Michelle, are you trying to tell me something? You're not—"

"Pregnant? Oh, no, not yet anyway. But David and I have talked about a baby. Actually, he's done most of the talking so far."

"Don't you want a baby, Michelle?"

"Well, sure . . . someday. But we've only been married a year."

"It'll change your whole life, you know."

"So I've heard. Maybe that's what I'm afraid of."

"You *are* afraid, aren't you? I thought nothing scared you."

"You kidding? After all we've been through, you know better."

"I know you've never run away from your fears."

"Is that what you think I'm doing now?"

"Are you?"

I ran my finger along the metal armrest. "I don't know, Jackie. I like kids, and I really do want a child of my own. But I'm not sure this is the time. I mean, I don't even *feel* motherly."

Jackie chuckled. "That comes when the nurse lays your baby in your arms the first time. All these incredible emotions hit you."

I caught the light and warmth in Jackie's eyes. I'd never considered her the maternal type either, so maybe there was hope for me. "You really do love being a mother, don't you, Jackie?"

Her eyes glistened. "It makes you more vulnerable than you can ever imagine, Michelle. Suddenly you're totally responsible for this helpless little person. You feel such an outpouring of love—it's almost physical—and yet you're overwhelmed too, knowing there are ties between you that will last forever. Raising a child is such a mixture of terror and ecstasy, but it's worth the cost, Michelle."

I felt a sob rise in my throat. "David wants a son so badly. And now, seeing little Stevie has only intensified his desire—"

"It has to be *your* desire, too, Michelle. When *you're* ready—"

"How do I know when I'm ready? Oh, Jackie, this probably sounds selfish, but all I can think about now is my writing career. I have so many ideas, so many dreams, so many projects whirling in my mind."

"David will understand. He's been supportive of your career."

I nodded. "But he's older than I am and ready for a family. He doesn't understand that a baby will end *my* career, not *his*."

"It doesn't have to be that way, Michelle. Knowing you, you'll find a way to write with a baby in one hand and a pen in the other. And even if you can't write for a while, remember, you can put a price on a book, but you can't put a price on a child."

"Oh, Jackie, you almost convince me."

"Oh, no, don't let me talk you into it. We're talking lifetime commitment here. I don't want you coming back in five years and saying, 'Look what you got me into!' " Jackie's attention was diverted by a sudden squeal. She looked over at Stevie standing by the pool and scolded, "Give the little girl back her rubber ducky, young man! You've got your own toys. And don't you dare spit water at that nice lady! You behave or I'm marching you right back to the cabin!" Jackie looked back at me and laughed. "See what you have to look forward to, Michelle?"

We were silent a moment before I asked, "Has it been easier since you and Steve went to live with your parents in Switzerland?"

"Well, Stevie rarely has trouble with his asthma anymore."

"That's great, but what I really meant was, what's it like living under the government's witness protection program?"

Jackie's face clouded. "I still hate the deception, the isolation. I don't know how I'd survive without my parents. They're so good with the kids, and I think they're even beginning to forgive Steve for his involvement with the cocaine syndicate. They see the toll it's taken on him to testify against the mob."

"The toll it's taken on all of you," I murmured.

"That's why I had to get away, even for just this short time, Michelle. You know me. I'm a free spirit at heart. I can't let the government or any syndicate rule my life. I'd rather die than live in fear." Jackie drew in a deep breath of resignation. "But I see now that I shouldn't have come on this cruise. It was a mistake. I may be putting other people's lives in jeopardy."

"Listen, Jackie. We have no proof that those threatening rhymes are anything other than a very stupid practical joke."

"Is that what you really believe, Michelle?"

"I'm trying to, Jackie. Until someone proves otherwise. David insists we go ahead with all our planned activities, so we'll go into Juneau this afternoon when the ship docks. Want to come with us?"

"You know I can't go ashore, Michelle. I promised Steve."

"I know. I understand. You're a brave lady, my friend."

Jackie twisted her wedding ring. "I do what I have to do, Michelle. God has given me the strength—and the peace."

"You've come a long way since college," I noted.

Jackie nodded. "I had no time for God then, but now I'm just so grateful that God has time for me. He's become so real to me this past year during all our difficulties—fleeing Solidad, resettling in Switzerland, having Rebecca, trying to make a new life without acknowledging our past, wondering if the mob would catch up with us."

I reached over and squeezed Jackie's hand. "My problems seem small now compared with yours. Just remember, I'm here for you."

Jackie smiled. "Michelle, I'm so glad we're together again."

"Me too. Besides David, you're the best part of this trip."

"Something else that's blessed me, Michelle," said Jackie, "is President Stoddard's devotions from 1 John. I've been so hungry for good teaching from the Scriptures. Steve and I don't have a home church, you know, so I really—" Jackie's words hung unfinished as a commotion erupted beside the children's pool. Stevie was chasing two little girls round and round, delighting in their squeals. Jackie jumped up and shouted, "Steven Turman—uh, I mean *Marshall*—stop that right now!" She looked back at me and shrugged helplessly. "See, Michelle? I can't even keep track of who we're supposed to be!"

All I could do was shake my head in mute sympathy.

As Jackie took little Stevie firmly in tow, I gazed around at the gorgeous scenery. The dark, looming mountains with their frosty caps cast a surrealistic mirror image in the chill sea, creating a crystalline wonderland. Utterly breathtaking! Suddenly I realized that the S.S. *Mendenhall* was slowly edging toward the dock in Juneau. I studied the colorful city couched against ebony, pine-studded hills. The clustered buildings looked like a finely crafted village laid out by a model railroad enthusiast. "It's incredible, Jackie. Such rugged, untouched beauty. I can't wait to explore Juneau!"

Jackie led Stevie over to the panoramic windows and pointed out the shoreline. "See that, Stevie? Isn't it pretty? That beautiful city is the capital of Alaska."

"Can we go there, Mommy?"

"We can't leave the ship, honey."

"Why not, Mommy?"

"We promised Daddy we wouldn't." Jackie turned to me. "Michelle, when are you and David going ashore?"

We're meeting Abigail and Seth at four for the flight to Taku Glacier Lodge for dinner."

"Can I go with Aunt Michelle and Uncle David?" begged Stevie.

"No, Tiger. You and I will go to the Lido Deck for ice cream."

* * *

Shortly after four, David and I and Abigail and Seth disembarked for our Wilderness Lodge Adventure. Gingerly we stepped from the ship's gangplank onto the sleek seaplane. Minutes later we were airborne. Our seaplane dipped low, winging in the shadows of snow-shrouded mountains where moose and mountain goats roamed freely on the sheer cliffs. Then we soared over a mass of solid, crusty glaciers with their emerald-lined crevasses and dusky-gray peaks. Forty miles north of Juneau, the pilot skimmed the verdant green wilderness and landed our plane on the Taku River. A few seals and land otters sunned on a nearby sandbar oblivious of the frigid air.

As David helped me step from the seaplane to the floating dock, we caught the tempting aroma of king salmon sizzling over alderwood coals on an open grill. Our path cut across a plush green lawn past the cook in his high-top chef cap. He grinned, flipped a fillet like a pancake, then basted the fish with a sauce he said was made of brown sugar, butter, dry white wine, and lemon juice. He nodded ahead toward the remote Taku Lodge. "Dinner in a few minutes," he said.

We strolled past a strawberry patch to the picturesque lodge, awestruck by the bleak beauty of the frost-riven mountains, the aqua-blue glaciers and lush forests surrounding us.

Inside, the main dining room boasted a large stone fireplace and a high cedar beam ceiling, its rustic walls decorated with bearskins and mounted animal heads. The smoky aroma of salmon filled the room.

When the hostess invited us to take our seats, I sat down beside Abigail and across from David and Seth at a table spread with golden-grilled salmon, homemade baked beans, sourdough bread, and pineapple-coleslaw salad. I turned to Abigail and noticed her childlike glow as she gazed across the table at Seth, her gray-blue eyes beaming. He flashed her a disarming smile.

I kept thinking, *Is this really my Hopewell English prof— the brilliant, sedate, always rational Abigail Chadwick?* I remembered her as unswervingly well-balanced and in control—an intensely dedicated person wrapped up in research and in the lives of her students.

But she sat now like a flustered schoolgirl caught in her first teenage crush. I studied the two of them. Would Abigail give up her 20 years of teaching at Hopewell for the inscrutable Seth Mueller? As much as I was charmed by Seth, I didn't fully trust him. Was his interest in Abigail monetary . . . or momentary? He arched a shaggy brow, his curious, cunning eyes as blue as the cloudless sky behind Taku Lodge. Then he tapped his fingers on the table and chuckled.

"Why are you laughing, Seth Mueller?" Abigail asked him.

"I was thinking about our junior year at Hopewell—when we met."

"In the school library?"

He nodded. "I was struggling with a term paper. Remember? Then I looked up and caught your eyes."

Abigail blushed, and I mused, —*He caught more than your eyes, dear Abigail. He stole your heart.*

Seth was saying, "I told Abigail, 'Term papers won't get me into pro tennis.' "

"You didn't whisper it either," Abigail reminded him. "You boomed out your frustrations for all the world to hear."

"And you went, 'Sh-h-h. Maybe I can help you.' After that, whenever I had to do a term paper, I went hunting for you, Abigail."

Abigail twirled the emerald ring Seth had given her in their youth. "That was such a long time ago," she sighed.

"Yeah," he agreed. "Twenty-five years."

But from the wistful look on Abigail's face, I knew it could have been just yesterday.

For a moment Seth was silent, his expression clouded. "I really did intend to keep in touch, Abigail, but the years just slipped by." Then, as he filled his platter, Seth turned to me. "I've been reading your book on Rob Thornton, Michelle. Abigail lent me her copy. I like your style." Between bites of succulent salmon, he went on. "How about it? Can you go back to Thailand with me? Say spend two or three weeks there?"

"Just like that?" I asked, snapping my fingers. "No preparation? Just hop a plane and go with you?"

"I'm serious, Michelle. You could do a human interest story on the refugee camps—not the filth and the pain, but the heart of it all, the people."

"You are serious!" I shot a hasty glance at David.

The scar along his chin pulsated. "Surely you're not simply interested in promoting Michelle's career?" he said coolly.

Seth put his fork down and rested his chin on his doubled fist. "No, it would be to my advantage too. I need the publicity. The book would serve as a fund-raiser."

"Then you see a book primarily as a means of raising money?"

"I'll do anything for funds to feed the world's hungry," Seth declared. "Play tennis. Campaign. Beg." His voice was sharp, his gaze suddenly cold. "Anything," he repeated.

For the past hour we had felt so relaxed—a glacier away from the pressing threats aboard ship. Now an uneasiness crept into our conversation, an unsettling mood dampening our conviviality. Seth was obviously a man of deep inner convictions, but he was also a private, guarded man. Had the news media been right? Was there a certain ruthlessness in Seth's approach to his missionary cause? An insensitive mannerism that drove people away? I sensed that in seconds Seth could be either victim or villain, friend or foe. Was Abigail's love for Seth so blind that she didn't know he had enemies?

David picked up the fish platter and abruptly forked another fillet. His resistance to Seth only spurred me on.

"Why a book on Thailand? That's not the only place you go."

"I know," Seth answered, more mellow now. "But you already have a special interest in that country. Wasn't that where they found your friend Rob Thornton?"

"Yes. In a refugee camp. He had escaped from Vietnam into Laos. But when he got deathly ill, a young Laotian girl risked her life by taking him across the Mekong River to Thailand."

"Then how about it, Michelle? Interested in going with me?"

Abigail smiled patiently. "Seth, don't push Michelle for a book now. I imagine she's more interested in the girl who rescued Rob, the girl he left behind." She looked at me. "A young Hmong girl, wasn't she?"

"Yes. I was just—I mean—I wondered—"

"If we could find her?" Seth pulled doubtfully at his mustache.

David slipped his arm around my shoulder. "Face it, Michelle. The chance of finding Liana is one in a thousand."

"It's more like one in 50,000 refugees," Seth added.

I heard their arguments, but the odds didn't dim my rising hopes. The spark was there. My mind was racing a thousand miles away, far from the wilderness lodge and our cruise ship—to Thailand. Maybe senators' row in Washington D.C. couldn't help Rob get Liana back—or wouldn't help him. But maybe I could. It would be a grand exchange—a book for Liana. If it worked, Seth would have more funds for feeding the hungry. And if Liana was somewhere in the refugee camp, I'd find her in that sea of hungry faces.

*   *   *

Abigail, Seth, David and I arrived back on board ship in time for a quick change before attending the evening program in the Golden Sails Lounge. Abigail was eager to get a good seat. "They're doing Tom Taylor's *Our American Cousin* tonight," she said excitedly.

Seth frowned. "Whose cousin?"

"It's a comedy—eccentric and melodramatic—but a comedy. You'll like it. I do, in spite of my rather proper scholarly image."

"That's the play they performed at Ford's Theatre the night Lincoln was shot," I said.

"The very same," said Abigail as we sat down in the second row.

A silhouette of Lincoln sitting in a cane chair appeared on the left side of the stage. A balsa wood replica of the presidential box was draped with an American flag.

Near the stage stood a huge bouquet of red roses in a translucent porcelain vase, displaying a gold banner that read, "Congratulations, Hopewell College—50 years."

I leaned over to Abigail and said, "Aren't those flowers beautiful? I wonder who sent them?"

"Perhaps compliments of the ship. Who else could afford them?"

I was about to suggest that someone back home sent them, but the ship's orchestra began to play "Hail to the Chief." I glanced around at the audience. The Thatchers were sitting in the front row just ahead of us, the Seatons to our left, and Cam and Stephanie Ellis just behind David and me. As the orchestra reached a crescendo, I heard Cam whisper something about not feeling well. I looked around.

"Cameron's ill," said Stephanie. "We'd better not stay."

"I'm so sorry," I murmured. They slipped out just as the orchestra hit the final notes of the anthem. The play began, but my thoughts were still on the Ellises. They seemed like such a sad couple. Strange that even a delightful cruise on a luxury liner wasn't able to lift their spirits.

I realized that the play was in full swing and I hadn't been paying attention. I listened. The plot was quite simple, yet charming in its own quaint way—a domineering mother scheming to marry off her daughter to a rich American backwoodsman. When she learned that the man wasn't rich after all, she angrily ordered her daughter to her room. Alone on stage, the frustrated suitor uttered a bitter soliloquy, calling the mother an old man trap.

As the audience tittered, a sharp explosion split the air. I lurched instinctively as the porcelain vase shattered, showering tiny shards of glass over the first few rows near the stage. Screams and cries erupted from the audience. Someone shouted, "It was just a blank—part of the program!" Someone else retorted, "That bullet was real. Look what it did to the flower vase."

I looked around, dazed by the sudden pandemonium, trying to make sense of what was happening. This was part of the play, wasn't it? A reenactment of the night Lincoln was shot? But no. Several people were leaving their chairs, heading for the exit. Others didn't seem to know what to do. Dr. Jason Thatcher was moving efficiently through the audience, murmuring reassurances, checking for injuries.

David was on his feet too, heading for the stage. I grabbed my purse and followed, wending through the buzzing, frightened crowd. I lost him momentarily, then found him backstage, already talking with the ship's entertainment director. The young man seemed as perplexed as everyone else. "I was supposed to fire the gun. This one, here." He held up a weapon for David to examine. "It's loaded with blanks. But before I could shoot, someone else fired. The stage lights blinded me, so I didn't see who it was. It all happened so quickly."

"You're certain that someone else fired?" asked David.

"Yes, sir. I didn't even have my finger on the trigger."

I glanced at David. I could tell he was wondering the same thing I was: Was this another bizarre warning to the Hopewell reunion? Another hideous reminder that someone was destined to die?

CHAPTER
EIGHT

As David and I walked back through the Golden Sails Lounge, I paused and picked up a long-stem red rose lying on the floor. The room was empty now except for stewards re-arranging chairs and sweeping up broken glass. They moved swiftly, silently under the watchful gaze of a ship's officer. The swarthy man's eyes blazed as he hurled orders in Italian, his words precise and demanding.

"It's a shame about the accident," I told the officer. "The flowers were so beautiful. It was kind of the captain to send them."

"Roses? Not likely the captain's gift," he grunted.

I touched the softness of a petal, then handed the rose to him.

He smiled tightly. "Are you one of the Hopewell alumni?"

"Yes, she's one of the honorees," David volunteered.

"Then perhaps you would like the rose, ma'am. We've thrown the rest away. They were mixed with glass, you know."

"Is the captain aware of what happened?" David asked.

"Yes, of course, sir. He was notified immediately. He's already conferring with your college president, Dr. Stoddard."

As David and I started to go, I turned impulsively and asked the officer, "What about the flowers? Who sent them?"

"They came from Miss Scarlett's Greenery in Juneau."

David and I walked back to our stateroom in silence. Once inside, David promptly locked the door. I had managed a bold facade for the ship's officer, but, in the privacy of our room, I began to tremble. "Someone could have been killed tonight, David. This thing is becoming more insidious all the time. It's not a game anymore."

"Someone sees it as a game, Michelle. Cat and mouse, with life-or-death stakes." David's brow furrowed. "If it were a simple murder plot, this—this stalker could have done the deed long before this."

"Even tonight. That bullet could have hit any one of us as easily as it shattered that vase. Obviously this madman—or mad woman—is determined to strike terror in our hearts before delivering his fatal blow."

David led me over to the little sofa beneath our window and pulled me down beside him. "Your hands are clammy, hon. I know you're frightened, but you can't let this whole thing get to you."

I snuggled against his shoulder. "Admit it. You're upset too. I'm just glad Jackie stayed in her room with little Stevie tonight."

"That's right—you said the Tiger's running a slight temperature. Maybe I'll go over and check on him."

I sat up and nervously smoothed back my tousled hair. "What if the warning was meant for Jackie? What if the cocaine syndicate has found out where she is and now they're closing in for the kill?"

"Michelle, darling, please don't borrow trouble—"

"Who's borrowing?" I countered, my voice shrill. "It just comes heaping itself in my lap uninvited!"

"We have no evidence that the threats are aimed at Jackie."

I wound a strand of tangled hair around my finger. "I'd never forgive myself if something happened to Jackie—especially since she came on this cruise just because I'm being honored."

"Really, Michelle, I—" An urgent knock on the door cut off David's reply. He strode over, peered through the peephole, then opened the door to my kid sister Pam. "Good timing," he told her. "I'm on my way to check on Stevie. Go on in. Michelle could use a little reassurance."

Pam was breathless as she stepped aside to let David pass. "Reassurance? That's what I'm here for!" She burst in, bristling with an electric air of fear and excitement. "You were there, Michelle, in the lounge—you saw those flowers—that vase explode—I was never so terrified! I thought, this is it—and can you imagine the irony? Being murdered on a cruise ship, of all places?"

"Pam, slow down. *Calm down!*" I exclaimed. "Here, *sit* down."

"Please, Michelle, don't hover over me like Mother does. I'm perfectly fine. I'm just upset. This crazy person—whoever it is— he must be after you and David—or Jackie—or maybe all of you!"

"Listen, Pam, just listen to me. We have no proof that he's after any of us." Even as I spoke, I knew I didn't sound convincing. I was mechanically mouthing what David had said moments before.

Pam stared defiantly at me, her hands on her hips, her dark eyes flashing. "You just tell me, Michelle—you tell me who else on this ship is more at risk than the three of you. Who else has an entire cocaine syndicate seeking revenge against them? Remember Morro Bay? Remember what happened on Solidad, your little Caribbean Paradise? Some honeymoon! You and David were nearly killed!"

"You don't have to paint such a dark picture, Pam."

"Who's painting? I'm frantic." She sat down and took my hand. "You're my big sis. How could I get along without you to heckle?"

"No one's going to hurt me, or Jackie, or anyone else."

"Can you be sure? Can you absolutely promise me?"

"Of course not, Pam. What do you expect me to do? There's nothing any of us can do but wait this thing out."

Pam stood abruptly. "Are you kidding? Sit around waiting? No way. I know what I'll do. I'll fight back even if you won't."

"What do you mean by that?"

"Nothing. I'll explain later. I've got to go."

"Go? Go where?" I asked as I walked her to the door.

"Nowhere. Back to my room. I'll see you tomorrow."

"David and I are going back into Juneau in the morning. Why don't you go with us? We could have fun and forget our worries."

Pam looked thoughtful. "Sorry, Michelle. I have other plans."

"You're turning down a helicopter ride? And white-river rafting on the Mendenhall River? That's not my bold, adventurous kid sister."

Pam was halfway out the door. "I'll explain later, sis. Bye!"

* * *

That night, even the gentle roll of the ship as it lay anchored in Juneau's quiet harbor didn't help me sleep. I tossed fitfully until dawn, then sat groggy-eyed through breakfast. Finally, I shook off my sleepiness in the chill wind as our tender sped across the lapping waters toward Juneau. David snapped photos with his Nikon camera, looking as untroubled and relaxed as the tourists around him.

"Sweetheart, look at the ship from here," he said eagerly.

I glanced back. The sleek vessel bobbed with queenly splendor in the harbor, a string of colorful flags flapping from her mast.

"What do you think, Michelle? Incredible, isn't it?"

"Dazzling," I said. "Magnificent." *And potentially dangerous*, I mused silently, remembering the threats and the shattered vase.

At the pier, David closed his camera case and smiled. "Before this day's over we'll know how Brett Seaton felt walking in space."

I frowned. "Walking in space? What do you mean?"

"We're going to walk on a glacier this morning."

"I thought we were taking a helicopter ride."

"Both. A glacier isn't exactly like walking on the moon, but—"

"We're hiking somewhere on a mass of ice—?"

"Don't worry," he grinned. "We won't walk far in moon boots."

Moments later, as David and I approached the blue-and-white helicopter floating in the bay, we spotted the Seatons waiting in line. "Morning. Looks like you're heading our way," said David.

"Wouldn't miss this trip for the world, David," said Brett.

"I'm excited too," said Candy, looking model-perfect in a smart jacket. "I love flying—flew for years as an airline stewardess."

"Until I rescued you." Brett gave her a playful hug.

"I'm still not sure you rescued me," she teased. "I've been grounded ever since. You know, cooking, dishes, housework, kids—"

"You know you love it. And you're a pretty *good* cook too."

"I was a good airline stewardess."

"Like I said . . . until I rescued you."

Her powder-blue eyes snapped. "The oxygen was low that day. I wasn't thinking straight."

Brett chuckled. "We were joy-flying when she proposed to me."

Candy arched her finely drawn brows. "I proposed to you?"

"Well, didn't you?"

"I was so dumbfounded I just repeated your question, 'Will you marry me?' Frankly, Brett, dear, I still say the oxygen was low."

The Seatons' tense banter was interrupted by the helicopter pilot's crisp instructions. "Here, folks, put on these warm ice boots. They'll help you keep your footing on the glacier." Then, as we boarded, he asked casually, "Have you people ever been airborne?"

"Airborne?" Candy repeated. "My husband thinks he invented flying. He has conveniently forgotten the Wright brothers."

Within minutes the roaring, whooping sound of the rotors drowned out our voices. The chopper rose slowly, gaining altitude past the barren, rocky sentinels toward the misty summits. An early morning sun cast a pink, ribboned glow over the mountain peaks and shot a blinding reflection off the glaciers. We caught a quick aerial view of our cruise ship in the channel, then soared toward our rendezvous with a fantasy-land of ice.

Below us, Mendenhall Glacier looked immense—like a steep, sprawling roadway of snow and ice forcing its way between mountains, bulldozing sheer granite, its icy sculptures splitting off into Mendenhall Lake, leaving jagged peaks of frosty, translucent blue.

Our copter quivered, its rotating blades whirling as we hovered above the glacier valley. Then we descended in a breathtaking swoop and touched down on the slick, spangled surface of the glacier.

Gripping David's hand, I stepped gingerly from the helicopter, awestruck by the vast, rugged fields of icy grandeur. Stretching as far as the eye could see was a silent world of savage beauty, a snow kingdom with great, yawning gaps and purple-shadowed crevasses. As a bitter wind whipped my collar against my face, I imagined an earthquake rumbling beneath us, collapsing the great luminous mass on which we stood. I wondered if we—and the copter—could be swallowed up by one of the ominous hollow caverns that split the ice. "David," I said, staring down into the bubbling blueness of one deep crevice, "what if we slipped and fell straight through?"

David straddled the jagged crevasse with his lanky legs as if to prove there was nothing to fear. "See, hon? Nothing to it. Just one big wintry playground. Disneyland can't match this!" He scooped up a handful of powdery snow and tossed it at me. Brett and Candace were pelting each other with snow too. Laughing breathlessly, I chased David around an ice mound until he stopped suddenly, caught me in his arms, and swung me around frivolously.

He set me down when we heard a loud whir overhead. The wind stirred to a frenzy as a second helicopter came in for a landing, its blades whirling. The door opened in the copter's belly and out tumbled several passengers bundled in heavy coats, scarves and moon boots. Immediately I recognized the Thatchers and the Ellises. Stephanie brightened and waved as I made my way toward her, shuffling cautiously in my thick-soled ice boots.

When I reached her, she was gazing around in wonderment, with tears in her eyes. "What's wrong, Stephanie?"

"It's just the beauty," she whispered. "The glacier—it's so majestic, so overpowering. I've never seen anything like it. It—it almost makes you think that—that maybe God really did create—"

"God did, Stephanie. He did."

Cam stood at her side, his sleeveless windbreaker open casually. "After this trip, maybe I can persuade Stephanie to go

mountain climbing with me. If she could forget the mosquitoes, she'd love it."

"I'll try, Cameron. I promise. The next time you go."

I turned confidentially to Stephanie. "I've read your poems—
the ones about your son. They were so touching, I cried."

Stephanie's eyes glistened. "Oh, Michelle, you really liked
them? Cam, did you hear? Michelle likes my poetry."

"Not those poems again," he muttered. "With all this talk of
poetry, you're going to have the Hopewell alumni getting the
wrong impression, thinking my wife is sending those threatening verses."

Stephanie looked horrified. "Cam, how could you even
say—?"

I patted her arm and whispered, "Oh, Stephanie, I never
even thought—I would never accuse—We'll talk about the
poems later."

Noreen Thatcher turned our way and said brightly, "So
you're a writer too, Mrs. Ellis! How utterly fascinating!"

I studied Noreen as she bubbled on about writers she had
met, her clear blue eyes matching the azure sheen of the
glacier. Noreen reminded me of Jackie—petite and elegant
even in her moon boots. Without skipping a beat, she changed
the subject to her husband. "Just think," she said, gesturing
dramatically, "Jason was so tired he wanted to stay on board
and miss this. But I insisted he come."

I looked over at Jason Thatcher a few feet away. He was
stooping down, staring into a deep, icy chasm. His dark leather
jacket hung loosely over his broad shoulders; his silver hair
blew freely in the wind. I glimpsed a desolate expression on his
chalky-white face as the troubled lines around his eyes con-
stricted. He looked like a man who wanted the fissure to split
wide open and swallow him. Finally, when he heard Noreen
calling, he straightened like a man too tired to go on, kicked
some loose snow into the frosty crevice, then lumbered solemnly back to the helicopter.

CHAPTER
NINE

Back in Juneau an hour later, David and I joined Brett and Candace Seaton for lunch at the Front Street Cafe. We downed cup after cup of hot black coffee as we chatted amiably, recovering from our chilling, exhilarating stroll on the glacier. As we warmed up, Brett became less reserved, more talkative, telling us of his years in the NASA program. He said seriously, "We knew the men and women who flew the Challenger. Some of them were personal friends." He looked away for a moment, remembering. "You can't work with men and dream with them and golf with them and not feel the loss when they don't make it. Lives snuffed out in a twisting, feathery cloud of smoke."

"How well I know," David said. He was silent a moment before asking, "What's your chance of getting back in space?"

"I expected to be part of the flight crew for the Discovery. But things didn't turn out. Now I'll have to wait my turn."

"Astronauts are always racing time," Candy said. "They've got experience going for them, but age working against them. We didn't think it would be this long after the Challenger."

"Then you're eager for Brett to be back in space?" I asked.

She laughed a sardonic little ripple. "It's fly with him, dream with him, or nothing."

"Candy's been more concerned since the Challenger disaster."

Candy's chin puckered. "I don't want to raise two small children without a father. Some of my friends are doing that now. And we used to visit over coffee and brag about our husbands and kids." She opened her wallet and handed David a snapshot of Brett and their two children. The boy and girl both looked like Brett, with jet-black hair, angular, woebegone faces and warm, dancing eyes.

"You have a lovely family," I said. "What darling kids."

Candy smiled. "Tricia is six—a shy little homebody. And Dana is eight. All he talks about is being a pilot like his daddy."

"You can see why Candy would like me home full-time. She would like me to quit NASA—permanently."

"I have a feeling you're not a quitter, are you?" said David.

"Not so far. But a dozen astronauts have left the program in the past two years."

"Out of fear?" I asked.

"No." Brett ran his broad hand through his dark cropped hair. "You settle that issue a long time before you go up in space."

"Brett already thinks he's immortal," Candy said bitterly. "I keep hoping they'll scrub all manned space flights—for good."

Brett glared at her. "Nothing was ever accomplished without risks, Candace. I'm determined to remain in the space program, danger or no danger."

"I thought you'd already flown a mission or two," I said.

"But I want to command a shuttle flight someday."

"He's not satisfied with working in Mission Control, communicating with flights in orbit." She twisted the wedding band on her tapered finger. "He always has to break the sound barrier himself."

"Don't give the ring back," Brett teased coolly. "Not here in front of our new friends." He uttered a hard little laugh, but Candy only looked away with a scowl.

In the awkward moment that followed, I asked, "But, Colonel Seaton, if you left the space program, what would you do?"

"Maybe go back to Patuxent River as a test pilot. Or back with the Atlantic fleet. Or maybe—maybe I'll come back to Alaska and be a bush pilot." He shoved back his chair. "More coffee anyone?" When we assured him we'd had plenty, he bounded toward the counter in quick, gliding steps, as if the cafe wasn't large enough to hold him.

While Brett was gone, Candy said, "I wish he would get out of NASA. He hasn't been the same since his mission was scrubbed. Sometimes I think he blames himself for the shuttle disaster, for not openly fighting some of the safety shortcuts and mechanical failures. I'm sick of hearing about Delta rockets and O-rings. I just want some peace and stability in our home."

"But Brett still needs you to believe in him," I said.

She nodded. "Maybe I'm still afraid of the unknown. Until the Challenger tragedy, I thought I had resolved all my fears." She sighed deeply. "As a kid I was afraid of everything, but my folks made me believe I could do anything, even fly. That's why I became an airline stewardess."

"So how did you and Brett ever get together?"

"For a while I had reservations about marrying a test pilot. But I fell in love with him. I especially liked his commitment. The first day we met, he asked me what I believed about God. I was shocked and told him so. Do you know what he said? 'I plan to marry you someday and I want to be certain you love the Lord.' "

Brett was back now with his refill. He swallowed quickly and set the empty cup on the table. "We'd better go, Candy. We need to pick out some souvenirs for the kids."

"And we should call my folks to see how the children are."

"Great. I'll tell Dana about our copter ride. He'll love it."

"And I'll tell Tricia about the baby seals we saw." Their eyes met for an instant, his piercing, hers filled with silent yearning.

As they left the cafe, I looked at David and said, "Candy makes Brett sound much less cocky then he wants us to believe. I wonder if he'll ever get a chance to command a shuttle?"

"He'll make it," said David. "The man's got guts. He's a risk-taker, not a quitter."

"But I'm not certain he's the hero you want him to be, David. Down deep I think Brett's an angry, depressed man."

"You writers," he winked, "always painting everyone with a dark inner soul. Next you'll tell me Brett sent the Hopewell threats."

I nudged David playfully. "Brett's not the type for poetry."

We were silent a minute. Then I looked earnestly at David. "Darling, let's never quarrel or bicker like the Seatons. Never."

"Don't look so fretful, sweetheart. We're not the Seatons."

"I know, but they seemed like such a perfect couple that first day—and now, it's obvious they've lost something in their marriage."

"Communication, for one thing."

"David, will we always be able to talk—really talk?"

"I hope so, hon. I'll fail you at times, but I won't mean to."

"But we'll always forgive each other, won't we, David?"

"That's the only way, Michelle. I can only tell you, if I had it to do over again, I'd fall in love with you in a second."

* * *

After lunch, David and I joined the Thaatchers and the Ellises at the pier for the tour bus to the Mendenhall River. When I learned we had a half-hour wait, I decided to make a side trip to the florist. David protested, but I assured him I wouldn't be long. I kept thinking there had to be a connection between the person who bought the bouquet of roses and the one who fired the bullet into the vase. Or was the one who purchased the flowers—and saw them destroyed—just another victim of the Hopewell stalker? The answers were there—somewhere.

I found Miss Scarlett's Greenery on Seward Street—an enchanting shop with flowers and gifts in the window. At the counter a pleasant young woman greeted me warmly. "Good afternoon. May I help you?"

"I just dropped by to tell you how beautiful the bouquet was—the one you sent to the S.S. *Mendenhall* for my college reunion."

She brightened. "How sweet of you. We enjoyed making up the bouquet. It's not often someone orders 50 roses in one arrangement."

"Well, you see, it's Hopewell's fiftieth anniversary."

"Yes, the customer told me that."

"Oh? Who sent them?" I asked casually. "The ship's officers?"

"No. The man was a passenger, I believe."

"One of the alumni? There are 250 of us traveling together."

"I don't think so. When he gave the order, he said he just wanted to do something nice for the college reunion on board."

"That makes it even more lovely, doesn't it? A stranger being so thoughtful." Suddenly I thought of Jason Thatcher and how troubled he had appeared at the glacier. He looked like a man with secrets. Was it possible that he had sent the bouquet? "Tell me," I said to the lady, "was the customer a distinguished man with silver-white hair? Was his name Thatcher?"

"He didn't give his name, but we did talk shop. He sounded like an ambitious, self-made man. Quite the entrepreneur, I gathered."

"How interesting." I glanced at my watch. "I'd better go. My husband will be furious if I miss the bus to the Mendenhall River."

The woman smiled. "Sounds like the gentleman yesterday. He was edgy, impatient to get back to his wife before she missed him."

"Really?" I said, but silently I mused, *I don't know any more about this man than when I came in—except that he's an ambitious, married flower-lover.*

I left Miss Scarlett's Greenery and, on impulse, sidetracked over to Franklin Street for a quick peek at the famous Red Dog Saloon. I knew David would never approve. I stole through the swinging doors and peered through the darkness at an old gold-rush dance hall with a bearskin rug on the back wall, flags on the ceiling, and sawdust on the floor. A young woman in red velvet played a tinny honky-tonk piano. Stifling a smile, I bought David a lacy red garter with the Red Dog logo. Then I strode back to the pier just in time to board the motorcoach. As David and I took our seats, Jason Thatcher leaned over and said, "I thought you went to buy some flowers."

"Oh, I got a garter instead," I said brightly. Looking puzzled, Jason cleared his throat and leaned back perfunctorily in his seat.

When our bus pulled up beside Mendenhall Lake, I spotted five large rubber rafts bobbing at the shoreline. We all piled out and donned purple-and-green ponchos, snugly fitting life vests, and knee-high Juneau sneakers. As we clambered down the rocky slope to the beach, I protested, "David, I don't want to go out in the middle of that lake in a rubber raft. What if it leaks? Or capsizes?"

Noreen and Jason caught up with us. "I heard that, Michelle," Noreen teased. "You and Jason are a couple of party poopers. He wants to sit this one out too."

As we approached the rafts, I decided that staying alone on this isolated beachhead with Jason Thatcher, so moody and remote, wasn't exactly appealing either. So I would risk it with David on the raft.

When we realized we needed two more people on our raft, David and I shambled over to the Ellises in our outrageous garb. "Come join the Thatchers and us," said David. "We have room for two more."

Cam scowled. "I'm not much for keeping company with doctors."

"Cam never goes to a doctor," Stephanie said hurriedly.

"Hey, come on, Cam," said David. "Jason's not the doctor on board. He's just one of us—one of the alumni."

"Please, Cam," said Stephanie, "I want to be with the Ballards."

"Okay," he relented, "as long as you two don't talk poetry."

I winked at Stephanie. "We wouldn't think of it, Cam. As long as you and David don't dwell on your Vietnam days."

He took his wife's hand. "We'll just talk about the Mendenhall."

"You mean, our ship?" I asked.

He nodded toward the massive ice fields. "The glacier . . . the lake . . . the river. We'll be in the midst of all three."

When we reached the Thatchers, David announced, "Well, we've got our ten passengers now. Let's cast off."

Thatcher nodded curtly at Cam. "Since you're the great outdoorsman, Mr. Ellis, white-river rafting should be to your liking." Jason's tone was less than cordial.

Cam's lips curled in a sneer. "True, Dr. Thatcher. And I trust that the invincible surgeon has no qualms about facing the rapids."

Stephanie gripped Cam's arm. "Cameron, not here, please. Don't start something."

He shook his arm free and stepped into the raft. "Come, Steph."

Noreen laughed uneasily. "Well, here we go, Mrs. Ellis. Don't we look lovely in our purple ponchos and man-sized rain boots?"

Stephanie returned a tight smile, then stepped into the raft.

I started to climb in ahead of David, but Kevin, the young oarsman with sun-bleached hair and bare, muscular biceps, stopped me. "Let's put your husband in the center for better balance."

"Better balance?" I exclaimed. "That'll put me right next to the water. If we capsize, I'm in first."

"Doesn't matter," Kevin grunted as he shoved the raft out into the water and sprang in. "We're packed as tight as oranges in a crate. If one goes over, we all go." Grasping the oars, he pulled away from shore with quick, smooth strokes.

Within moments we circled the lake, then scudded in front of the cloud-rimmed glacier, caught in a chilling wind that swept low off the ice fields. The biting breeze tangled my hair and stung my cheeks. "Kevin, where's the river?" I asked, my teeth chattering.

"Behind us. On the other side of the lake. But I'm giving you an up-front view of the glacier first."

We were barely bobbing in the water now. "I like this spot out here," said Kevin. "I've lived in Juneau all my life, grown up in the shadow of the Mendenhall, but I never get over the sense of wonder and power it gives me. I wanted you to see it— feel it!"

Slowly Kevin maneuvered the raft back toward the middle of the lake, rowing with powerful strokes, propelling us across the water to a distant cove. As the soundless wind churned the water, the raft glided in a rhythmic, backward motion toward the Mendenhall River.

For a time we drifted lazily with the bends and curves of the tree-lined river, bobbing along the gentle swells like buoyant ducks. Then suddenly we were scooped up with the main current. We dipped with the waves, dodging slick boulders and uprooted trees.

Our exhilaration mounted as we nosed toward the first rapid. We plunged headlong into a spumy wall of water, then Kevin whipped us around a jagged rock, hitting it with a glancing blow. We sideswiped another rock, then took the rapids broadside, careening crazily into the turbulent white foam. I screamed as frigid waves swept over me, waterlogging my poncho and boots. Before I could catch my breath, we hit another huge swell that sent us pitching wildly into the debris lining the shore.

As Kevin frantically worked the oars, I looked over at Cam Ellis, beside David. Cam was in his glory, thriving on the excitement. His eyes danced and his bearded jaw was thrust forward, catching the foamy spray as we rode with the current. The Thatchers huddled together in front of us, their arms bent protectively, warding off the onslaught of rushing water as we buffeted the rapids and veered around the serpentine river. As the glacial waters sprayed my face, I burrowed my head against David's shoulder. Halfway around the next cove, the waves eased, and I began to believe that we might make it out alive. "Never again, David. Never again," I cried.

"Sorry, here we go again, Michelle," warned David. "The next rapid is just ahead."

Even though David held me tight for the rest of our frenzied, surging white-water ride, I was trembling inside, drenched to my skin. Finally, in desperation, I tugged off a boot and dumped the water back in the river. I was still pulling my Juneau sneaker back onto my numb foot when we hit the last two rapids. "Another five or ten minutes and we'll be back on shore," said Kevin.

It can't be soon enough for me, I mused silently.

When we finally hit the beach, Cam and Stephanie Ellis climbed out of the raft and walked on ahead of us without a word. The Thatchers, David, and I struggled wearily up the hillside toward the bus, yanking off our life preservers as we went. At the top of the hill we slipped out of our drenched ponchos and sat down on the fallen timbers. I tried to pull off my wet boots, then said in exhaustion, "David, please help me."

He knelt and pulled them off. "Your feet are cold, hon."

"Like icebergs. I've got half of the Mendenhall in my boots."

Noreen had already slipped on her stacked heels and was gazing in a hand mirror, touching up her makeup.

Making conversation, I asked, "How did you ever fit a vacation into Dr. Thatcher's busy schedule?"

Noreen glanced at her husband, her eyes twinkling. "Jason just needed one more thing to fill his 40-hour days. Imagine, this week we've actually slept in. Usually Jason's up at four every morning and off to the hospital by five."

"I told you, Noreen, that's going to change. I'm going to spend more time at home now."

"Good," she said. "Then our next 25 years will be even more special." She lifted her hand to her lips and blew him a kiss across her long, slender fingers.

Jason dropped his rain gear on the log beside him. "There's no guarantee of another 25. We're getting older."

"Nonsense," she scoffed. "We're just beginning to live. The kids are almost grown, and you're at the height of your career."

Jason reached out and locked fingers with his wife, but his smile was restrained. "Sometimes I feel like I'm at the end of my career." He turned to David and me. "Just for six months I'd like to do nothing else but relax. Choose a hobby and go for it."

"You've been pursuing hobbies all your life, Jason. Hiking. Photography." She dropped her mirror in her purse. Looking at David and me, she said, "Most of Jason's hobbies have been for our girls. He took up skiing to be with them. Joined the PTA when they were little. Studied French with Karen so she could pass the course. His latest venture is building a sound room in the garage for Susan."

"Susan's 19, our music bird," said Jason as he helped Noreen up. "In fact, she's studying music in Europe this summer."

"What about your other daughter?" I asked as we waited in line to board the bus. "What is she doing this summer?"

"Karen's trekking all over Europe with her friends. She's like no one else in this family—stubborn, free-spirited, not at all concerned about overachievement."

"She'll make it, Noreen. She has the potential. She just has to find herself in this mixed-up world we live in."

"Jason believes if you give them a solid biblical background, they'll do fine. I worry a little more, especially with Karen. She's so lovable, scatterbrained, vulnerable. She's barely 17 and staying in shoddy little hostels, only God knows where."

"That's just it, Noreen. God does know where. I had to give her Europe this summer. It was the one thing she wanted."

"Yes, I know. You acted as if your life depended on it."

Crinkly smile lines fanned around Jason's eyes, softening the deep weariness in his face.

Noreen smiled. "Susan and Karen are Jason's whole life."

"The *three* of you are my whole life," he told her.

Our conversation ended as we boarded the motorcoach and rode back toward downtown Juneau, stopping briefly at the Visitor Information Center near Mendenhall Glacier. "Say, Michelle, I have an idea," said David. "Let's get off here and take the hiking trails by the glacier for a good look at Mount McGinnis and Bullard Mountain."

"Oh, no, David! How will we get back to the ship?"

"They say the city bus comes within a mile of the glacier. It'll be a nice little walk."

"But after our helicopter ride and raft trip, I'm exhausted!"

"Hon, you can catch up on your sleep when we get home. But, tell me, how often can we see scenery like this?"

David was right. So I argued away my exhaustion, reminding myself that, being younger, I should have no trouble keeping pace.

As we started to get off the bus, David looked over at Cam and Stephanie Ellis. "Hey, you like hiking, Cam. Care to join us?"

"Not this time. We've got tickets for the Lady Lou Revue, and I'm taking in the Red Dog Saloon before we head back to the ship."

"Please, Cam," said Stephanie, "don't overdo it. You're not used to drinking, you know."

"Don't nag me, Steph. Who said anything about drinking?"

Minutes later, as David and I began our hike just past the visitors' center, I said, "It sounds like Cam has a recent drinking problem. Do you suppose it relates to the son they lost?"

David shrugged. "The Ellises never said they lost a son."

"But Stephanie's poetry says so."

David's tone turned serious. "The more we learn about the Ellises, the less we know. But one thing is certain. I want to be Cam's friend. He's such a troubled man, a loner, he really needs a friend. And if I can help him spiritually, I'd like that too."

I looked up at David. "That's what I love about you, darling."

He smiled and took my hand protectively, then led me up the rocky nature trail that wound toward the glacier. I had convinced myself I could keep up with David, but after an hour on the hiking trails, I knew my weariness couldn't be argued away. As we returned to the information center, I collapsed on the steps and barked, "After all our hiking, there's no way I can walk a mile to the bus."

David scanned the long, empty highway and shook his head.

"We're stuck here in this wilderness," I lamented, near tears.

A strange masculine voice broke in. "Excuse me. I'm a police officer. You folks need some help?"

David and I turned to face a tall, slender man with twinkling eyes. A smiling woman with a softly rounded attractiveness stood beside him. "We're the Bomans," he said. "Walt and Peggy. You two from the ship?" When David nodded, he said, "It's a long walk back. If you like, we could drive you right to the harbor."

"You don't know how glad I am to hear that!" I sighed in relief.

Peggy offered her hand in greeting. "Welcome to Juneau."

As we walked to their car, David and I introduced ourselves. Peggy stared at me in astonishment. "You're Michelle Ballard? Didn't you write that book on the POW—*A Vietnam Legacy*?"

"She's the one," said David proudly.

"Oh, your book was wonderful!" Peggy clasped her husband's arm. "Walt, this is Michelle Ballard, an author. I have her book at home."

Walt smiled at me. "I'll bargain with you. You stop by the house and autograph your book and we'll show you around Juneau."

"I'd love to . . . and we'd love to see Juneau—*by car!*"

The next two hours were delightful as Walt and Peggy drove us around Sheep Creek, Last Chance Basin, the Treadwell Historic Mining Area, and Douglas Island. "You can't drive far around here," said Walt. "There are just 60 miles of road from one end of Juneau to the other. We love it here, but this country is very inhospitable. If you go out in the cold, you'd better know what you're doing."

As we wound around Thunder Mountain, Walt shared some Alaskan folklore. "Back around 1880, the Sitka Mining Company funded teams to go out and stake new claims. Two fellas named Joe Juneau and Richard Harris found gold right here at Gold Creek. Other miners came flocking and that's how Juneau got its start. Of course, it was called Harrisburg at first, but when Harris left town, the people named the place after his partner, Joe Juneau."

"Fascinating," I said. "Can we see Gold Creek?"

"This is it," said Walt, pulling to a stop in a desolate stretch of wilderness flanked by craggy mountains and towering spruce. "The mine's over there in the side of the mountain. Want to see it?"

David was game, so the four of us hiked over the rocky, muddy trail, stumbling over twigs and jutting stones until we reached the deserted mining camp. We crossed over a rough plank bridge that spanned a shallow, bubbly creek where prospectors once panned for gold. We passed an old steel train car corroded with rust, its narrow benches eerily vacant and streaked with dirt.

We walked a few steps farther. "This is a ventilation shaft," said Walt. Rotted timber framed the crude doorway to the abandoned mine. A few weatherworn boards with rusty nails defied entry.

I peered between the boards into an abyss of blackness. "It sounds . . . haunted. Like something alive crying deep inside."

"Nothing so mysterious, Michelle. Just the wind whistling through the tunnel—a constant breeze, 15 miles an hour. The mine's eight levels deep, but this tunnel's only five feet by eight."

"Does anyone go into the mine anymore?" asked David.

Walt nodded. "A few people have. I'm no spelunker, but they tell me there are rooms in this mine as large as a coliseum, with ceilings 40 to 50 feet high. Big enough for two football fields."

"That's incredible," I murmured, shivering as cold tentacles of dampness enveloped me. My thoughts rolled like a videotape, spinning back a hundred years, replaying bygone days when the cry for gold drove men to Alaska. I could envision a bewhiskered Dick Harris and Joe Juneau, their eyes glittering and gleaming like the gold nuggets they sought. I could hear the raucous cries of the rough-and-ready men who followed them. And I could picture them at night in the gold-rush trappings of frontier saloons with honky-tonk pianos and gaudy chorus girls toasting their fame and fortune.

As my imagination soared, I could smell a smoking locomotive rattling over the rusty rails, hauling cars full of miners through an ancient mine honeycombed with miles of winding tunnels. I could see the noisy, heaving train carrying the men farther and farther down the mine shaft toward darkness and dreams. I wondered how many men who sought fame and fortune found it? And how many men died trying?

"Michelle, Michelle," said David, his voice sounding ghostly hollow from the mine shaft, "come back from never-never land."

"I—I was imagining what it was like when the mines were active."

"I thought so. But listen to Walt. He says Juneau may be mining again in another five years—if gold prices accelerate."

"You mean there's still gold there?" I asked in surprise.

"Yours for the digging. It just isn't profitable to mine yet."

David touched my arm. "Listen, Michelle, if we don't get back to the ship soon, we'll be walking to Skagway."

We took one last, lingering glance at the Gold Creek mine, then turned and walked back down the boulder-strewn trail to the car.

"Is it true that there are big brown bears in these parts?" David asked as we climbed into the vehicle.

Peggy chuckled. "Bears? There sure are. Tell them, Walt."

He nodded. "We have black bears in Juneau and brown bears on Admiralty Island. Sometimes when food is scarce they come down into town and eat the garbage. We police end up chasing the critters, shooting firecrackers at them from our shotguns. Would you believe, those bears get so they recognize our unmarked police cars! They're smart. You don't want to mess with a thousand-pound brown bear," he said as we drove back toward town.

"And they can outrun a quarter horse," said Peggy.

"You're kidding!" I exclaimed. "They look so cumbersome."

"Fact is, they're unbelievably agile," said Walt. "When I go hunting, I can hear a deer approach, but not a bear. In spite of their massiveness, bears move soundlessly."

"Have you actually encountered a bear?" David asked.

"Once. This big, shaggy bear and I just stood there eyeballing each other. When he raised up on his haunches, popping his jaws in aggravation, I knew I was in trouble. Like lightning, this crusty old bear made a false charge at me, running 40 miles an hour. Scared me silly! Then he just stopped in his tracks and lumbered away."

"I'm glad I wasn't there," said Peggy as we drove down Franklin Street toward the pier. "I would have had heart failure for sure."

Walt squealed to a stop near the dock. "I think we made it in time. Your ship's still there."

The S.S. *Mendenhall* sat in the harbor, gleaming against the exquisite Juneau sunset. The last tender bobbed at the pier, waiting to take us back to the ship. But, somehow, I felt strangely reluctant to leave our new friends. As David and I said good-bye to the Bomans, I hugged Peggy, then told Walt,

"Thanks for making our visit to Juneau so special. We'll never forget it!"

With one last wave at the Bomans, David and I bounded across the dock to the tender. We boarded just as the engine revved and sat down breathlessly by Abigail Chadwick. "Just made it!" I exclaimed.

Abigail frowned. "But Seth didn't. He's late. The tender's leaving without him."

"Where is he?" I asked.

"He told me he had a last-minute errand to run and to go on without him. David, can't you get them to wait?"

"I'll try, Abigail, but we've already shoved off."

I clasped Abigail's arm. "Wait! Isn't that Seth running along the pier toward us?"

"He'll never make it," said David.

"Tell the crewmen to stop!" cried Abigail.

Seth ran like a sprinter, gaining momentum as he closed the gap between dock and tender. Then, with the agility of a long jumper, he took a flying leap into the boat. Two crewmen caught his arms and yanked him forward, breaking his fall. He was breathing heavily as he dropped onto a bench across from us.

"Well, Seth Mueller, I hope your last-minute errand was worth it," Abigail scolded. "You could have killed yourself."

Seth thrust a shock of wind-tangled hair back from his forehead, then gave Abigail a boyish, triumphant grin. "I did it for you, Abigail." He removed a book from his jacket and handed it to her. "Sorry, I didn't have time to gift wrap it."

With exquisite care, Abigail turned the hardbound, gilt-edged volume over in her hands. "*The Best of Robert Service*. Oh, Seth, he's one of my favorite poets. I don't know what to say."

"I noticed you admiring it in that bookstore. I wanted to get you something you liked so you'd remember our time in Juneau."

Their eyes locked fondly. "I'll remember, Seth. Always."

CHAPTER
TEN

As our tender drew near the ship, I noticed another shuttle boat unloading just ahead of us, bobbing beside the enormous S.S. *Mendenhall*. From the string of lights that illuminated the ship, I spotted my sister Pam working her way cautiously up the gangplank, a tall, strapping man beside her. They were holding hands.

Something inside of me shouted, *No!* But I could tell by the startled expression on David's face that I hadn't made a mistake. Silas Winters, the charming, elusive DEA agent from the Caribbean, was boarding the ship with Pam.

"Oh, David," I cried, "no wonder Pam wouldn't join us on the raft ride today. She must have been on a rendezvous with Silas ever since we hit Juneau." I felt a momentary sense of rage and indignation against my sister. "Now I understand why she's been so secretive these past two days."

David took my hand. "Stay calm, Michelle, until you have a chance to talk with Pam and hear her side of the story."

As soon as David and I boarded the ship, he took our things to the stateroom while I sought out Pam. I confronted her in the main lobby where Silas was registering at the purser's desk. "Why is Silas here—now of all times?" I demanded.

"Why not? He's taking the rest of the cruise."

"Then you invited him to join you, didn't you"

Pam's eyes flashed. "Sure. I'm bored. I wanted some company. This ship is filled with nothing but the newly wed and the nearly dead!" She drew in a sharp breath. "Besides, I told you I was going to do something about those threatening messages. Who can protect us better than Silas Winters"

"We don't need a drug enforcement agent involved. This whole thing may not even be drug-related. Admit it, this was just an excuse to be with Silas again. So why all the secrecy"

"Hold it, big sis. I didn't want to rock your boat, knowing how you feel about Silas."

"What do you mean? I don't feel anything."

Tears sprang in Pam's eyes. "That's just the trouble. I do." She whirled around defiantly just as Silas turned from the purser's desk. He took several swashbuckling strides and gathered her into his arms. An agile six-footer in his early thirties, Silas was as dashingly handsome as ever, with his Grecian, suntanned face, aquiline nose, and trim brown mustache. His shrewd deep-brown eyes softened as he gazed down tenderly at Pam.

After a moment, he turned tentatively toward me and said, "Hello, Michelle. You obviously weren't expecting me."

Before I could reply, the purser called out, "Mr. Winters, I almost forgot. I have a message for you."

Pam looked up curiously. "What could it be"

"Agency business, no doubt." He excused himself and steered Pam back to the desk.

David arrived back from our stateroom with our jackets. He took one look at me and knew I was upset. "Come on, Michelle, we can talk with Pam and Silas later. Let's go out and watch the ship sail from Juneau. It'll be wonderfully romantic."

We strolled outside to an open deck where a crisp breeze pummeled us and the twinkling lights of Juneau winked a sweet farewell. As I stood by the railing close to David and felt his strong arms around me, I relaxed a little. "It isn't fair, David, Pam not telling us about Silas."

"Would you have approved"

"Not really. I'm so afraid those two are getting serious."

"Not *getting*, Michelle. They already are. Pam was smitten from the moment she met Silas in the Caribbean last year."

"I knew she and Silas were corresponding, but I had hoped—"

"That they were just pen pals"

"Really, David! This isn't a time for humor."

"Then how about romance" he murmured, kissing my hair.

I sensed someone approaching and drew away.

"I hope we're not interrupting," said Silas as he and Pam joined us at the rail.

David turned and extended his hand. "Nice to see you again, Winters. What brings you all the way to Alaska?"

"Actually, the agency sent me to Juneau. But if you mean who brought me to the ship, Pam did."

"We were surprised, of course," I said pointedly.

He tapped the rail uneasily. "Apparently Pam didn't tell you I was in Juneau."

"No. She forgot that little fact."

"Frankly, Michelle, until today I didn't plan to sail with the ship. Pam and I were just going to spend time together in town. Of course, the agency had already advised me that Jackie Marshall was on board. That was cause for concern. But then when Pam told me about the anonymous tape-recorded message and the other threats against the alumni, I decided to cancel my flight back to the lower 48 and come on board the *Mendenhall* instead. It took some doing in Juneau—phone calls to headquarters and a few hours of reshuffling funds and arguing with the shipping company before I—"

"Then you've been in Juneau awhile?" David asked.

"For several weeks. Working on a cocaine bust."

"An odd spot, isn't it?" I asked. "There are no roads into Juneau for drug deliveries."

"But there are plenty of planes and ships. We finally traced the deliveries to crew members on a cruise ship. They made their purchases in ports like Seattle or San Francisco, boarded with shopping bags, and made their sales in Juneau. No questions asked. No immigration."

"Clever," David said.

"A devious plan," Silas admitted, "but last month a couple of teenagers overdosed. That's when the DEA stepped in."

"And the crew members? Did you arrest them?" I asked.

"We're still tracking them down."

"On the *Mendenhall*? Then you *are* on agency business!"

"Relax, Michelle. I'm just here at Pam's invitation."

I nodded, but I wasn't convinced. Silas had deceived us once before in the Caribbean, working secretly for the DEA. Could he have been planted on board the *Mendenhall* to hunt down drug-trafficking crewmen? Or did he have some inside information? Was the international cocaine syndicate once more seeking revenge against David, Jackie, and me? If so, that enlarged the danger. Our stealthy adversary could be anyone on board ship. In fact, someone among the Hopewell alumni could actually be a hit man for the syndicate.

The questions and suspicions roiled in my mind, but I couldn't voice them tonight, not with Pam nearby. But I vowed to seek Silas out privately tomorrow. I needed answers, and I had a feeling Silas was just the man to see.

* * *

During the night the ship cruised up Lynn Canal and docked just before dawn at the charming gold-rush town of Skagway. But when I woke early Thursday morning, rustic locales and Klondike miners were the farthest things from my mind. I was more determined than ever to talk to Silas Winters. If necessary, I'd scour the ship to find him.

But as it turned out, Silas found me as I was sitting on the open deck watching David and Seth Mueller play shuffleboard. He sauntered over and squeezed my shoulder. "Truce" he said.

"Truce," I agreed.

He shoved his hands in his pockets. The wind caught his hair and tousled it, giving him a vulnerable, boyish look. "I don't want to spoil your trip, Michelle. You know that, don't you"

"I know. I just worry about Pam."

"Pam? Or *Pam and me*"

"Truce," I repeated.

He sat down in the lounge chair beside me. "Michelle, believe me, if Pam would marry me today . . . If it helps, I do love her."

"I know."

"Pam would never be happy with my career. I'd be gone a lot."

"And she wouldn't know where."

"That's right."

"I'm not sure Pam could handle knowing you were in danger, wondering if you were dead or alive."

He flashed a wry half-smile. "She could always pray."

I turned to face him. "But, Silas, think of it. If you don't believe . . . or won't . . . and something happens to you . . ."

"I'd be lost."

His words shocked me. "You mean you actually believe—"

"No. That's how you and Pam believe. Frankly, I'm not sure about God yet. I don't want to play religion just to get a woman."

"Pam wouldn't want you to."

Silas frowned. "Sometimes I think there's too much against us."

"Do you mean me"

"Well, that's true. Pam respects your opinion. But it's something bigger. God, maybe. The way I figure it, Michelle, Pam's got to want me for myself, not just because I believe in her God."

"Do you mind if I keep praying for you"

He glanced toward the shuffleboard court, ignoring me for a moment. "Good shot, David," he called. David waved back.

Silas avoided my eyes. Finally he said, "I wish I could tell you I don't need your prayers, or anyone else's. But I have a feeling I do. A crazy business, isn't it"

I studied him curiously. "You mean your job"

"No. Life." He sat forward and cracked his knuckles. I thought perhaps he was going to leave. Instead, he looked at me and said, "Michelle, yesterday you said you thought the drug administration put me on board ship. But, like I said, I just wanted to spend some time with Pam. But that message I received last night . . ."

"Yes, I remember. Go on."

"I did some informal checking on my own. I've got inside connections, you know, so I decided to check out the passengers who took out hefty insurance policies for this trip. I'm talking big bucks."

"Since when have you been interested in the insurance business"

"I'm not. But I wanted to take some precautions—you know—run some checkpoints with our special passenger on board."

"You mean Jackie Tur—" I caught myself and said *Marshall* instead. "But how can you possibly check 700 passengers"

He dismissed the question with a smile.

"So what did you find out" I asked.

He lowered his voice a notch. "From the information filtering in, I've come across three passengers with—shall we say—*unusually generous* policies who are with the Hopewell tour group."

I chuckled. "Silas, a lot of people who take trips think travel insurance is like a rabbit's foot. It's their security for getting back home again."

"Does David believe in a rabbit's foot"

"What's that supposed to mean"

"Are you aware that David took out a large policy in *your* name, Michelle"

"I—I—"

"You didn't know! Well, he's the beneficiary if anything happens to you."

"I don't like what you're implying, Silas."

"It's not what I'm implying. It's what others might think."

"So who are the other two carrying large insurance policies"

"Seth Mueller, for one—the famous tennis pro."

"Really? That's Seth Mueller playing shuffleboard with David."

"I know. That's why I'm here. I'd like to meet him."

"And is David the beneficiary on the other two policies"

"You know he isn't."

"Then who is"

He drummed his fingers on the metal arm. "One beneficiary is a lovely lady and the other's a starving world."

"A starving world" I echoed. "Wouldn't that be Seth's policy? Who else would be trying to feed the world"

I looked out across the deck. Abigail Chadwick was strolling our way, waving to Seth Mueller, her gaze candidly adoring. A wild, insane idea raced through my mind. Had Abigail taken out a large insurance policy? Just last night she had said that her love for Seth seemed so futile. Was life futile too? Had this exquisite lady come on board to give the love of her life one more chance to respond? Could she—who spent her years delving into centuries-old romantic literature—be suicidal? Had she taken out a life-insurance policy to feed the hungry—a final gift to the man she deeply loved?

Stop it, Michelle, I scolded silently. *You're letting your writer's mind carry you away with absurd imaginings.*

"An attractive lady, isn't she" said Silas, following my gaze. Abigail smiled fleetingly at us, then took a deck chair on the other side of the court. Silas watched her appraisingly.

"She's a friend of Seth's," I said, "and wishes she were more."

"I know," said Silas. "I've learned quite a bit about her—a doctorate in literature from England, a college professor at Hopewell for many years. She influenced the nomination of Seth Mueller as one of the four honored alumni, and I suspect she would do anything—anything to cover for the man."

I eyed Silas warily. "Do you trace everyone like that"

"No. I've just made it my business to know pertinent facts about Hopewell's honored alumni—and anyone involved with you four."

"Do you know that much about Seaton and Thatcher too"

"Enough to know that Jason Thatcher holds the third multi-figured policy. Everything he owns is heavily insured—his home, his medical practice, his wife and kids, and especially his own life."

"Very interesting. But do you really think these policies have any bearing on the weird messages we've been receiving"

"With Jackie Marshall on board, I'm making it my business to find out. We never approved of her taking this trip. We can't protect the Marshalls when they go against our efforts."

"Kind of like with God," I said softly. "He can't always protect us when we go against Him."

"Please, Michelle, no sermons. I'm serious."

"So am I. Besides, Silas, Jackie flew into Vancouver. She never touched the U.S. mainland. She refuses to get off at any port and she and Stevie will fly back to Switzerland from Canada as well."

"Yes, I'm here to make certain she does."

"Then you are here on agency business."

"Not in the way you think. It's just that the threat against the Hopewell reunion could be aimed at Jackie."

"Not likely," David interjected as he slipped up beside me, breathless, his face glowing with sun and perspiration. He wiped his brow. "The threats seem to be aimed directly at the *honored* alumni."

"It could be a decoy," said Silas.

David sat down beside me. "We've thought of that. For a while it seemed that Michelle and I were the only ones taking the threats seriously enough to want to solve the mystery."

"Yes, Pam tells me that President Stoddard has been keeping it low-key. Pam is irritated with everyone trying to play it safe, ignoring the threats. She's especially worried about you, Michelle."

"There are a lot of strange things happening on this cruise," David agreed, his gaze taking in Seth and Abigail engrossed in conversation nearby. "I, for one, am glad you're with us, Winters."

Silas nodded. "There are a lot of things to clear up—"

I turned on David and feigned annoyance. "That's right, David. Tell me, did you take out an e-nor-mous insurance policy in my name"

"Did I what"

"You heard me," I pouted. "Did you take out a policy on me"

He shrugged. "Well, I signed something. I asked my secretary Mitzi to get the tickets and insurance. I just signed the papers."

"Well, David," I said huffily, playing my petulance to the hilt, "if something happens to me, you'll be a very rich man."

"I'm already a very rich man," he said dryly.

Silas broke in, "We'll have to check it out, you know, David."

David's eyes flashed; his words exploded, "You'll have to *what*"

"It's just routine, David. . . ."

"I don't even have a copy of the policy with me."

"Take my word for it, David," said Silas. "It was sky-high."

"And you would get every penny, David," I jibed.

He reached over and pulled me out of my lounge chair into his lap. "I can't help what that scatterbrained Mitzi does, but heaven knows I don't want to lose you, my sweet, infuriating Sherlock."

Silas wasn't warming to our humor at all. "Tell me, David, do you know of anyone who would want to harm Michelle"

Impulsively I blurted, "Of course! David—when he loses at chess!" I could have bitten my tongue the minute I said it. "I'm sorry, darling. I was just trying to be funny."

"Who's laughing" David countered, releasing me. "So what are you saying, Silas? That I'm a suspect in this crazy plot"

"You and I know differently, Ballard. But all I can do right now is offer my help—unofficially. So far there's no proof that the threats are drug-related or aimed at Jackie or any of you. But perhaps the three of us can do some sleuthing on our own."

"Then we're not crazy for thinking something is out of kilter"

"Pam's convinced something will happen to one of the honored alumni or Hopewell guests. She doesn't want it to be her sister."

"And you can't risk it being Jackie Marshall," I said.

He eyed me impassively. "That's about it."

CHAPTER
ELEVEN

After lunch I left David playing tennis with Seth while I went back to the stateroom for a nap. I shed my shoes and dress and lay down in my slip. Slumber swept over me like a great, rolling wave.

David woke me an hour later. "You feeling okay, hon?"

I sat up and shook my head groggily. "I'm just wiped out after our big day in Juneau yesterday. Did you and Seth have a good game?"

"Good from his viewpoint. He won." David sat down beside me and rubbed my neck. "You feel like traipsing around Skagway?"

I smiled grimly. "Actually, I feel like I could sleep for a week, but then I'd miss most of the cruise."

"I could go ashore with Seth and Abigail and let you sleep."

I nudged him teasingly. "You kidding? Me sleep while you have all the fun?"

David chuckled. "I'm not sure that being a third wheel with Seth and Abigail is my idea of fun."

"David, shame on you. I thought you liked Seth and Abigail."

"Don't get me wrong. I do." He leaned over and kissed the back of my neck. "But I'd rather spend the day with you."

"You will," I smiled impishly. "In Skagway."

He sighed. "Yeah, well, that would be nice too."

I slipped away from David, went to the bathroom mirror, and peered at my smudged makeup and pale complexion. What had happened to my rosy cheeks and healthy glow? Splashing cold water on my face, I asked, "Did you and Seth have a good visit?"

David ambled over to the sink and watched me blot my face with skin freshener. "Yes and no. Seth did most of the talking."

"Really? What about?"

"The usual—his world-hunger programs. And you."

"Me? You mean the book he wants me to write?"

"Bingo. But I gave him a clear perspective on the subject."

I stared at David's reflection in the mirror. "You did *what*?"

"You know. I let him know it just wouldn't work right now."

My voice took on an emotional edge. "Who says it won't work?"

David rubbed my shoulders but I stiffened against his touch. "Michelle, you know perfectly well—we've talked about it—"

I toweled my face. "*You've* talked about it, David."

"What's that crack supposed to mean?"

"It means in your mind it's a foregone conclusion that I won't write Seth's book, and I won't go to Thailand. I'll stay home and be a dutiful little wife."

The muscles in David's face hardened. "I once thought that's what you wanted." He turned to go, but I caught his arm.

"Wait, David, we can't leave it like this—the two of us at each other's throat. Can't you understand where I'm coming from on this?"

"That works two ways, Michelle. I want a wife, not a foreign correspondent."

"Haven't I been a good wife to you, David?"

His expression softened. "Better than I deserve."

"Then why can't you trust my judgment about my career? Why can't you trust me to do what's best for us, for our marriage?"

"Maybe it scares me a little to see us wanting separate things. I don't want our marriage relationship to become just an afterthought to you, a convenience, like congenial roommates."

"Really David, we could hardly be considered mere roommates!"

"What I'm saying, Michelle, is that when it comes to a family, I want the whole ball of wax—a loving wife, a comfortable house, children to come home to—"

I eyed David sharply. "That's what this is really all about, isn't it? Children! You're saying no to this book to punish me for not wanting a baby."

David threw up his hands in exasperation and stalked out of the bathroom. "You said you wanted to talk, so I told you how I feel. I try to be honest and you launch a full-scale attack."

I followed David over to the sofa. "I'm not attacking. I'm just trying to understand what's happening to us. Why can't we agree on anything anymore?"

David sat down. "I'm willing to work out a compromise."

I sat on the opposite end of the sofa. "Compromise on a baby? I can't be just a little bit pregnant, David. It's all or nothing."

"That doesn't mean your career has to end."

"Doesn't it? I'm not Superwoman. I'm smart enough to know that a baby is a full-time job. Something would have to go. I would never neglect our child, so it would have to be my writing."

"I'm sorry you see having our child as making such a sacrifice."

"Oh, David, it won't be someday. But right now—"

"Right now you'd rather trot off to Thailand with Seth Mueller."

"Are we going to talk rationally or hurl insults?"

David put his head in his hands. We were both silent now, absorbed in our own thoughts. Finally David looked up at me and remarked, "No one ever said it would be easy."

I stared at him. "What?"

"Marriage. Society, Women's Lib, even the churches haven't figured out just what husbands and wives are supposed to be doing these days. Why should I presume to have the answer for us?"

"Are you saying there are no solutions? Isn't that fatalistic?"

"Oh, there are answers, Michelle. The Bible is full of answers—guidelines for right living. The principles are there, but God leaves it up to us to apply them to our own lives. There's no verse to tell us whether you should go to Thailand or get pregnant."

"So how do we know what's right, David?"

He managed a crooked little smile. "I suppose we could ask God. Pray about it. The two of us."

"We do pray, David. Almost every morning, even if it's just a few words."

"Sometimes that gets to be as much a habit as grabbing toast and coffee and throwing you a good-bye kiss," said David.

I smiled in spite of myself. "Oh, so now I'm just a habit?"

"A wonderful habit. One I never want to break."

"Same here," I whispered, with feeling. "So do we pray?"

"Now? After our squabble, I don't feel very righteous."

"Me neither." Gently he pulled me over beside him and cleared his throat. A minute passed before he spoke, his voice low and gravelly. "Lord—our Father—I'm a little embarrassed to talk to You right now. In fact, I don't want to do the talking at all. I've said too much already. I've been caught up with what I want, what I think is right for Michelle and me. Now I just want to listen—hear what You want for us, what You expect of us. Even before we are each other's, we are Yours."

For several minutes we sat together in the quiet of our stateroom, sharing a wordless communion with the Lord. I didn't know what to pray for, or what to hope for, so in the soundless, cloistered room of my mind, I uttered, *I love You, Jesus. Give me Your will, Your best, even if I don't know what it is.*

Finally, David stirred and kissed the top of my head. "Know what, darling? We have only a couple more hours to see Skagway."

I stood up and smoothed my slip. "Give me 20 minutes to fix my face." I started for the bathroom, then looked back at David. "Nothing's resolved, you know. You still want a son, I still want my career."

"I know, sweetheart. We don't need the answer as long as we both keep our hearts tender before God—and tender with each other."

I brushed my hair back from my forehead. "It sounds so simple, doesn't it, David? Why is it so hard to live?"

The two of us promised to tuck our differences and our separate hopes and dreams away for a few fleeting hours when we disembarked at Skagway—a picturesque village wedged between towering mountains.

The depot wagon—a rustic, horse-drawn buggy—met us at the pier and clippity-clopped us a quarter mile into the frontier town with its wooden boardwalks and gravel streets. The main street summoned nostalgic images of the past. Quaint, turn-of-the-century buildings resembled a movie back lot for filming an old-time Western. Skagway was a living ghost town with a rowdy, flamboyant gold-rush flavor. The residents, dressed in flannel shirts and gingham dresses, rode by on buckboards and waved merrily, their pride in their town obvious in their healthy, glowing expressions.

Our driver—a young man in a black Lincoln suit and high-top hat—filled us in on Skagway's history. "The town was founded in 1888 by William Moore, a ship's captain. We were the last outpost for the gold seekers bound for the rich Klondike fields. It was a treacherous 600-mile journey over the mountains to the mine."

"What was it like during the gold-rush days?" I asked.

Our jocular driver chuckled. "History has it we were a rip-roaring boomtown teeming with gold-hungry prospectors, gun-toting ruffians, and cancan girls."

"When did you come to Skagway?" asked David.

"I was born here," said the fellow proudly. "As a matter of fact, my great granddad was one of the 20,000 fortune-seekers who set out with high hopes and an old mule. The poor animal was loaded with supplies for the winter. The mule died on the way, but Gramps made it back in one piece. He used to tell us how tough it was, how the carcasses of men and animals littered the trail. Thousands died of exposure and starvation. The irony is, when Gramps finally reached the Yukon, most of the land had already been claimed."

"Then he never found the gold he was after?" I asked.

"Nope. He ended up broke. What he didn't lose on Dead Horse Trail, he lost to wine, women, and song in the Skagway saloons." He flicked the reins, urging the horses onward.

"When the boom ended, Skagway dwindled to what it is today—800 people or so. But we're proud of our history."

Our friendly, talkative driver wound down finally as we reached the Visitor Center—a timeworn building with a rough-hewn facade made of 20,000 pieces of driftwood. "You folks might like to take in the Soapy Smith matinee. Soapy was the infamous bad man of the Klondike. He ran Skagway with six-gun ruthlessness, but he got his just dues in a final duel with the town marshall. They wiped each other out."

By the time our driver dropped us off at the pier, David and I were caught up in the excitement and romance of the gold-rush era. Our argument of the morning was forgotten, or at least submerged for the moment. We were laughing like frolicking children as we climbed the gangplank and headed for the Sea Breeze Dining Room for dinner.

Later, with the first twilight glow of evening, the *Mendenhall* set sail, cruising leisurely in the fading rays of daylight down the lovely, pristine Lynn Canal. Arm in arm, David and I watched the rustic town and forested coastline recede into the distant mist. Dreamily, we went in and joined my sister Pam and Silas Winters in the Golden Sails Lounge for a lilting, bombastic salute to musical comedies. Afterward, the three of them headed for the midnight buffet while I returned to my stateroom for a little extra beauty sleep.

When I woke at dawn the next morning, David's side of the bed was empty. The covers were rumpled, his pajamas tossed over the headboard. "Don't tell me he's already out jogging on the sun deck," I muttered into my pillow. I rolled onto my back and began to feel the power of the engines beneath me, the ship rising and falling with the gentle ocean swells. Without warning, a swift, violent onslaught of nausea punctuated the rocking motion. I stumbled out of bed and bounded into the bathroom where I spent several ghastly moments retching into the bowl.

I knew if David found me like this, he would confine me to our stateroom with hot tea and lemon. He'd worry about flu or a virus when I knew it was a simple case of *mal de mer*. I had to get out, go somewhere for help.

I was perspiring as I pulled on my silk dressing gown and peeked out the door. The corridor was empty except for our young steward balancing a pile of clean linen. He grinned, then looked quickly away. I slipped out and scurried down the hall to Pam's room. I turned the knob and tapped lightly, then knocked more persistently. Pam yanked the door open and stared in annoyed wonderment at me. "Good grief, Michelle, what do you want at this hour of the morning?"

"I'm sick."

"You look terrible."

"I *feel* terrible."

Pam pushed back her sleep-tangled hair. "Tell David."

"He's jogging on the sun deck."

"At five in the morning?"

"He likes to see the sun come up."

"It's still the middle of the night to me."

"Please, Pam. You're a nurse. Help me."

She pulled me inside, grumbling, "Even as a nurse I never liked the night shift."

Another wave of nausea washed over me. I ran for the bathroom. "I'm going to be sick again!"

Pam switched on the bathroom light. "You *are* green."

"I'm seasick." I leaned over the sink, dry gagging. "But if I don't stop this, I'll never talk David into another cruise."

Pam slapped a cool, wet cloth on my forehead. "Here, sit on the john," she urged. "We'll use the waste basket for an emesis bucket."

"I fail to see the humor," I muttered.

As Pam turned off the faucet, we heard Abigail stirring. "What's wrong, Pam?" she called.

"No problem," said Pam. "Just my big sister being a big baby."

When I glanced up to protest, I noticed that Pam had the strangest expression on her face—half impish, half astonishment.

"How many times have you been seasick, Michelle?" she asked.

I gripped the basket. "Two or three, I don't remember."

"You were okay the first night out?"

I nodded.

"Very interesting," she said, drawing out the words. "If you were prone to seasickness, I doubt you would have weathered those first few hours at sea."

Abigail joined us, standing barefoot in the bathroom door-way—my old college prof in a sheer pink nightgown and pink plastic hair rollers. "You were a little ill that night in the storm," she said.

"And the last few mornings," I moaned, reaching for the dry saltine Pam offered. "I felt nauseated, but not this bad."

"The ocean's smooth today, Michelle."

"So I get sick on gentle swells."

"Abigail," said Pam, "hand me that sweat suit in the corner."

"The one you didn't hang up last night?" she asked sweetly.

"Probably the one Pam borrowed from me," I said. "I haven't found my teal pantsuit since she was in my cabin two days ago."

Moments later Pam tossed the teal pantsuit in my lap and wrenched the wastebasket from my hands. "Put that on, big sis. We're going to see the ship's doctor."

"That's a good idea, Pam," said Abigail. "He can give Michelle something—medication or one of those patches behind the ear."

"No shot," I protested, wriggling into my pantsuit.

"I didn't have a shot in mind, big sis. We're going for a pregnancy test."

I almost vomited again. "Pregnancy test? David'll have a fit!"

"You've always said he wants kids."

"He does," I croaked, "but not on vacation."

"That's crazy, Michelle."

"Crazy or not, that's what he said in Solidad when he thought I was pregnant. He said, 'Not here, Michelle. Not on our honeymoon.'"

"Well, if you're pregnant, big sis, the honeymoon is over."

"Would you please stop calling me *big* sis!" I said shrilly.

She brushed my damp hair from my face and handed me some mouthwash. "So if you're pregnant, Michelle, how did it happen?"

"Really, Pam, you're a nurse. You figure it out."

"You know what I mean. I thought you were being so careful."

"I was," I said, burying my head in the basin again. Then, coming up for air, I said, "I know what happened. David had just brought home 11 red roses . . ."

"Eleven? Why not a dozen?"

"We just needed 11. He gives me a rose for each month we're married."

Pam shook her head wearily. "Heaven help him when you reach your golden wedding anniversary."

I couldn't even laugh. I was gagging again.

"So what about the 11 roses?" Pam prompted.

"It was the same day I found out about the Hopewell cruise. We'd had a little quarrel—"

"You two? Quarrel?"

"About having a baby."

Pam pursed her lips, half-amused. "Do I dare ask which side you were on?"

"If you must know, I voted for waiting a few years. But then the news about the cruise just bowled me over. . . ."

Pam wiped my forehead again. "You're not making much sense, you know. What do roses and a cruise have to do with getting pregnant?"

"I'm trying to tell you. I ran into David's study and confronted him with the brochure about Hopewell's honored alumni—"

"He was supposed to keep intercepting the mail," said Pam.

"I know, but he forgot, what with the roses and all." I made my way out of the bathroom, weak-kneed, and collapsed on the sofa.

Pam followed, carrying the wastebasket. "So, okay, you burst into David's study. Then what?"

"Well, I—I was so excited about the cruise, I just—you know—just got carried away."

Pam shook her head. "Say no more, big—uh, I mean, sis. A moment of passion will do you in every time."

"You make it sound so cheap and tawdry."

"Not cheap. Great. I like the idea of being an aunt. It may be the closest I get to a baby of my own." Pam turned to Abigail. "Now, if you'll excuse us, we'll finish off this rude awakening with a doctor's visit."

I groaned. "I can't be pregnant, Pam. I'd know, wouldn't I?"

"You'll know in an hour or so."

"But Seth wants me in Thailand and I've almost convinced David!"

"Thailand can wait, but this baby won't," said Pam.

"You make it sound like a proven fact," I countered.

"You bet," said Pam with a gleeful grin. "In fact, Aunt Pam is already thinking of names. Like Pamela—after me—if it's a girl!"

As Pam pushed me out the cabin door, Abigail reached out and squeezed my hand helplessly. "Do you want me to pray that it's just seasickness, Michelle?"

CHAPTER TWELVE

When Pam and I reached the doctor's office, I was almost relieved to find the door locked. "I should have realized," said Pam, "the doctor's not going to be in at 6:00 A.M. Maybe we can call the emergency number."

"It's not necessary, Pam," I insisted. "I'm feeling better already. I'm sure it was just a simple case of seasickness."

Pam eyed me suspiciously. "And it only strikes you the first thing in the morning? Well, you'd better come back during office hours and have a pregnancy test anyway—just to be sure."

"All right, Pam. If it'll make you happy, I'll do it. But later. Maybe tomorrow. David and I are spending today looking at Glacier Bay. It's the highlight of our whole cruise and I'm not going to spoil it fussing around with a pregnancy test."

"You still look a little green around the gills," said Pam.

"Don't worry. I'll cover it with foundation and blush."

"That might help your color, but it won't erase the nausea."

I wrinkled my nose at Pam and turned away. "I'm not pregnant!"

"Don't be too sure, big sis!"

I hurried back to my room and managed to shower and dress before David returned from jogging. When he finally burst in the door, breathless and perspiring, he asked, "What got you up so early, hon?"

"You wouldn't believe me if I told you."

"Well, I'd better get my shower over before breakfast. I'm starved. How about you?"

I clasped my stomach in misery at the thought of food. "All I want is a cup of hot tea."

David pulled off his jogging sweats and threw them on the bed. He gave me a half-amused smile. "I ran into Stoddard up on the deck. He asked me if you were writing another novel—a mystery."

"Why would he want to know that?"

"It had crossed his mind that these Hopewell threats were a hoax, maybe part of your research for your next book."

"He was kidding, I hope!"

"I think so, but I couldn't help feeling there was a nugget of doubt in his mind. He did mention how you were into things all the time at Hopewell—little jokes and pranks. He said with you and Jackie on board, anything was possible."

"Then he wasn't kidding! He must really suspect me! Next thing you know he'll have a crew member tailing me!"

David squeezed the back of my neck as he headed for the shower. "I wouldn't have told you what he said if I thought it would upset you. I thought it was kind of funny myself."

I sat down weakly on the bed and shook my head in despair. "How can I possibly face Stoddard or the other alumni if they think I'm involved in this crazy mess?"

"No one's accusing you of anything, Michelle," David called through the open bathroom door. "I think President Stoddard is just desperately looking for an easy solution to this thing. He'd be delighted if the threats were a simple prank by an ingenious author working out a mystery plot."

"Well, they're not, and I hope you told him so."

"I told him you were going to turn this thing into the best mystery ever, rivaling Robert Ludlum or John MacDonald."

I darted into the bathroom. "David, you didn't! Tell me you didn't!"

David grinned. "I didn't, darling. I came to your rescue like a knight in shining armor. Stoddard ended up apologizing for even suggesting the possibility." David was still chuckling as he slipped into the shower stall.

I went back to the bed and sat down, nursing my wounded spirit. I could hear David whistling above the sound of running water. Moments later, he poked his head out from behind the curtain. He was dripping water on the floor. "It doesn't matter what Stoddard or anyone else thinks. Pranks or not, I love you, Michelle Ballard."

He disappeared back behind the curtain, but before I could look away, he poked his face out again. "Still upset?" he asked.

"I'm just embarrassed, hurt. Having President Stoddard even joke about me doing something that malicious—"

"Forget it, Michelle. I can think of more important things to do." He smiled impishly. "Want to join me? The water's fine."

*   *   *

Two hours later, the S.S. *Mendenhall* had already picked up the park rangers and was cruising deep into Glacier Bay as David and I finished a light breakfast. We went back to our stateroom, bundled in our warmest clothes, then made our way up to the observation deck where dozens of passengers lined the railing, snapping photos or videotaping the glaciers.

I gazed around in wonderment at the phantasmagoria of ice and snow—mammoth crystalline glaciers couched among lofty, ice-clad mountains, their snowy peaks melting into the milky-whiteness of the sky. I slipped my hand over David's arm as a hint of sunlight cast a luminous sheen on the overcast heavens. "The glaciers—they're so immense—so incredible. Pictures just don't do them justice."

"Maybe not," he smiled, "but I'm going to take plenty anyway."

We walked over to the rail and found a spot beside Jackie and Stevie. Our greetings were bright and brief as we turned our attention back to the icy grandeur around us. I looked down into the jade-green water dotted with ice floe. The floating islands ranged from ice cubes to boulder-size chunks. "David, the sea looks like a giant slush. Can you imagine taking a big straw and stirring it around?"

"I'm not *that* thirsty," he quipped as he focused his camera.

"Oh, David, I am. I could drink in this scenery all day!"

Our ship moved slowly, serenely through the opalescent water like a soundless phantom in a glassy, frost-bound kingdom. The regal glaciers rose up skyscraper-high from the sea, their sculpted cliffs and deep fjords dazzling in countless shades of aqua blue and chalky gray. The rugged glaciers loomed close, rising up in sheer ice walls, so close I felt as if I could reach out and touch them. Solid and massive, they looked like sleeping giants or prehistoric animals slumbering in the bay. As we glided through the ice-choked waters, I felt dwarfed by nature, caught in a breathtaking wilderness that whisked me back in time to the chillingly mysterious Ice Age.

"Look, David—this beauty—it's as if time just began."

"No," he said thoughtfully, "it's more like the cycles of history have ground to a halt. Life stands still, unchanging, eternal."

"It's true, David. This place gives me such a feeling of stability, of permanence, of peace. I don't want to leave."

Even as I spoke of the tranquillity of Glacier Bay, I heard a distant cracking sound followed by an echoing roar. David whipped his camera in place and snapped a picture as a monstrous chunk of ice calved off from the frosty glacier and thundered into the bay. At the instant of impact, a miniature tidal wave swept our way, sending three seals shimmying across an ice floe into the icy waters. As an avalanche of ice plunged from the fractured glacier, two bald eagles took flight, winging majestically over our ship.

"Jackie," I cried, "wasn't that spectacular?"

"Breathtaking!" she exclaimed. Then, leaning down, Jackie asked little Stevie, "What do the glaciers look like to you, honey?"

In his buoyant child's voice, he squealed, "Like Sno-Cones and bubble-gum ice cream!"

David bent down and scooped Stevie onto his shoulders for a better view. "There's more than ice to see, Stevie. You look real close and you might even see a bear!"

"A big, scary bear?" cried Stevie.

"You bet—a black or brown one or maybe even a rare blue one."

"There aren't blue bears, are there, Mommy?"

"Must be—if David says so, Stevie."

"I've never seen one," said David, "but that's what people say."

After a few minutes Stevie's lower lip protruded. "I want to see a bear, Mommy!"

"Just keep looking at the mountains, honey."

"Uncle David promised me a big bear!"

"What about that snow-carved figure down there?" I suggested, pointing to an iceberg that resembled a large white polar bear.

"Mrs. Marshall, would your son settle for a mountain goat?" asked a deep, resonant voice from behind us. "There's one on that barren cliff to the right."

I whirled around at the familiar voice, embarrassed to see President Stoddard and his wife, Rachel, sitting in deck chairs nearby, lap robes wrapped securely around them. President Stoddard was out of his element in a heavy wool hunting jacket, a navy-blue sun visor shoved back on his high forehead. Even from where I stood, I could see his shrewd twinkle. He held out binoculars in his long, knuckled fingers. "Here, let the boy look at the mountain goats."

As I walked over and took the binoculars, a hint of a smile pursed Stoddard's lips, as if he were swallowing his dry sense of humor or privately wondering how my mystery research was coming.

I turned my attention back to Stevie when I heard him beg, "Can I pet the baby goat, Mommy?"

"Look, Tiger," David exclaimed, pointing, "there's a harbor seal on that slab of ice!"

Stevie aimed his binoculars at the seal and squealed delightedly.

I smiled inwardly at the eager twosome—David, so tall and strappingly handsome, and Stevie perched proudly on his shoulders, his chubby fingers clutching the huge binoculars. David was so good with kids. Would I ever have his special knack, his easy way of making them laugh? If David had his way, I'd find out soon enough. I winced, remembering the pregnancy test Pam insisted I take. *What if? . . .*

* * *

We'd been at the rail for over an hour when Silas Winters and my sister Pam sauntered our way. "Can we chat awhile?" Silas asked, beckoning us over to one side.

"Talk? Here on the deck?" I glanced around uneasily. Was anyone watching? Candy Seaton was visiting with Jackie. Brett was pointing out the seals to young Stevie. Cam and Stephanie Ellis stood at the rail nearby, their attention focused on the glaciers.

I turned back to Silas. He was saying quietly, "I talked with Captain Pagliarulo last night and offered my services regarding this Hopewell problem. Unofficially, of course. I cleared it with my agency first, naturally. They agreed, since there's the remote possibility of a drug connection. Or a syndicate involvement. Or even retaliation against Jackie Marshall." He gazed around covertly. "The captain and I figure if we combine our ideas, we'll come up with some viable theories. We'd like to force this fellow out into the open and wind this thing up before we dock in Vancouver."

"Does the captain know you're telling us these things?" I asked.

Silas flashed an elusive smile. "Yes. It's a little unorthodox to involve passengers in this sort of intrigue, but I told him we worked together in the Caribbean. I vouched for you both. Told him you were absolutely trustworthy."

"I'm glad the captain's finally taking some action," said David.

"Actually, Captain Pagliarulo has been investigating this situation since the night someone fired a shot into the vase of roses. He immediately tightened security and notified authorities that there could be trouble on board."

"I haven't noticed any extra security," I told him.

"You won't see it," said Silas, "but you can be certain it's there." As we ambled back over to Jackie, Silas added, "Let's keep this thing confidential. As far as everyone else is concerned, I'm just another passenger—Pam's friend. In fact, she's already introduced me to several of the alumni."

Without warning, just as we reached Jackie, Cam Ellis burst between David and me and barked, "What's going on over here? A Hopewell prayer meeting?"

Silas chuckled. "You kidding? Not me, man. I'm not exactly on speaking terms with the Man upstairs." He held out his hand to Cam. "We haven't met yet. I'm Silas Winters. I boarded in Juneau."

"I noticed." Cam's brow arched suspiciously. "My name's Cam Ellis. This is my wife, Stephanie," he said, drawing her to him.

"Silas is a friend of my sister, Pam," I told the Ellises.

"More than friends." Pam took Silas's arm possessively.

Silas bent over, kissed Pam's lips, and drawled, "Much more."

"Since you're new on board, Mr. Winters," said Cam, "you probably haven't heard about all the trouble Hopewell's having—"

"Trouble? Tell me." Silas played his ignorance to the hilt.

With relish Cam told Silas about the threats against the four honored alumni. "No one knows which honoree is the intended victim, but the notes say one will be dead by the time this cruise is over."

"Which one?" asked Silas, giving Cam his full attention.

"Who knows?" said Cam. "From what they say, the only thing the four of them have in common is this Hopewell honor."

"And right now the honor isn't very comforting," I said dryly, slipping my cold hand into David's warm, protective one.

Brett Seaton, standing now beside Jackie, leaned back against the rail and eyed Cam curiously. "I still say it's no big deal, Ellis. Nothing has happened since the vase shattered in the Golden Sails Lounge. And that was likely just a freak accident."

"Just coincidental that the flowers were for the Hopewell anniversary?" Candy challenged her husband with a grimly bemused smile. "And you think we're not dealing with an insane man?"

"I think the threats are more the deeds of an angry man than an insane one," said Cam. "Maybe I'm playing devil's advocate, but I think we need to understand this person's motives."

"Motives?" Jackie countered, drawing Stevie over beside her. "Only an emotionally disturbed man would threaten the lives of innocent people."

"Perhaps it's the only way he can see that justice is done," Cam shot back, his voice suddenly raw with emotion.

"Justice? What kind of justice, Mr. Ellis?" inquired Silas.

As I looked around from face to face, I was alarmed by the agitated expressions. Why was Silas Winters allowing this conversation to get out of hand? Was he deliberately egging us on? Searching for motives, as Cam had suggested? Silas's gaze lingered appraisingly on Cam. Then he looked down at Pam and winked. "Let's go grab a bite to eat, sweetheart."

"And miss the rest of the glaciers?" Pam pouted. "No way."

"Why don't I order lunch inside on the sun deck?" said David. "For all of us. How about it, folks? We could warm up a bit."

"You go ahead," said Brett. "Candy and I'll stay out here and face the wind awhile longer."

I snuggled into my coat, warding off the chill as David beckoned to a young steward. "Can you have some lunch ordered up to the sun deck for us—say," he glanced around, "say for eight of us? You can charge it to my stateroom . . ."

"No charge for the food, sir," the young man answered as David tipped him generously. "I'll have sandwiches and salad on the sun deck for you in about 20 minutes."

A half hour later Cam still looked disgruntled as we sat munching our sandwiches. He looked over at Silas. "What kind of work do you do, Mr. Winters?"

Silas drained his piña colada. "I travel a lot. This job. That job. Europe. The States. Grenada."

"He was the concierge in the Caribbean when we met," said Pam.

Silas eyed Cam curiously. "What business are you in, Ellis?"

Before Cam could reply, Stevie bounded over to Silas and held out his hand for the slice of fresh pineapple in his empty glass. Silas gave him the fruit and Stevie darted back beside his mother. Cam followed the boy's antics with somber eyes. Was he thinking about the son he had lost—if indeed my suspicions were true?

After several long moments, Cam raised his gaze to Jackie. "I notice that you never leave the ship, Mrs. Marshall. Is it because of the threats to the alumni, the danger we're all facing?"

Stephanie patted Cam's arm. "Oh, Cameron, let's not spoil this beautiful scenery by discussing unpleasant things."

Cam bristled. "Stephanie," he said sharply, "let's face it. We're all in danger on this ship. Why shouldn't we talk about it?"

Stephanie crept back into her shell, too intimidated to finish her lunch or even look my way. I felt sorry for her, angry with her unfeeling husband. "Cam," I said gently, "you know President Stoddard asked us to keep things as low-key as possible. He doesn't want us to raise unnecessary alarm."

"But murder demands a hearing," Cam argued hotly.

"There's been no murder, Cam," I said emphatically.

"Not yet. But if somebody doesn't do something soon, there will be. Mark my words." Cam pushed his plate aside and leaned back in his deck chair. Even the beauty of the surrounding fountainheads of ice couldn't dispel Cam's sullenness.

The minutes ticked away. Five. Ten. Fifteen.

I was irritated by Cam, but I pitied him too. I thought again of Stephanie's poems and was convinced that Cam's inner turmoil was caused by the death of his son. But how would the others know the reason for Cam's pain and anger if he wouldn't tell them?

One by one our group disbanded. Pam and Silas excused themselves and walked off, hand in hand. Jackie led an animated little Stevie back out to the observation deck, reminding him of how much the glacial mountains resembled the Swiss Alps back home.

"What about it, Cam?" David asked. "Are you warm enough to go back out and get some more pictures? Maybe a shot of a bald eagle."

Cam slouched in the deck chair, his eyes closed. "I'll just rest here awhile, David," he said without looking up. "Stephanie, you'll stay with me, won't you?"

She sat down in the chair beside him and rested her hand on his, her face settling into an expression of pained resignation.

* * *

That evening, after a full day of watching the glaciers, I was ready to turn in early. I'd started this busy Friday at dawn with a violent attack of nausea; now, at shortly after ten, I was finishing the day with an inexorable wave of exhaustion. I'd never felt more weary. I sank into a deep, welcome sleep as soon as I settled between the smooth sheets. My dreams were filled with ice kingdoms and snow princesses and glittering rainbows with tiny, plump cherubs that all looked like little Stevie. David skated through the dream, gathering the cherub babies, calling them all his sons. . . .

The telephone jangled in the deep, dusky silence just before dawn. I jumped up, fumbled for the receiver, and mumbled a fuzzy hello. After a moment, the low, muffled voice of a man intoned:

Just beyond the windswept sea
cold, cruel death awaits for thee!

Terror-stricken, I slammed the receiver back into its cradle and woke David. My heart hammered as I choked out the words, "David— another message! The same man—that deep, sinister voice—oh, David, the death threat—it's aimed at *me*!"

CHAPTER THIRTEEN

Grinding his jaw tightly, David grabbed up the phone, dialed Silas Winters, and spoke briefly, tersely. Then, covering the mouthpiece, he said to me, "Thatcher and Seaton received the same warning. Silas still has to check with Mueller, but I assume he got a call too. That means no one's out of the running yet."

"What a quaint way to put it," I said grimly.

David hung up the phone and took me in his arms. "You're sure it was the same man who made the taped message Stoddard played?"

"Positive. And it was the same ominous tone I heard in the library when the man said, 'I will hunt you down. I will have my revenge.' There's something familiar about his inflection. I have a feeling I'd recognize the man if he spoke in his normal voice."

"Then he could be someone we're associating with every day."

"Oh, David, that's what gives me the creeps."

The sharp contours of David's face hardened. "Maybe we should cut short our cruise. Pack up and fly home from the next port."

"We can't, David. If we panic and run, so will everyone else. Then this deranged person—whoever he is—wins."

"It's either that or go on as if nothing's happened."

I shivered involuntarily. "I guess we have no other choice."

That morning, as our ship cruised around Hubbard Glacier at Yakutat Bay, David and I went up to the Sky Room for the usual Hopewell devotions. President Stoddard had obviously heard about the latest telephone threat because he prefaced his sermon with a message directly to our unknown terrorist.

"Whoever you are—if you are in this room—please come, seek me out, let me pray with you. God offers you love and forgiveness—and a better way to handle your problems than with hateful threats."

There was a long moment of silence as everyone stole furtive glances around the room. As I quietly scanned the faces around me, I wondered, What secrets do they hold? Is our anonymous adversary among them? Is it someone I know and trust? The more I pondered, the more suspicious I felt—of *everyone*! No wonder Stoddard, in his own helpless paranoia, had suspected me!

I felt relieved when President Stoddard finally launched his devotional message. The entire mood in the Sky Room brightened as his resonant voice boomed, "Can you believe it—the beauty and splendor of Glacier Bay yesterday?" As everyone applauded, Stoddard continued, "It was as if all of nature was shouting about the majesty of God. Bald eagles soaring skyward. Puffins playing on an iceberg. A school of sea lions diving and swimming in those ice-clogged waters. Nature was alive yesterday. And why not? The Creator of the heavens and earth—and of those fantastic, icy, blue-rimmed wonders— was there with us. Reminding us of Himself."

Stoddard paused and rubbed the bridge of his ruddy, pronounced nose. "What about it, dear friends? Is your heart bursting with joy toward your Creator? Are you winging like the bald eagle? Carefree as the sea lion? As trusting as the puffin? 'Beloved, what manner of love the Father hath bestowed upon us that we,' not the eagles or puffins or sea lions, but we human beings 'should be called the sons of God.' And when we see Him in His indescribable beauty—a beauty far surpassing Glacier Bay—'we shall be like him; for we shall see him as he is.' "

President Stoddard squared his broad shoulders and raised his well-worn Bible. "Beloved, if we have this hope in us, then we will desire to be pure. We will love, forgive, and rise above any threat that hovers over us." He glanced out the Sky Room windows where the weather was gloomy with low-hanging clouds. Yesterday's mirror-like sea had become frothy and foamy as the waves crested and broke. Stoddard's voice was confident as he declared, "We can face every storm with the courage of those who walk with God!"

Without warning, a resounding, stentorian voice cut through Stoddard's words. "Any storm, President Stoddard?"

We all turned to stare at Jason Thatcher. His face looked haggard, distorted; his eyes riveted on Stoddard. "What about the storm of dying, sir? What about that?"

"Through any storm, Dr. Thatcher," Stoddard repeated kindly.

Jason cleared his throat with a rare nervousness. "President Stoddard, I've spent my whole career in life-or-death situations; my adult years teaching Sunday school classes—teaching men and women to trust God. But I have avoided the issue of dying like a staph infection in the surgical suite."

"You know the Lord, don't you, Thatcher? You've had a personal encounter with Him? You believe in life after death—?"

"Ever since my boyhood."

"Then what is it that troubles you?"

"The act of dying. I've never been able to prevent it. I've never been able to tell anyone exactly what happens."

Stoddard gave a quick, little chuckle. "You mean between the moment of dying and the golden streets of glory?"

"Something like that, sir."

"Are you looking for a pat, scientific answer to feed man's soul, Thatcher? Or are you wondering if there is a river to cross or a mountain to climb or some final, lonely tunnel?" When Dr. Thatcher didn't answer, Stoddard went on. "We know certain things, Jason. We know that God keeps His promises. That to be absent from the body is to be ushered into the very presence of God. We know that the Savior will stretch out His nail-scarred hands and welcome us home."

"I've taught all of that, sir. I've reassured my patients again and again, but you can't give false hope . . . and sometimes you get backed up against a wall with no way out. What do you do then?"

"You trust," Stoddard answered simply.

"Trust?" Thatcher's ashen face twisted slightly. "Do you think I can look at a patient—at an emaciated, dying man and simply say, 'Trust'?" Jason pivoted, gazed around entreatingly at the audience, then turned back to Stoddard. "Perhaps I'm playing devil's advocate, but I have to have answers. For my patients, for myself."

"We understand, Dr. Thatcher," said Stoddard placatingly. "Perhaps another time we can—"

"No, you don't understand," Jason shot back. "I'm sick of walking into a hospital room, patting a patient's bony shoulder, and suggesting chemotherapy or surgery when I know nothing is going to salvage the man." He ran his fingers through his cropped mane of silver-white hair. His voice rode the edge of hysteria, desperation. "President Stoddard, do you know what it feels like to realize you're not going to be here tomorrow or next week or next month? I deal with such realities all the time. People think of surgeons as cold and indifferent. But, sir, I have never performed surgery without agonizing in prayer and without offering to pray with my patients."

"That's commendable, Dr. Thatcher. That's as it should be—"

"Is it?" Jason retorted. "I've been searching my own soul. I walk in and tell a young man that he's in the homestretch; it's over for him. Essentially I'm telling him to go home, tidy up his affairs, and wait to die. Is that it? I've done my duty? The man wants to live. Grow old. Retire. Watch his kids and grandkids grow up. He wants to hold his wife's hand for another 30 or 40 years."

I could tell that President Stoddard was growing increasingly ill at ease. "We can certainly sympathize, Dr. Thatcher—"

Jason slumped back in his chair. "I'm sorry, sir. I got carried away. It's my problem. I'll work it out."

Stoddard's gaze was caring now, intent. "You're wrong, Dr. Thatcher. You have just invited us to share your problem, and God's Word challenges us to carry another man's burden as our own." He paused and the silence in the room was startling.

When he spoke again, his voice was hoarse. "Jason, when my wife and I lost our only son many years ago, no one knew what to say. We wanted answers. No one had them. Our faith was shattered. Then my father arrived. He didn't have any answers either. He didn't even have any advice to offer. He simply put his arms around my wife and me and loved us, day after day, week after week. Then one day I realized, with a first stirring of joy, that I was beginning to heal."

Stoddard fixed his gaze on Jason. "I have no answers for you, Jason. Only God has the answers. All I can say is reach out to your patients. Take their hand. Put your arm around them. Just walk with them one step at a time. Let God do the rest."

He held his Bible open. "As I said before, 'Behold, what manner of love the Father hath bestowed upon us, that we should be called the sons of God.' Jason, dwell on that love. The Father loves you. The Son loves you. The Spirit indwells you. Bathe yourself in His love and forgiveness, and you'll be prepared to face your patients." Slowly, in a deep, rich baritone, Stoddard began to sing, "What a friend we have in Jesus . . ."

After President Stoddard's closing prayer, Cam Ellis stole out of the Sky Room alone. As the rest of the alumni slipped quietly out the door, David leaned over and whispered, "I'm going for a game of tennis with Seth and Silas. But first I'll see if Cam wants to join us. I know you wanted to talk to Stephanie before lunch."

I nodded and walked on quickly, catching up with Stephanie just ahead of me. "Finally we have a chance to talk about your poetry," I told her with enthusiasm. "Your style is so fresh—"

She looked up, her eyes brimming with tears. "Oh, Michelle, I—I just—" Suddenly, she began sobbing uncontrollably.

"Stephanie, I didn't mean to—what's wrong?"

"It's all—all so overwhelming—" she blurted.

I slipped my arm around her supportively and led her to a quiet corner in an empty lounge. When we were seated, facing each other, I said gently, "You've been needing to cry for a long, long time, haven't you, Stephanie—ever since the death of your son?"

"You know?" she sobbed. "Oh, I wanted you to know."

"I knew from your poetry, Stephanie. You made Rodney so real to me. I wept with you when I realized that you had lost him. But why? Why haven't you told us? Just in these few days we've become good friends. David and I want to share your pain."

"Will you still be our friends when I tell you that Cam and I never even went to Hopewell?" she asked. "We're—we're not even Christians." She wrung her hands nervously. "What President Stoddard said—I never heard such things before. Rodney tried to tell us. He went to Hopewell for a while. But Cam and I wouldn't listen."

"Then your son was a Christian?"

"He—he said he was. But then suddenly he dropped out of Hopewell and transferred to Stanford. After that his faith didn't seem to matter anymore, especially when he began law school. Then during this last year Rodney let a wall go up between us."

"I thought your husband and son were great friends," I said.

"They were close. Rodney went into law to please his dad. He was such a sensitive boy; he hated confrontations with his father. But all he really wanted to do was write music."

"Then he was a musician?"

"He never studied professionally, but he used to sit alone in his room, strumming his guitar, writing sad little ballads. In the end I think our plans for him overpowered his own dreams. We loved our son, Michelle. Maybe we just loved him too much."

I touched her hand kindly. "Can a parent ever love too much?"

"I don't know. Right now I'm so confused about everything, even God." Her sad little smile flickered and faded. "President Stoddard talks about being certain—but I don't know anything about God for certain. Oh, Michelle, I have no peace. I have no peace."

Gently I said, "Only with God's forgiveness, Stephanie, can you ever find peace."

Stephanie dabbed at her eyes. "I have no right to forgiveness, Michelle. I—I mocked Rodney's faltering faith. And now he's gone. If Stoddard is right about heaven, where is my son now?"

I studied Stephanie's stricken face, weighing my response. How could I reassure her when I didn't know what Rodney believed? I didn't want to shortcut the sovereignty or mercy or judgments of God. I knew only that God had known Rodney Ellis from the foundations of the earth. He knew what choices Rodney would make and how young he would be at his death. "Stephanie," I began, "I believe someday God will give you peace about your son. He knows you're broken, hurt, confused. He wants to welcome you, love and forgive you, and give you peace."

"It sounds wonderful," she murmured. "Perhaps some-day . . ."

"Why not now?" I asked softly, not wanting to rush God's miracle in Stephanie's heart. "You'll never find a better place or a group of people who loves you more."

"But I'm not worthy of love, Michelle," she said quietly. "I haven't been honest . . . with you, with Cameron, with any-one."

"What do you mean, Stephanie? Honest? About what?"

She swallowed a sob. "The way my son really died. I've always told people he died of pneumonia."

"Are you saying that's not how he died?"

"That's what his death certificate says—and what Cam believes to this day. It's what I thought at first too. But it's not true."

"What happened? Weren't you with him when he died?"

"No. He was living in San Francisco. He called us from the hospital and insisted there was no need for us to come out; he was getting better. He even had his roommate Kent call to assure us he'd look after Rodney until he got back on his feet. And Rodney promised his dad they'd still take their hunting trip this summer." Her voice wavered. "The next thing we knew, the hospital called to tell us our son had died. We were devastated. It seemed so senseless, so unnecessary—a healthy, strapping boy dying of pneumonia these days."

"But you said he didn't die of pneumonia."

"That's right. But I didn't learn the truth until a month after Rodney's death. I flew out to California to collect his things and sell his car. Cam wouldn't go—he couldn't accept the fact that Rodney was gone."

"That must have been difficult for you, making the trip alone."

"Yes, but I wanted to talk with Kent. He was the last one to see our son alive. I wanted to know everything—why Rodney hadn't sent for us. Whether death came easy. Why the doctor—." She choked, then started again. "I wanted to know why the doctor couldn't save him. Oh, Michelle, I had a hundred burning questions."

"And did it help to talk with Kent?"

Stephanie's lips trembled; her eyes flashed. "I wish to heaven I'd never seen that young man. What he said nearly killed me. I'll never forget him declaring, 'Mrs. Ellis, I loved your son.' "

Stephanie's words left me chilled. "Don't go on," I murmured. "You don't have to tell me."

"Oh, but I do. I shall lose my mind if I don't share this burden with someone. When Kent said those words, I was glad my son was dead. I was glad he could never shame his father and me."

"You don't mean that, Stephanie."

"I did at that moment. I started pounding Kent's chest with my fists. He grabbed my wrists and said, 'Mrs. Ellis, I'm sorry. If it hadn't been for me, your son would still be alive. But like it or not, I loved Rodney.' I told him I didn't want to hear anymore, but he said, 'Yes, you will hear. You'll hear what Rodney couldn't tell you himself because he wouldn't hurt you for anything in the world.' "

Stephanie paused, overcome with emotion. Wordlessly I reached over and slipped my arm around her. "I'm so sorry, Stephanie."

Her voice broke as she continued, "Kent told me how hurt Rodney had been. He turned down a hunting trip with his dad because he was so ill; he refused to let us visit him; he was too proud to send for us even when he was dying. I realized what

Kent was really telling me about Rodney when he said, "Mrs. Ellis, your son had . . . AIDS."

For a moment neither Stephanie nor I spoke. Her breathing was labored; she twisted a tissue into a ragged white snake.

"Are you saying Rodney did die of pneumonia . . . as a result of AIDS?" I asked.

Stephanie nodded. "Rodney kept hoping it was a lung tumor. He even saw a specialist, but there was no hope." She wept softly again. "Kent told me that all Rodney ever wanted to do was make us proud of him. Imagine, living like that and wanting us to be proud of him. At least Kent had the decency to tell me that Rodney moved out of their apartment almost a year ago, saying he was going to try to find God again. But when he got sick, he moved back with Kent."

"Then Rodney never found his peace with God?" I asked.

"Not if you believe Kent. He says there's no welcome mat out at the churches for homosexuals."

"I can't speak for the churches, Stephanie, but I can tell you that God offers forgiveness of sin to anyone who comes to Him in repentance. A person may not find a comfortable seat in a church pew, but he can find forgiveness and a welcome mat at the foot of the cross."

Stephanie looked skeptically at me. "A welcome even for Kent?"

"For Kent. For Rodney. For you. For me."

"Maybe God can forgive, but I can't. I feel such rage against Kent. I remember when it was time to say good-bye to that young man, he offered to shake hands. Instinctively, I pulled my hand away. I felt if I touched him, I'd be contaminated. I never extended Kent one moment of forgiveness, one moment of mercy."

"What about Rodney?" I asked. "How do you feel about him?"

"I don't know, Michelle. All I know is that if my son was willing to die alone so that he wouldn't shame Cam and me, I can't betray him. I've vowed to carry Rodney's secret to the grave. But these last few days I realized I couldn't bear this pain alone any longer."

"And you've never told Cam how Rodney really died?"

"I couldn't, Michelle. It would kill him. Cam hasn't been himself since Rodney's death. He keeps threatening a lawsuit against Rodney's doctor for malpractice. He refuses to admit that our son is dead. Cam never drank before, but now—he's drowning his sorrows. I can't reason with him. His grief and bitterness are out of control."

"Then with all you've been through, Stephanie, how did you happen to come on the Hopewell cruise?"

"Actually, the brochure came in the mail addressed to Rodney. Cam said we should go on the cruise in Rodney's place. He said the college had once been part of our son's life, a part we deliberately rejected. I reminded him that Rodney left Hopewell under unpleasant circumstances—something he would never talk about—but Cam said the trip might help us understand that part of our son's life. It might show us what drew him to Hopewell in the first place. I thought the trip would help Cam, but it hasn't. He's more troubled than ever."

I squeezed Stephanie's hand. "Maybe David could talk to Cam."

"Oh, no, Michelle. Promise me you won't tell him what I've said. Cam must never learn the truth about our son."

"Stephanie, I think Cam needs to know. And perhaps he needs professional help—serious counseling before it's too late."

"Please don't say that, Michelle. I love Cam. He's all I have left. I don't want anything to happen to him."

"Then can you and I talk again, Stephanie? Pray together?"

She stood up abruptly. "I can't, Michelle. If I believed in this Jesus of yours—and oh, I'm so afraid that God is speaking to my heart—it would be the last straw for Cam. I'd lose him forever, and I've lost too much already." She turned, tears streaking her face, and ran from the lounge.

CHAPTER
FOURTEEN

For the rest of the day I couldn't get Stephanie out of my mind. She carried such a secret burden of grief over her son. How long could she endure such heartache alone before it broke her spirit completely? I wanted to go to her and offer my comfort, but I'd said enough for now. Meanwhile, I would keep her in my prayers and give her some time and space before seeking her out again.

I spent Saturday afternoon in the lounge watching our ship head into an oncoming storm. High, foamy waves sprayed the bow of the ship as we rolled and dipped with the turbulent sea, until it seemed the waves and horizon met in a crashing crescendo. The rain pelting the windows matched my own somber mood. I wanted to run to David and tell him all I had learned about the Ellises, but I'd promised Stephanie I'd keep her bitter secret.

As I sat gazing out at the rough, wind-tossed sea, I heard a melodic voice behind me say, "They tell me the storm won't last forever, but I'm not so sure."

I whirled around and looked up at Jackie with a sigh of joy. "I've been looking for you, Michelle," she said. "Come help me pick out a gown for the Hopewell reception tomorrow night."

"Sure, be glad to," I said, standing up. "Where's Stevie?"

"Your dear David offered to take him while I shop. Wasn't that sweet of him? But you know those two—they're best pals."

"I know," I smiled. "David won't let me forget it."

As Jackie and I walked down one deck to the gift shop, I asked, "Are you eager to get home to Steve and the baby?"

"Yes, I think about them all the time. Stevie really misses his dad. That's why I'm so glad David's spending time with him."

"Oh, David adores little—" Before I could utter the words, I spotted David and Stevie heading for the stairwell in their swim trunks and terrycloth robes, towels tossed jauntily around their shoulders. "David, you two can't swim in this kind of weather!"

He stopped in mid-step and steered Stevie over to us. "No fear, my dear. We're swimming in the heated pool, not the ocean."

"But the water will be sloshing all over the deck."

"Sounds like fun," he grinned, winking down at Stevie.

Stevie's eyes sparkled as he took David's hand. "Mommy, me and David's going swimming."

The pride in Jackie's eyes matched Stevie's. "I see. You will be careful, won't you, David? He thinks he's a little fish, but he's just learning to swim."

"Is Steve teaching him?" I asked.

"Yes. Steve has so much time on his hands, he has little Stevie into every sport in town—skiing, sledding, mountain climbing—"

"How are the work opportunities in Switzerland?" asked David.

"Not good for an American on the run. Steve can't even claim his work experience. This witness protection program —it's a whole new life-style. No history. No background. It's no way to live."

"Look, Jackie," said David, "I have friends with Hewlett-Packard. They have a European office. I could put in a good word—"

Jackie interrupted sadly, "How can you lend a helping hand, David? You aren't even supposed to know us. We don't exist anymore, remember?" Her voice wavered. "What Steve wants— what we both want is to come home again. Sometimes I think it's worth the risk."

"Well, if you do, I can offer Steve a job at my computer design company in Irvine—in sales, if he'd like."

"You'd trust him that much?"

David smiled. "What are friends for?"

"If we come back," said Jackie, lifting her chin stoically, "it won't be with the government's approval or blessing. We don't know what mob reprisals we may face. Would you risk be-friending us then?"

He squeezed her shoulder reassuringly. "The offer still stands."

"Thank you, David. You don't know how much you and Michelle mean to me." Jackie leaned down and brushed a hurried kiss across Stevie's cheek. "Now go on, you two, and have a good swim."

Jackie and I spent the next two hours in the gift shop as she tried on every size 5 evening dress on the rack. She finally settled on a pale lime-green silk sheath. I bought a necklace and earrings to go with my own dusky rose evening gown.

Throughout Saturday night and Sunday I tried to keep my mind on the Hopewell banquet. It was to be the highlight of our cruise. Mentally I rehearsed what I would say when President Stoddard called me to the podium to accept my award. But in spite of my resolves to keep my thoughts lighthearted and positive, a hint of nausea and lingering depression brought back the pregnancy test I hadn't taken and Stephanie's desolation over her dead son.

After chapel on Sunday, as the *Mendenhall* cruised north-ward through the Gulf of Alaska toward Prince William Sound, Jackie and I went to the ship's beauty salon to have our hair done. Half of the Hopewell women were there, talking giddily about the upcoming banquet. Even Erma Moosenbocker was there, sitting wedged in a narrow chair, her curlered head under a dryer. She crooked her little finger my way in a tentative wave, so I ambled over and sat down beside her. Her voice boomed over the roar of the dryer. "Michelle, can you hear me? Listen, I have a whole shopping bag full of your books. I lugged them home from the bookstore and I lugged them onto the ship. About wrecked my back in the process. In fact, I fall over them every morning when I get out of my bunk."

"My books? I don't understand."

Her round, red face puckered slightly. "I gotta confess, Michelle. All during the cruise I've been watching you and trying to work up the nerve to ask you. Will you—you know—

autograph them? They're for my folks and my Aunt Gertrude and my cousin Harry and—"

I broke into laughter. "Oh, Erma, I'd be delighted to autograph the books. Just bring them by my room anytime."

Erma beamed. "Thanks, Michelle. Everyone'll be thrilled to know I'm friends with a celebrity." She paused, eyeing me with careful scrutiny, and said, "You know, Michelle, you've grown up a lot. You're not that uppity, annoying little sprig you used to be."

I stood up and patted her arm. "Thanks, Erma . . . I think."

That evening David and I arrived at the lavishly decorated banquet hall shortly before seven. Already the sprawling room was filling with couples in their finest dress—men in stylish black, gray, or white tuxedos or dinner jackets, women in gorgeous, flowing pastel gowns or cocktail dresses. The linen-draped tables were laden with flamboyant arrangements of succulent food and glistening ice sculptures. Waiters in black tie and tails darted through the crowd offering hors d'oeuvres and exotic fruit drinks.

I looked around for familiar faces. Brett and Candace Seaton looked breathtaking together, he in his full dress uniform, she in a silver-sequined gown; my sister Pam and Silas Winters stood off in one corner, exchanging yearning glances; Abigail was obviously in her glory with Seth Mueller, her official "date" for the evening. When I spotted the Thatchers talking with the Ellises, I nudged David over, intending to join their conversation. But when I heard Cam Ellis goading Dr. Thatcher, I decided to keep my distance. Still, I couldn't help overhearing their whispered, volatile exchange.

"Hey, Thatcher, you had quite a pity party for yourself in devotions yesterday. So you've lost a few patients, huh, Dr. Thatcher?" Cam said in a low, needling voice. "What's it like, Doc? Do you really lose sleep over it, or do you just go on to the next patient? Does it break your heart, or did your heart turn to stone years ago?"

"I die a little with every patient I lose, Ellis," said Jason.

"Really, Thatcher, aren't you being a little melodramatic? Disappointed over losing a patient, perhaps—but dying over it?"

"Dying more than you know, Ellis."

"Dying?" Cam mocked coldly. "You're wrong. I *do* know. But I wasn't sure until now that *you* knew, Dr. Thatcher."

Jason's eyes narrowed. "You only *think* you know, Ellis."

Stephanie tugged angrily at Cam's arm. "That's enough, Cam."

Noreen Thatcher looked in bewilderment at the two men. "I honestly don't know what you two are talking about," she tittered.

Signaling David with my eyes, I stepped back into the crowd, hoping Stephanie hadn't spotted us. But within moments she came bustling after us, exclaiming, "Oh, David, Michelle! Please, come join us. Cam so enjoyed talking with you the othher day, David."

While David sauntered over to chat with Cam, Stephanie motioned me over to a private corner. "I just had to talk to you, Michelle," she said breathlessly. "I want you to know—it's because of you—what you said—I've been thinking, praying, and agonizing over everything—my life, Cam, our son, his death. And this morning it was so clear to me—my need of Christ. I—I prayed and invited Him into my life, Michelle—and you were right. He is real, and He just wrapped me up in His love. It's so incredible—"

I clasped her hands. "Oh, Stephanie, I am so happy for you! Does Cam know yet?"

"Oh, no, not yet. I just can't tell him, Michelle."

"But he's bound to find out sooner or later."

"I need time, Michelle, and so does Cam. Someday . . . when he's not so upset, so on edge . . ." She looked away wistfully.

"Well, at least you and I can talk and pray together, if you'd like—maybe in the Sky Room after devotions each morning."

Stephanie and I visited a few moments more, then I excused myself and went over to Abigail and Seth. Abigail's face had the fresh, rosy glow of a child on Christmas morning, her eyes dancing with star shine and dreams. She held Seth's arm as if she intended never to let him go. "This is the most magnificent night of my life," she whispered when Seth turned to speak to someone else. "You are looking at a happy, happy woman, Michelle."

"Does this mean—are you talking about something permanent?"

"Oh no, Michelle. Tonight. *Tonight* is the rest of my life! No matter what else happens, I've had these moments with Seth."

"That's a wonderful attitude, Abigail, but I'm sure this is only the beginning." I turned and caught David's eye across the room. He was still talking with Cam. He winked at me and I blew him a kiss.

Abigail smiled knowingly. "Well, Michelle, who are you flirting with now?"

"My husband," I replied with an impish grin.

Suddenly President Stoddard's voice boomed over the microphone: "Welcome, Hopewell alumni and honorees. It's time to sit down for our anniversary dinner. Please find your places and join me in a prayer of gratitude for God's 50 years of blessings on our college."

After the prayer, David and I sat down at the front table reserved for the honorees. Seth Mueller and Abigail sat beside us, the Thatchers and Seatons across from us, the Stoddards at the end.

Waiters served succulent medallions of filet mignon with mushroom caps and béarnaise sauce, topped with fresh jumbo shrimp. It looked like a king's feast, but after a few bites, my stomach turned to butterflies. I told myself I was simply nervous about having to stand up and give a speech. My queasiness had nothing to do with the slim chance that I might be pregnant. *I am not pregnant*, I reminded myself emphatically.

When it was time for dessert, the lights dimmed, the music resounded, and the waiters marched in triumphantly, balancing silver trays of flaming baked Alaska high in the air. The fiery ice cream mounds were breathtaking but—surprisingly for me, a lover of sweets—not the least bit appetizing.

At last Stoddard stood and, drawing himself up to his full Lincolnesque height, walked to the podium and said, "Ladies and gentlemen, this is the moment we have all been waiting for. It's time to present our awards to Hopewell's four honored alumni. But first, let us reminisce a little about Hopewell College's illustrious 50-year history." He smiled slyly. "I don't suppose any of you here remember all 50 years, although I daresay there are a few of us who remember quite a few decades." He chuckled to himself, then launched into a half-hour recital of personal and professional recollections.

David was shifting restlessly when President Stoddard finally announced, "Now, Hopewell alumni and friends, it's time to introduce our honorees. Each will receive a fine plaque with his or her name and accomplishments etched in gold. Our first honoree is astronaut Brett Seaton, a man who has been like a son to me since his first days at Hopewell."

Brett, in beribboned full Marine uniform, moved with broad, gliding steps to the rostrum, then turned and flashed his disarming smile. For a moment I thought he would salute. He stood ramrod straight—one of the elite breed, as Candy had said. Then with an almost chauvinistic air, he spoke briefly of his military career, his family, his dreams. As he concluded, he said, "I want to thank Hopewell for honoring me when I spent so little time there. But the principles I learned at Hopewell and in the Stoddards' home strengthened my faith—and carried me safely through combat and on into the space program." He looked down at the plaque in his hand, then fleetingly at Candy. "Someday I expect to ride a shuttle again and be there when NASA establishes the first space station. I'll take this plaque with me and leave it there as my token of appreciation to Hopewell and my deep gratitude to God."

When President Stoddard called Seth Mueller to the platform, he handed Seth a plaque and a sealed white envelope. "Go ahead and open it," Stoddard said. "It's from all of us—an alumni gift for your ministry of feeding the hungry. We want you to know, Seth, that God cares about the starving millions even more than you do. When He called you to this ministry, He promised to supply your needs. Promotionals, fundraisers, TV talk shows—they have their place, but we want you to expend your energy on the work at hand—feeding hungry bodies and hungry souls."

Seth stared at the check with genuine boyish delight. "Ten thousand dollars? I—I'm overwhelmed. I don't know what to say."

"Your face says it all, Mr. Mueller. We're proud of you—proud of your victories on the tennis court but even more pleased with what you are doing in Africa, Thailand, and around the world."

"Ladies and gentlemen, I—I—" Whatever Seth had intended to say was momentarily forgotten, lost to the emotion of the hour. His cockiness was gone; there were tears in his eyes. "Your faith in me means everything," he murmured. "I get so caught up in chasing after publicity and amassing funds, as if feeding the hungry depended solely upon me, on my efforts. But how can you tell people about God when their stomachs are hungry? I know what it's like to be hungry—physically, spiritually. Maybe that's why I become so obsessed with raising funds and seeking publicity for my projects. To tell you the truth, I almost missed the bus for this cruise because I was hounding a TV producer in Seattle about doing a telethon. I even tried to convince an airline stewardess to let me call ahead from the cockpit." He held up the check with obvious pride. "This is more than just a gesture of kindness from you people; it's a reminder that God must be in charge and not Seth Mueller, and that the ministry belongs to all the people, not just to me."

A ripple of applause rose from the audience.

Seth looked at his plaque, then gazed down fondly at Abigail. His voice was tender as he said, "I travel around the world and have no home of my own, no place to hang this honor, but I want someone very special to keep it for me for the day I come home." He extended his hand. "Abigail Chadwick, please come join me on the platform."

Abigail looked up in surprise and mouthed, "You want me?" Slowly she slipped out of her seat and walked up beside Seth.

"Abigail, for most of these people you have been their college professor, but to me you have been a lifelong friend and devoted supporter." He pressed the gleaming plaque in her hands and said, "I want you to hang this in your office at Hopewell, and someday I'll come back for it." With a gallant flourish, he leaned over and kissed her soundly on the lips.

The audience exploded in applause. Happy tears rolled down my cheeks. I knew that this was Abigail Chadwick's finest hour. She was no doubt happier receiving Seth's plaque than she had been receiving her doctorate degree or the scholarly honors that hung on her wall. She was blushing like a new bride as she took her seat.

But the lively mood changed dramatically as President Stoddard called on Dr. Jason Thatcher to take the stage for his award. Jason moved with the slow, weary reluctance of an old man. He was still the same attractive, meticulous physician with dapper, silver-white hair, but his usual verve and spirit had vanished. His sturdy hands trembled slightly as he gripped the rostrum. Wrinkles, worry lines, and age spots shadowed his finely chisled features. I hadn't realized before how old he looked, how defeated. He wore the same morose, melancholy expression I'd noticed that day he had stood on the Mendenhall Glacier, staring down into the deep, icy crevasse.

President Stoddard eloquently praised Dr. Thatcher's medical achievements in the field of thoracic surgery, then handed Jason the plaque. Jason cleared his throat nervously. "I don't really deserve this award. I'm only a man—a very human man, with frailties and struggles like everyone else. But I deeply appreciate the kindness of Hopewell College toward me." His voice broke. With inexpressible sadness, he added, "Sometimes a surgeon thinks he can play God, but even a surgeon must learn to accept his losses as well as his successes. And I've had my share of losses." He looked as if he were about to say something else, then thought better of it. With a final quiet thank-you, he left the stage and returned to our table.

I offered Jason a reassuring smile and was still feeling a heart-wrenching ache for him when I heard President Stoddard call my name. As I promptly made my way up to the platform, Stoddard announced, "Michelle Merrill Ballard is our only woman honoree. Since leaving Hopewell as reigning popcorn queen a few short years ago, Michelle has distinguished herself as a bestselling author."

Stoddard went on for several minutes with glowing accolades, then, with wry, twinkling eyes, he handed me not only a plaque, but also a thick hardback book with a colorful dust jacket showing a tropical Caribbean island. I stared at the book in astonishment as Stoddard continued, "We arranged with Michelle's publisher to have available tonight a large quantity of her new novel, *Storm at Tamarind Bluff*. I stayed up half the night reading it; it's superb."

I clutched the book in my hands and exclaimed, "How did you ever manage this? I haven't even seen a copy of this new novel myself!"

"I know," said Stoddard. "Your husband helped me arrange with your publisher to ship us the first copies hot off the press. We have a table set up so you can autograph a copy for each guest here."

"Thank you, President Stoddard," I said, sounding giddy as a child at a circus. "And you too, David. I must admit you keep our marriage one surprise after another." David winked at me as laughter rippled over the audience. I held my novel up high. "I've been waiting for weeks to see this book. Isn't the cover great? I love it." I paused, swallowing the emotion welling in my throat. "This book is such a part of me, just like *Vietnam Legacy* was. The only thing better than seeing my books in print is knowing that I'm sharing them with you, my Hopewell friends—and with others like you around the world whom I'll never have a chance to meet."

I set my book on the podium and held up the exquisite gold plaque. "Thank you, Hopewell College, for honoring me. I didn't earn this alone. If it hadn't been for my beloved David and his best friend Rob Thornton, there wouldn't be a first book. And if it weren't for my esteemed professor and friend, Abigail Chadwick, there would probably be no books at all. Maybe I should give this award to Abigail, but since Seth Mueller has already given her his, I think I'll keep this one for myself. Thank you, everyone."

Amid a burst of applause, Stoddard took the microphone and said, "Will the four honored alumni and their guests join me at the dessert table as we cut the cake?"

We made our way over and circled the table as the chefs brought in a huge white cake with 50 flaming candles and a gold banner declaring, "Congratulations! Hopewell's 50th Anniversary." President Stoddard raised his arms and led us in singing the familiar, lilting refrains of Hopewell's alma mater. Then he took the sterling-silver serving knife, drew in a deep breath and blew out the candles, and cut deeply into the cake.

Suddenly, like a shroud dropping over a corpse, the room was thrown into blackness. A hundred frightened voices punctuated the first moments of stunned silence, all buzzing at once: "The lights—who turned off the lights?—where are you?—stay where you are—the switch—someone find the switch!" Pandemonium reigned as the room remained swathed in shadows. Several women screamed; people milled around, speaking in hushed, urgent voices, shoving and bumping into one another. I reached instinctively for David and sank against his chest. I heard little Stevie cry out, "Mommy, Mommy!"

Then Silas Winters' powerful voice broke across the banquet hall. "Everyone, please listen. Everything's all right. Stand still. Stay calm. We'll have the lights back on in just a moment."

Even as Silas spoke, the room was flooded again in light. I looked around, blinking. Everything seemed undisturbed. I sighed in relief. Perhaps it was simply an accidental power failure after all.

"We were just cutting the cake," said Stoddard nervously. "Come on, folks. Gather around. Be happy! We're having a party!"

The crowd clapped vigorously and broke into laughter, releasing tensions and shaking off the breath-clutching claws of panic. I looked up at David and smiled grimly as we headed over to my book table. "My hand's trembling so; how will I autograph 250 books?"

"Let them eat cake," quipped David as he sampled Hopewell's confectionary masterpiece.

I gazed with pleasure and wonderment at the autograph table stacked high with my books. I took the first shiny volume off the top and ran my hand over its smooth surface. Then I opened it gently so that the spine wouldn't break. Turning to the title page, I noticed a folded sheet of stationery tucked inside. "Look, David, President Stoddard must have left me a note." I opened it and scanned the brief rhyme, my amusement somersaulting into sheer terror as I read:

Death is an honored guest here too.
Shortly he'll claim one of you.

CHAPTER
FIFTEEN

Wordlessly, my heart hammering in my throat, I handed David the threatening note.

"What's wrong, hon?" he asked, taking the paper. "You look like you just—" He read the rhyme, then cast a quick, darting glance around the room. "Did you see anyone here by your books, Michelle?"

"No, David, it must have been planted when the lights were out."

"Or before the banquet even began."

"But who did it? The stalker must be someone right here in this room with us, David—one of the Hopewell alumni."

David tucked the note in his pocket. "Let's keep quiet about this for the moment, Michelle. I'm going to show the note to Silas."

"You want me to autograph books like nothing even happened?"

"Yes, until Silas and I can confer with Stoddard. Silas may want to bring the party to a prompt conclusion, but we've got to handle it carefully. We don't want to stir up unnecessary panic."

I shuddered. "If you want panic, I've got enough for everyone."

David squeezed my hand reassuringly, then strode off to talk with Silas and Stoddard. Minutes later, President Stoddard stepped to the microphone and announced, "Attention, folks, we'll be winding up our celebration a little early so you can get a good night's sleep for our day in port tomorrow. And don't worry. We'll see to it that you get your autographed copy of Michelle's book later."

Back in our room, David and I talked until after midnight

about the latest threat. "I think some wacko is getting his kicks by spoiling everyone else's cruise," said David. "He's too cowardly to show his face and confront anyone, or to do actual violence."

"The only problem is, David, if you're wrong, it'll be too late . . . for somebody. And, remember, the note was left in *my* book."

"I know," said David. "That's why I've asked Silas to keep an eye on you when you're out of our stateroom. He promised he would."

True to his word, Silas—and Pam—showed up at my door before breakfast the next morning. "Sorry, Silas. David's out jogging."

"I'm here to accompany you to the infirmary," he announced.

"Infirmary?" I echoed, baffled. "Why? I'm not ill."

Pam stepped forward and gave me a knowing smile. "We were going to see the doctor about your seasickness, remember, Michelle?"

"It's much better, Pam," I insisted. "Hardly noticeable now."

"We'd better be sure. Come on, sis. Doctor's in his office at eight. And we dock at Valdez at nine, so we'd better hurry."

I went reluctantly, not wanting to make a fuss before Silas. I was relieved that he stayed outside while Pam and I went in. We had hardly sat down in the waiting room when the nurse appeared and asked brightly, "You're Mrs. Ballard, here for your pregnancy test, right?"

"H—How did you know?"

"I phoned ahead," said Pam. "Told her we were coming."

"Please come with me, Mrs. Ballard. It'll only take a minute."

With a sigh of resignation I followed the nurse down the hall to the consultation room. I was back with Pam in five minutes.

"Now that wasn't so bad, was it?" she asked with a grin.

"This is a big waste of time, dear sister," I said coolly.

"Don't kid me," said Pam. "You're dying to know the truth."

I crossed my arms obstinately. "Well, we'll know in 20 minutes, and I hope then you'll stop hounding me about babies."

She grinned gleefully. "I'll help you think of names."

"Really, Pam, I would think you have more important things to worry about—like you and Silas. He's nothing but trouble."

Pam frowned. "That's a low blow, Michelle. Silas is doing everything he can to protect you and Jackie and—"

"I'm not questioning his professional integrity, Pam. It's his personal life—the two of you together. There's no future for you—"

Pam's face settled into a defiant pout. "How would you know?"

Soberly I said, "I went through the same thing myself with Scott. I know you could never be happy with a man who doesn't share your faith, who's skeptical of the God you cherish."

"Maybe he'll change. Don't you believe in miracles, Michelle?"

"Not miracles bought at the price of disobedience. If you marry him, your disobedience might keep him from ever coming to God."

"Who's talking about marriage?" countered Pam.

"I've seen that look in your eye. You're in love with Silas."

Pam's lower lip trembled. "I hate it when you sound so pious, Michelle, especially when you're right. I do love Silas and he loves me. But he won't keep me from loving God. He knows how important my faith is to me. He just doesn't want me to force God on him."

I slipped my arm around Pam. "And you think you could make it work that way? The two of you going in different directions?"

Pam blinked back tears. "I—I know what the Bible says, but I love Silas so much, Michelle. I don't think I can let him go." She took out a tissue and dabbed her eyes. "It's not fair, big sis," she sniffed. "This was supposed to be your moment of truth, not mine."

"Don't worry, mine's coming," I said as the nurse approached.

"Mrs. Ballard, the doctor will see you now. Right this way."

My heart was pounding furiously as I sat down across from Dr. Becker—a smiling, gray-haired physician old enough to be my father. "Well, Mrs. Ballard, I think I have good news for you."

"Good news?" I chirped. "Then I'm not—?"

"Yes. Yes, indeed, you *are* pregnant, Mrs. Ballard."

I sat back, stunned. "Are you sure?"

He sat forward, his hands folded on the desk. "I see that this is something of a surprise. You did tell me you're—*Mrs. Ballard*—?"

I felt my face flush. "Oh, yes, I'm married. And I—I know my husband will be absolutely delighted with this news. It's just—"

Dr. Becker patted my hand. "I understand. You're a new bride. You feel as if you're still on your honeymoon. A baby means change."

"Lots of changes," I murmured, "and I don't mean just diapers."

He chuckled. "Well, I'm sure you'll cope very well, Mrs. Ballard. We'll do an exam now, or if you prefer, you can see your own physician as soon as you get home. He'll prescribe vitamins and give you further instructions. . . ."

"I'll wait until I get home," I murmured. But all I could think of was, *A baby. I'm going to have a baby. I'll be someone's mother!* Numb and incredulous, I returned to Pam in the waiting room.

She jumped up eagerly. "So what's the news, big sis?"

"Don't call me *big sis*," I winced. "I'm going to be getting bigger every day!"

Pam swung me around. "Then it's true—I'm going to be an aunt!"

"And I've got to figure out a way to balance books and babies."

Pam eyed me curiously. "You're not happy about being preggers?"

"Ambivalent is more like it. Truth is, I'm scared spitless."

She grinned. "You'll make a great mommy. Just wait and see."

Silas was waiting for us just outside the infirmary. "You get something to take care of that seasickness, Michelle?"

"No, Silas. I'm afraid I'm in for a long siege."

"Well, they say it doesn't last forever."

"No," I mumbled under my breath, "just nine months."

When Pam, Silas, and I returned to my stateroom, David was back from jogging and ready for breakfast. There was no way I could tell him now about the baby. In fact, how could I tell him at all? He'd know I wasn't happy. It would hurt him to see the doubt and confusion in my eyes. How could I make him understand my mixed feelings?

* * *

We ate a hurried breakfast as our ship eased through the serene waters of Prince William Sound and docked at the quaint alpine town of Valdez. As Pam and Silas and David and I stepped off the ship, we gazed around at towering mountains with a Swiss-like grandeur—high, snow-carved peaks and rugged fjords edging pristine, sapphire waters. Although Valdez itself was marred by storage tanks, pipelines, and oil freighters, the busy city was couched amid cascading waterfalls and spectacular rock formations. It was a fascinating community that had survived a devastating earthquake and two "boom towns"—a frenzied gold rush at the turn of the century and a wild rush for oil in the 1960s. Today Valdez was the southern terminus for the Trans-Alaska Pipeline.

The four of us strolled around town, wandering through the curio shops, stopping for coffee and fresh pastries at a tiny restaurant that resembled a Swiss chalet. We spent an hour browsing in the downtown museum among the exhibits and memorabilia that chronicled the mid-sixties earthquake and the town's early years. I studied photos of houses and cars literally swallowed by the earth, plunging into monstrous fissures. "Can you imagine such a tragedy?" I said softly. "You have to admire the indomitable pioneer spirit of these people. It says here that after the earthquake they simply moved to higher ground and started over, rebuilding their entire city."

We left the museum at 11 A.M., grabbed a light lunch in town, picked up a toy oil freighter for Stevie, then headed back to the ship. Jackie was out on the deck leaning against the rail, gazing wistfully up at the majestic, picture-postcard mountains. I joined her while David took Stevie to the Lido Deck for ice cream. "Wish you could have gone with us into Valdez, Jackie," I said.

"Me, too. But I promised Steve I'd stay on board, remember?" She sighed pensively. "I sure wanted to go into town. It reminds me of home. Valdez is called the 'Switzerland of Alaska,' you know."

"You're really missing Steve and little Becky, aren't you?"

"More so today than ever." She turned and looked earnestly at me. "I've done a lot of thinking and praying on this cruise, Michelle. And I've had to admit some important things to myself."

"You mean about Steve and you?"

She nodded, her flawless, model-perfect face clouding slightly. "Ever since Steve's trouble with the law and the cocaine trial, I've stayed with him because I felt he needed me. But this trip has made me realize for the first time how much I need him. I love Steve so much, Michelle. I can't wait to get back to him and the baby."

At the mention of the word *baby*, I flinched. Jackie noticed. "What's wrong, Michelle? You look a little pale."

"Pale? I'm afraid that's not all I'm going to be, Jackie."

"What do you?—are you saying?—you're not pregnant?"

I nodded. "That's what the doctor said this morning."

Jackie hugged me joyously. "Oh, Michelle, that's terrific!"

"I wish I felt that excited," I mumbled. "I haven't even had the courage to tell David. I've spent the whole morning in Valdez arguing with myself. I just don't want to be pregnant, Jackie."

She smiled warmly. "You'll find the right moment to tell David. And don't worry, Michelle. A time will come when the baby won't be just an abstract idea to you; you'll think of *him*—" Jackie's eyes twinkled. "You'll think of him as a real person, and then the baby will suddenly be the most important thing in your life."

Just sharing my news with Jackie was somehow comforting. We spent the rest of the afternoon chatting and reminiscing, safe in the tranquillity of a friendship that neither time nor distance could shatter. Our sweet ambience matched the serenity of Prince William Sound as we cruised toward the sheer ice summits of mammoth Columbia Glacier. We inched daringly close to the face of the cliff as huge pinnacles of ice creaked and crackled and thundered into the Sound. Then the ship's engines went dead. Only the lapping of icy waters against the bow of the ship broke the eerie silence.

Jackie and I gazed around in fascination at nature's wonderland. Gulls, puffins, and black-legged kittiwakes swooped playfully overhead; a frisky seal caught a ride on a floating iceberg; and porpoises swam and dove gracefully beneath the ice floe.

By dinnertime, the S.S. *Mendenhall* had reached its northernmost point and was turning south, back through the Prince William Sound, heading toward open sea. As our ship moved against the shadow of the coastline under a vaulted, Prussian-blue sky, we steered a clear course over the wind-rippled sea toward home.

Late that evening, when David and I were alone at last, I decided I must tell him now about the baby. I dressed in my shimmering peach nightgown and slipped into bed beside him, cuddling against his muscular chest. For several minutes I lay still, staring into the darkness, weighing my words. They had to be just right. I had to sound positive. Finally, gathering my courage, I said, "David, I have something important to tell you." I paused. He was silent, apparently waiting for me to continue. "I just found out this morning, David," I went on softly, hesitantly. "I—I'm pregnant. I know you're glad—it's what you wanted—but I'm scared. I know we'll work it through together, but I'm going to need your help, David."

I waited for my husband's eager response, for him to gather me into his arms and tell me how happy he was about the baby, but all I heard was his deep breathing followed by a sudden loud snort. David was snoring! Grabbing my pillow and pulling it around my head, I muffled a crowing retort. Hilarious irony!—should I laugh or cry?— the news David had been waiting for, and he never even heard me!

CHAPTER
SIXTEEN

After breakfast and devotions on Tuesday morning, David and I went up to the sun deck for a game of ping-pong. We planned to spend a leisurely, snail-paced day relaxing and playing, since our ship would be at sea until Thursday morning. I welcomed a chance to unwind a little, read a book, and maybe even catch a few rays of sun. It was a perfect day to spend on the enclosed sun deck. Rare beams of sunshine broke through the mildly overcast sky. The sea was calm with a mirror-like translucence, unusually placid for the Gulf of Alaska.

Just before lunch, David suggested we go out on the promenade deck for a casual stroll. Halfway around the ship, we stopped at the fantail to watch the skeetshooters. "Look, David," I said, "Cam Ellis and Jason Thatcher are playing. Shall we join them?"

"No, Michelle, I think this is the wrong time to intrude. From the look on Cam's face, he's not *playing*. He's *fuming*."

We stood off to one side and watched unobtrusively as Dr. Thatcher raised his gun and fired at the clay pigeon flung in the air. We heard a piercing crack. He aimed again. Fired. Again! Fired.

"Bull's-eye! You hit all three," the cruise director declared.

Jason turned and handed the shotgun to Cam. "Let's see what kind of a marksman you are, Ellis."

Cam lifted the weapon to his shoulder and smirked, "I can shoot the cork out of a champagne bottle, Thatcher."

"Or explode a porcelain vase in a single shot?" charged Jason, his tone low and accusatory.

One after another, clay targets sprang from the trap, hurtling heavenward like birds in flight. As Cam fired, a rapid succession of sharp popping sounds fractured the air. In my mind's eye, I could picture the cork in Cam's imaginary champagne bottle shooting sky-high, puncturing the filmy clouds, and the chimerical bottle drifting down unbroken into the sea.

"Can you top that one, Thatcher?" Cam challenged.

"Maybe." Thatcher eyed Cam with cold condescension. "When are you going to tip your hand, Ellis? You might have perfect aim, but you're a coward at heart."

"A coward, am I?" Cam sneered. "At least I don't hide behind a medical degree to cover up murder, Dr. Thatcher."

"You don't know what you're talking about, Ellis."

"Don't I? I know enough to put you away for good, doctor."

Jason's eyes narrowed shrewdly. "Then it's your move, isn't it, Mr. Ellis? What on earth are you waiting for? Vengeance is yours. Go on. Be quick about it. You'll be doing me a favor."

"Checkmate, Dr. Thatcher," said Cam, aiming his gun out to sea and shattering another spiraling clay pigeon.

"Don't be too sure, Ellis. Sometimes the game plan changes—the hunter becomes the victim." With a curt nod, Jason pivoted and stalked away. Cam fired one more round at the clay target, then set the shotgun down and walked briskly after Thatcher.

I gripped David's hand. He smiled faintly, but I knew from the expression on his face that he was baffled, concerned. We left the fantail, took the stairway down, and cut across the open deck to the stern of the ship. "We should go to lunch, Michelle," David said finally. "I want to talk to Silas about Cam and Jason."

"You go ahead, David. I really don't feel up to eating. I'll just stay out here for a while."

"You're sure? I don't like leaving you alone."

"I'll be all right. You go on. Meet me up here after lunch."

David frowned, kissed me lightly on the cheek, then left. I stood alone, leaning against the railing, the crisp sea breeze brushing my face, my coat collar turned up. I didn't like what I was thinking. Thatcher. Ellis. Their constant clashing. I couldn't even share my innermost fears with David. I had promised Stephanie.

A sudden firm hand gripped my shoulder. I whirled around. "Oh, Silas, you startled me. Shouldn't you be at lunch?"

"David asked me to keep you company." He stood with his casual, confident air, his thumbs hooked on the pockets of his wool jacket.

"Really, Silas, I'm not afraid. I feel better in the fresh air."

"Same old seasickness, eh?" When I didn't answer, he added, "Pam tells me if we get married, I'll be an uncle within the year."

I glared up at him. "She had no right to tell you that."

"I guessed anyway. Actually, it didn't take a mathematical genius to figure out that seasickness doesn't last nine months."

"I'm beginning to think everybody knows but David," I lamented, "and, would you believe, he fell asleep when I tried to tell him!"

"Don't sweat it, Michelle. I won't tell anyone. Frankly, I was just checking out how you feel about my marrying Pam. But I can already tell by your expression that you're still opposed to the idea."

"It's nothing personal, Silas. In fact, you grow on a person."

"Then it's the same old problem—my not believing as you do?"

"Please understand, Silas. I really care about you. But I just wonder what it's going to take to convince you that God loves you."

"Pam loves me. Isn't that enough?"

"Are you saying Pam has decided to marry you?"

He flicked his sunglasses back on the bridge of his nose. "Pam won't give me her final answer until the end of the cruise."

"Saturday then? That soon?" Fighting the lump in my throat, I gazed out at the gentle swells. The hazy sun splattered miniature rainbows on the crest of the waves. I looked back at Silas. "I'll be glad for Saturday too. We'll be safely in Vancouver—home free."

"It's not that simple, Michelle. When we dock in Vancouver—in the excitement of leaving the ship, our mysterious stalker could carry out his threat and be lost in the crowd before we know it—"

I shivered. "Silas, you scare me."

"I don't mean to, Michelle. I'm just cautious. No one is safe until we know who's behind this madness. I'll be glad to get Jackie Marshall off the ship and safely on her way back to Switzerland."

"Have you pinpointed anything yet, Silas? Found any clues?"

"The DEA has been running dozens of checks for me. I'm in constant ship-to-shore communication with the agency."

"So what have you found out?"

"Not much—that Horace Stoddard is facing forced retirement in two years—Hopewell keeps its faculty on the lower side of 65. He's not happy about it, but he's not mad enough to kill anyone either."

"But someone is."

"Yes, I know. We're investigating ties between passengers. There's a link somewhere. It eludes me now, but I'll figure it out."

"Before someone gets killed?" I asked.

"That's my job, Michelle, but I admit I'm running into plenty of dead ends. Seth Mueller made his enemies at Wimbledon and he's infuriated heads of state in his missionary endeavors. But every dime he collects goes toward feeding the hungry." He leaned against the rail. "And Thatcher. We've run checks on his medical colleagues and his patients. But there's nothing to go on. No one on board has ever even been his patient."

"What about Colonel Seaton?"

"He has a good track record, and he's well-liked at NASA." Silas looked out at the gently shifting sea and pulled his collar up against the biting wind. "Actually, Seaton's wife—"

Silas's words were slashed by a sudden outburst of enraged masculine voices. We turned sharply and looked up at the fantail. Two men—tall and strapping, their fists clenched—stood on the veranda beside the railing arguing heatedly. I recognized Dr. Jason Thatcher's silver-white hair and Cam Ellis's rough-hewn beard.

Their voices grew louder, their words fiery, impassioned. Jason demanded, "Go on, make your accusation, Ellis! Say what you've been waiting to say!"

Cam's anguished sob ripped through the bone-chilling air. "You killed my son, Thatcher! You killed my only son!"

The two men began to scuffle, their bodies locked in bitter combat. One man thrust the other against the rail, pressing him backward over the frigid, fathomless waters. For long, harrowing moments, they teetered precariously in murderous, vise-grip tension. I tried to shout, but my mouth had turned acrid, dry as cotton; my senses reeled.

Suddenly, Silas broke away from me, sprinting across the weathered deck, bolting up the narrow stairway two steps at a time. Quelling my immobilizing terror, I darted across the deck after him. As I scaled the stairs, I lost sight of the three men momentarily.

Breathless, I reached the top step and stared in horror as one man toppled over the rail and plunged into the yawning ocean below. His raw shriek and my own scream blended in the frost-fettered air as I shouted, "Man overboard! Man overboard!"

CHAPTER SEVENTEEN

I stood mesmerized, caught in a nightmarish freeze-frame of time: A flailing Silas Winters plummeted downward like a fallen mariner trapped by the haunting siren song of the deadly, seductive sea. Silas's twisted body split the swirling waters with a thundering explosion of frothy, engulfing waves.

"Do something! Somebody do something!" I screamed.

Jason Thatcher stared down, stock-still, his powder-white face contorting with astonishment, his blanched knuckles gripping the rail. With the instinctive agility of an untamed animal, Cam Ellis sprang into motion, grabbing the nearest life buoy and hurling it vigorously toward Silas. The orange ring fell short of its mark. I could see Silas bob in the dark indigo waters, then go under and burst to the foamy surface again, thrashing in the eddying swells as the ship moved steadily, relentlessly away from him.

"Cam, he can't reach it! He can't reach it!" I shrilled.

Cam seized my arm in his powerful hand and pulled me toward him.

I jerked away, fearful lest I be his next victim. "Don't touch me. Leave me alone!"

His face twitched reflexively. "I'm not going to hurt you—"

I stared around in abject terror as a crowd converged and a deck officer vaulted our way. "Did someone jump? Did you see him?"

"My friend—he fell overboard. Please, you've got to save him."

"I notified the bridge the moment I heard your 'man overboard' cry," said the officer.

"That's all?" I rasped. "Aren't you going to rescue him?"

Three long blasts of the ship's whistle muffled his answer. "Ma'am, the captain's notifying the Coast Guard in Sitka.. . . A Mayday signal has gone out. . . . We'll be turning the ship around."

Even as he spoke, I felt a sudden, violent lurch of the *Mendenhall* as the enormous vessel veered to the starboard side. I was thrown against the deck officer as lounge chairs toppled and tables slid on the sun deck below us. Passengers swayed and grabbed for support, clinging to the rail, grabbing nearby pillars and posts.

"What's happening?" I cried, clutching the officer's arm.

"The ship's turning around, taking a reciprocal course back."

"Will we make it in ti—"

"Michelle!" David's alarmed voice severed my words. I wheeled around and opened my arms to him. He gathered me against his chest, then drew back and eyed me anxiously. He was breathless, his dark hair windblown. "Michelle, we felt the ship lurch in the dining room. Dishes, trays of food crashed to the floor. People were panic-stricken. I was afraid something had happened to you."

I pointed blindly toward the water. "David—it's Silas. Silas Winters. He fell overboard." I nodded toward an ashen Thatcher and a somber Cam Ellis. "They were quarreling again, David. Silas went to help. I didn't see what happened. I just saw Silas fall."

Bracing himself against the rail, David scanned the vast cobalt sea. The ship swung back hard, its engines groaning, its enormous bulkhead creaking as it churned the waters, reversing course.

"You won't see anything from here," said the deck officer. "Follow me to the bow. We're using the Williamson Maneuver to retrace our route." As we bounded after him, he said, "See? We're backtracking in our own wake."

"What about a life boat?" I cried. "Silas will drown before—"

"The man-overboard squad will lower away as soon as we're dead in the water. Dr. Becker will be with them."

I gazed out over the ship's bow. "Can they make it in time?"

"We don't have long in these cold waters," the officer admitted. "Temperature's mid-forties. We've got 20 to 25 minutes at the most, if the fellow has a strong constitution."

"If anybody can make it," said David, guiding me to the front rail, "Silas Winters can. He swam like a fish in the Caribbean."

"I'm afraid these aren't Caribbean waters," said the officer.

I clasped David's hand, my hopes wavering. "Silas was alive when he hit the water. I saw him bob to the surface."

Suddenly, with an apprehensive shout, my sister Pam broke through the crowd and came dashing up to us. "David! Michelle! They say—somebody—fell overboard. Is it anyone we know?"

David slipped his arm around Pam's shoulder. "It's Silas," he said in his deep, precise voice. "He tried to stop a fight between Dr. Thatcher and Cam Ellis."

Pam bolted from David's embrace and stared down at the rolling sea. She leaned over the rail, her arms outstretched, and shrieked his name over and over. "Silas! Silas! My Silas!" The bleak, frost-nipped wind blew her words back with a distant, mournful whine.

She whirled around, her eyes glazed with horror. "No, please, it can't be! Where is he, Michelle? He's gone!" She stumbled and collapsed in my arms, her usual expression of childlike innocence splintered with pain and remorse. "Oh, dear God, he's lost forever! It's all my fault!"

"They'll find him, Pam. I promise they'll find him."

David touched my arm. "Look, Michelle, out at the horizon."

We pressed against the rail, straining our eyes against the hazy sunlight shimmering on the waves. I was aware suddenly that the ship's engines were eerily quiet. We wafted gently, our vessel dead in the water, enveloped by a ghostly stillness. Minutes later, we saw the motorized rescue boat cruising toward a bright, bobbing object. "I see the orange life ring, David, but where's Silas?"

"There's something out there a few yards from the ring."

Pam trembled in my arms. "Oh, God, please let it be Silas!"

We kept our eyes on the rescue boat as it steered past the life ring toward the dark speck in the water. For long, nerve-wracking moments we watched as the six-man crew in orange life vests clustered on one side and hauled a slack body into the boat.

"I think they've got him, Pam," said David.

"Tell me, please, is he alive?"

"I'm sorry, Pam. I can't tell from here."

The crowd flanking the rail remained raptly silent as the lifeboat circled and sped back through spumy whitecaps to the *Mendenhall*. Minutes later we heard the creaking sound of the ship's davits as eager crewmen vigorously raised and secured the life boat.

"Do you see Silas?" Pam cried. "Is he moving?"

David steered us through the gawking throng just as sturdy, muscular crewmen lifted Silas's limp body from the rescue boat onto the stretcher. Silas was wrapped like a monk in dark blankets so that only his chalky white face showed. He was semiconscious, shivering convulsively. The words *he's alive* shot through the crowd like an electric current.

Pam lunged instinctively for Silas and buried her head against his chest. "I'm here, Silas, I'm here!" she wept as she kissed his purplish, ice-blue lips. "Please don't die. I love you so much!"

Dr. Becker climbed from the rescue boat and signaled two crewmen. They gently drew Pam away. "I'm sorry, miss," the grim-faced physician intoned, "we need to get him to the infirmary."

"I'm going with you. Silas is the man I plan to marry."

The doctor hesitated. "Are you sure you want to go in?"

"Yes, I'm a nurse," Pam said, rallying.

Dr. Becker nodded brusquely. "Then hurry."

As the crewmen hoisted the stretcher and carried Silas to the infirmary, the deck officer tapped me on the shoulder. "Excuse me, ma'am, you're wanted on the bridge. Captain would like to see you."

"Me? Why?"

"You witnessed the accident."

"But I wasn't the only one. There were two men—"

"Yes, ma'am, I know. Dr. Thatcher and Mr. Ellis."

"Have you talked to them? They can tell you what happened."

"I'm afraid not, ma'am," said the officer. "It's rather perplexing. I looked all around, telephoned their rooms, and checked with other passengers. No one's seen them. Looks like they just disappeared."

CHAPTER EIGHTEEN

Ten minutes later, with the ship heading south again, the deck officer led David and me into the private, imposing Command Bridge with its panoramic span of windows and sprawling, complex instrument panels. The officer on watch nodded as we entered, but the quartermaster kept his eyes riveted on the automatic gyropilot. I gazed around in fascination at the radar system, the barometer, the fire alarm control panel, and a dozen other mysterious instruments. The rectangular room was immaculate, with padded chairs and round stools, large metal cabinets, and utilitarian brown carpeting.

Captain Pagliarulo, in his official headgear and spotless navy blue uniform, stood beside the charting console, staring out at the ocean. He was a robust man with a commanding, authoritative stance. After a moment, he pivoted solemnly and said in his thick Italian accent, "Thank you for coming, Mr. and Mrs. Ballard."

"The deck officer said you wanted to see me," I managed.

"That's right," he said with a tight little smile. Captain Pagliarulo had a full face, wide bulbous nose, and a square chin. Shaggy brows and unruly gray sideburns lent a subtle irony to his otherwise impeccable appearance. "The man who went overboard—Mr. Silas Winters—I understand you know him well."

"We've known him a year. My sister and Silas are good friends."

The captain nodded. "Mr. Winters and I are slightly acquainted also."

"Yes, he told me so."

"We've notified his family of the accident." The captain paused and eyed me directly. "I am told you were with him when he fell."

"Just before that," I said. "We were chatting on the sun deck. And then—then we heard Dr. Thatcher and Cam Ellis quarreling on the fantail. Before I knew it, Silas was running off to intervene . . ."

The captain's expression remained stern. He stood ramrod straight, his eyes on the sea, his hands folded behind his back.

Finally a seaman approached. "Sir, they have found Dr. Thatcher."

"Ask him to come to the bridge immediately." Turning back to David and me, Captain Pagliarulo said, "Mr. Winters is fortunate, you know. A lesser man could have died in those waters, or broken his neck in the fall."

"Then Silas is going to be all right?"

"We'll know his condition after Dr. Becker finishes examining him. But now I need to know what happened. Was Mr. Winters involved in the fight?"

"I don't know. The three men were out of my sight for a moment as I ran up the steps to the fantail. When I reached the deck, I—I saw Silas. He was falling." My voice caught. "It was awful."

"Mrs. Ballard, did you see one of the men push Mr. Winters?"

"No. I told you, he was already falling. Jason and Cam—they'd have no reason to hurt Silas. He was just trying to help."

"Then you believe it was an accident?"

"I don't know what to think, sir. Like I said, I didn't see—"

"Yes, I understand. I want you two to stay. Hear what Thatcher says." With that, Captain Pagliarulo lapsed into silence as we waited for Jason. When Dr. Thatcher arrived minutes later, Noreen was with him. Jason looked pale, drawn. He refused to look my way.

"Thank you for coming, Dr. Thatcher," said the captain. "I've been talking with the Ballards about the overboard incident. Naturally we're all very concerned."

"How is Mr. Winters?" Jason asked in a solemn, pinched voice.

"We have no word yet, Dr. Thatcher." Captain Pagliarulo nodded toward the log. "According to our notations, Mr. Winters went overboard when he tried to stop a quarrel between you and Mr. Ellis. I find it surprising that a man could simply tumble over the rail without some propulsive force."

"That's what happened," said Jason. "Ellis and I were having a private argument. There was no need for Mr. Winters to interfere."

Noreen stepped forward. "I'm sure Mr. Ellis was the aggressor. He's been insufferable to my husband since this cruise began. It's not like Jason to be involved in a fistfight. He's a very controlled man—and a highly esteemed surgeon, as anyone among the Hopewell alumni can readily testify."

"I am not casting aspersions on your husband's character, Mrs. Thatcher. I am just trying to get a clear picture." The captain paused. "So, Dr. Thatcher, you had no quarrel with Mr. Winters?"

"None whatever. As I said, Cam and I were having a gentleman's disagreement. A very private matter. Things got out of hand. Ellis backed me against the rail. Then, out of the blue, Winters charged at us. On impulse we stepped aside . . . and Winters toppled over."

"Cam Ellis was trying to throw Jason overboard," Noreen charged. "I know it. Tell them, Jason. Don't protect that horrible man."

Jason recoiled, his expression doleful. "Please, stay out of it, Noreen."

Captain Pagliarulo walked over to his log and made another notation. "Stay available, Dr. Thatcher. We'll talk again."

"What do you mean, captain?" Noreen asked with a hint of indignation. "We are free to come and go, aren't we? We plan to go ashore in Sitka on Thursday."

"That's fine, Mrs. Thatcher. I'll be speaking to Mr. Ellis and Mr. Winters . . . assuming he recovers. If there's any change in plans, I'll let you know."

David and I left shortly after that, still as puzzled as before over the circumstances that led to Silas Winters' fall. I wondered, *Did the captain have the same questions I had? Was it truly an accident, or was it one more assault in the diabolical plot that had shadowed our entire cruise? Was Silas Winters the intended victim? Had someone known all along that he*

would board in Juneau? Or had Silas, by a fluke of circum-
stances, saved the intended victim from a watery grave? If
Ellis and Thatcher were truly in a struggle to the death, which
man was the victim and which the assailant?

Before returning to our stateroom, David and I stopped by the infirmary. The nurse offered no prognosis on Silas, except to say that he had been given an IV and oxygen and the doctor was doing all he could. Pam was with Silas, she added. Refused to leave, in fact.

"Please tell my sister we'll be back after dinner," I told her.

After a light seafood dinner, I sent David to the evening talent show with Jackie and little Stevie while I returned to the infirmary to check on Silas. The nurse promptly summoned Pam for me. She came out of the consultation room sipping a cup of black coffee.

"How's Silas?" I asked.

"Alive, thank God." Pam's face was stained with tears, her makeup blotchy. "He's suffering from shock and hypothermia, but he's coming around now, responding, and his color is better."

We both sat down. I shook my head in relief and murmured, "Thank the Lord. I prayed so hard . . ."

"Me too," said Pam. "I thought I'd lost him."

"Have you talked to Silas? Asked him what happened?"

"No, he's been out of it, groggy. I don't want to upset him. He's sleeping now. That's why I grabbed some coffee."

"You're not staying here all night, are you?"

"I won't leave his side, sis. I can't leave him. Ever."

I reached over and brushed her hair back from her forehead. "I wish I knew what to say to you, Pam. But right now I'm having a hard time dealing with all that's happened myself. Shell shock, I guess."

"I'm not surprised," said Pam. "You saw Silas fall."

I shivered involuntarily. "I won't forget that grisly sight for the rest of my life, Pam. I'm just glad Silas has a second chance—"

"It's a second chance to find God, if he'll see it that way."

"And if he doesn't?" I asked softly.

"I don't know, sis. When I was sitting by his bedside just now, Silas held my hand so tightly, and he kept mumbling over and over, 'I need you, Pam.' He's never needed me before, Michelle. How can I walk away from him? That could turn him completely against God."

I gazed levelly at her. "Pam, do you really want a man who could never be your spiritual helpmate, who would have absolutely no faith to share with his children—*your* children?"

Pam drew away, stiffening her shoulders as her lower lip settled into a pout. "Don't preach to me, Michelle—not now, not tonight."

"You know I don't mean to, Pam. I don't have all the answers either. I haven't figured out yet how to tell David about the baby."

Pam looked up wide-eyed at me. "Oh, the baby! I nearly forgot. Are you terribly disappointed about being pregnant, Michelle?"

I shrugged. "I've hardly had time to think about it. It's not real to me yet. I guess it'll take awhile to get used to the idea."

Pam managed an ironic smile. "About nine months, they say." She took one last sip of her coffee, then stood up. "I've got to get back to Silas, big sis; I want to be there for him when he wakes up."

I stood, too, and embraced her. "Call me if you need me."

Tears rimmed her eyes. "What I need is for you to find out why this happened," she said, barely suppressing her bitterness.

"Pam, the investigation's in the captain's hands," I told her.

"Maybe so, but don't let Dr. Thatcher and Cam Ellis off the hook, Michelle. Make them tell you, sis. Don't let them out of your sight until you learn the truth."

Minutes later, as I returned to my stateroom, I knew Pam was right. With Silas out of commission, who else would relentlessly seek out answers and pin down Thatcher and Ellis for the facts? The captain was investigating the incident, of course, but his official inquiry would likely be routine . . . and confidential.

With only a few days of the cruise remaining, someone had

to decipher this deadly riddle before another unwitting victim suffered. But who was foolhardy enough to play detective in the face of murderous threats and improbable accidents?

I sighed knowingly. *I was.*

CHAPTER
NINETEEN

On Wednesday, as our ship continued cruising south toward Sitka, I went up to the sun deck looking for Cam Ellis. I was near the pool when I spotted Seth Mueller heading my way in that audacious, egotistical stroll of his, a tennis racket slung casually over one shoulder. I realized again what an attractive man he was, solidly built, still youthful. "Good morning, Michelle," he said as he reached me. "I'm late for an appointment with your husband."

"I know. David's already out on the tennis court."

"Practicing?" he chuckled, brushing his hangdog mustache. "Why don't you come watch me win?"

"Another time. I'm looking for Cam Ellis."

"I just saw Cam go into the pub on the Lido Deck."

"This early in the morning?"

"Maybe he didn't look at his watch." Seth started to leave, thought better of it, and said, "Have you thought any more about writing my story? I could book you on my flight to Thailand."

"Thailand's out, Seth," I answered, thinking about the baby. "But I really would like to write your story."

"David's being a spoilsport, eh? I'll talk to him again—"

"No, please don't. But why don't you send me tapes and pictures? Maybe we could work out a book from this end."

He shook his head. "You have to see the refugee camps yourself. I can't paint them for you; you've got to see them, feel them."

"Then write the book yourself. You've been there, lived it."

He laughed uproariously. "Me, write a book? Michelle, I hardly ever wrote a research paper in college without Abigail's help."

"All right, Abigail could go with you and do the research."

Seth was suddenly pensive. "I can't see Abigail over there in that kind of setting. She's so—" He groped for words.

"Gracious? Ladylike? Delicate?" I offered.

"Yes, like a bone china cup—exquisite, lovely, fragile. There is so much pain and dying in those camps. Abigail's safe right where she is on the Hopewell campus. Shielded."

"Have you ever asked her to go with you? Given her a choice?"

"I'd like nothing better. But it's too late. Come on," he said abruptly. "I'll walk you up to the Lido Deck."

Seth left me at the pub. I peered into the dimly lit room. Cam sat alone at a corner table, nursing a drink. I walked over and took the chair across from him, uninvited. He looked up at me in surprise as a passing bar steward asked, "May I get you something, miss?"

"No," I answered quickly. "I just want to talk to Mr. Ellis."

"You're not afraid of me this morning?" Cam asked cuttingly.

"No. And I'm sorry about yesterday. I overreacted when you touched me. I was stunned. Silas Winters had just gone overboard."

"I know," said Cam. "I just wish Winters hadn't interfered."

"He saw trouble brewing and was just trying to help."

Cam tipped his glass and swallowed. "Help? Ha! Now the captain's watching my every move. He talked to me last night, you know."

"Yes, he said he would. He talked to the Thatchers, too. Noreen insists her husband never gets angry."

Cam Ellis rubbed his neck. "These bruises are not the result of a controlled, peace-loving man, Michelle."

"Cam," I said gently, "what really happened yesterday?"

Cam drained his glass and slammed it on the table. "Your friend Silas was in the middle of things before we realized it.

Then he took a wallop meant for Thatcher or me. I'm not sure which one of us struck the blow. All I know is, suddenly, Silas just went reeling backward and toppled over the rail."

I wanted to say, *It couldn't have been that simple, Cam. The rail's too high. Silas wouldn't be that clumsy.*

But the steward was back at our table. "Will that be all, sir?"

Cam nodded. He signed the tab, then gazed back at me, his eyes piercing, direct. "You saw what happened yesterday, Michelle. Why are you asking me about it?"

"Actually, I didn't see—" I wanted to cut off my words immediately, but it was too late.

A slow, twisted grin cut across Cam's bearded face. "Then you really don't know anything at all, do you, Michelle?" He stood, helped me to my feet, and added, "You will excuse me, won't you? I need to get back to Stephanie. She's been under the weather lately."

"I'm sorry to hear that," I said quietly. "Please tell her I said hello. I haven't seen her since the Hopewell reception."

"To be quite frank, I think she's had enough of discussing poetry and religion," said Cam. "You have her rather upset."

"Upset? Really? I never meant to. Would you tell her I'm having tea on the Lido Deck at four and I'd like her to join me?"

"I'll tell her, but don't count on her being there."

* * *

At four, as I sat on the Lido Deck sipping hot tea and sampling a fruit pastry, Stephanie Ellis slipped into the seat across from me. "I'm so glad to see you," I said. "I wasn't sure you'd come."

"Cam isn't happy about it, but I just had to see you and find out how Mr. Winters is. I keep hearing rumors—"

"He's better. My sister Pam's been at his bedside since he was rescued, and I stopped by the infirmary to see him this morning."

She smiled. "I'm relieved. I was so worried. . . ."

I offered her a pastry. "I've been wanting to talk to you."

She stirred her tea methodically. "Talk? What about?"

"Nothing. Just chat. I'm concerned about you, Stephanie."

"Don't be. I'm doing okay. Inside, in spite of everything, I'm at peace now. I don't understand it, but it's there."

"I'm glad. I was hoping we could talk and pray together."

"I'm not sure that would be wise, considering Cam. . . ."

"Have you told Cam about your new faith?"

"No, I didn't have to. He guessed. He said there was something different about me. I think it frightened him. He said this was the same way Rodney had been before all the trouble started."

I turned my teacup slowly. "Please, Stephanie, don't let Cam or anyone else steal the joy God has for you." As I gradually shared with her my own early walk with God—the blessings, the learning experiences—the worry lines in her face softened.

"Will you keep in touch with me, Michelle, so that I can grow too? I don't know anyone I can talk and pray with back home."

"We can telephone," I said, "and see each other when I visit my folks. They live near you. If it's all right, I'll have Mom call you. You'll love my mother. She makes knowing God seem so easy."

Stephanie and I were on our second cup of tea when I brought up the conflict between Cam and Dr. Thatcher. "Did they know each other before this cruise?"

Stephanie's face clouded. I could feel her drawing away from me, her eyes growing distant. "They never met until we boarded."

"Then why are they so antagonistic toward each other?"

"I—I can't talk about it, Michelle."

"That doesn't make sense, Stephanie. If there's something wrong, maybe David and I can help."

Her voice quavered. "I told you before, Cam hates doctors."

"Do you know what Cam and Dr. Thatcher were arguing about?"

Stephanie looked away. "What difference does it make now?"

"If they haven't solved their misunderstanding, it may come up again. The next time, it could be even worse. Something could happen to Cam or to Dr. Thatcher. You don't want that, Stephanie."

"You know I don't," she said, her voice taut with emotion.

"Then what are you going to do about it?"

"Pray, Michelle," she whispered. "You've taught me to pray."

I sighed, then reached over and squeezed Stephanie's hand. "We'll both keep praying, Stephanie. I promise."

* * *

At 8:00 A.M. on Thursday, the *Mendenhall* dropped anchor at Sitka. As David and I prepared to go ashore, I said casually, "Hope you don't mind. I bought tickets for the Zodiac Raft Ride."

He looked questioningly at me. "You did what? You told me you'd never go on a raft ride again."

"I know, but I was concerned when I heard that both the Thatchers and Ellises are going."

He gave me a whimsical grin. "Are you playing Sherlock again?"

Feigning surprise, I drawled, "Me, David? Me—play detective?"

Minutes later, we joined the crowd at the disembarkation door and took the tender over to Sitka—a lovely, scenic port town with verdant rain forests and sprawling, rock-strewn beaches, its harbor framed by the towering, snow-tipped Mt. Edgecumbe, a dormant volcano.

We spent an hour walking around town, visiting the Centennial building where Czarist Russian dancers swooped and swirled, their sprightly Cossack performance depicting Sitka's colorful past. At times we were only steps behind the Thatchers. They seemed content to walk alone. We followed them into the Sheldon Jackson Museum by the waterfront but lost them before we reached St. Michael's, an onion-domed Russian Orthodox cathedral in the center of town. I was fascinated by St. Michael's collection of religious artifacts—wedding crowns, old-fashioned vestments of elegant brocade, precious jewels, and rare icons. We browsed through the New Archangel Trading Company and the Totem Gift Shop, where I purchased some Russian nesting dolls, seaweed art by local artists, several pewter figures, and handcarved totem poles. At MacDonald's Bayview Trading Company, David bought me some Baltic amber and an exquisite 300 dollar Russian lacquer box illustrating an old Slavic fairy tale.

We joined Cam and Stephanie Ellis for a sandwich and coffee at the Bayview Restaurant. Stephanie forced a bright, bubbly facade, but Cam maintained an undercurrent of sullen reserve. When I told them we would be accompanying them on the raft trip to the wildlife refuge, Cam muttered, "I hear Thatcher's braving the trip too."

After our brief lunch, the four of us made our way back to the harbor, crossing over the rocky shoal to the pier. There was a steady, cold drizzle now as we boarded the *Baranof Queen*, a privately-owned fiberglass sport vessel with three crew members, a pilot in the wheel house, a small galley, and a narrow walkway around the boat. One crewman was already serving cheese, crackers and salmon caviar as we pulled anchor and cruised out into Sitka Sound. David and Cam took heaping platefuls, then the four of us sat down on a padded wood bench inside, two rows behind the Thatchers.

The waters were choppy with whitecaps, the swells mounting dramatically as the mizzling rain became a downpour. The *Baranof Queen* plowed through the rough, surging waves of the open sea, rising and falling like a roller coaster out of control. The smell of our fish snacks mingling with our topsy-turvy motion turned my stomach. I clutched my motion-sickness bag, praying I wouldn't have to use it, and wondered if Sherlock Holmes ever endured such nausea-inducing misery for the sake of a mystery.

A youthful, stubbly-chinned seaman teetered down the narrow aisle passing out rain ponchos, orange life vests, and cumbersome rubber boots. I struggled into my poncho and vest and nearly upchucked as I leaned down to pull on my boots. I thought darkly, *If Thatcher or Ellis pulled anything now, I'd be absolutely no help!*

One by one, people stumbled to their feet and wended their way out to the open walkway for some fresh air. I watched as Dr. Thatcher went over, pushed aside the heavy sliding door, and stepped outside. Cam's eyes followed Jason's every move. After a moment, Cam stood quietly and slipped out onto the walkway beside Thatcher.

I turned to David. "I've got to go out for some air—now!"

His gaze settled on Jason and Cam. "Watch out for those two."

"That's what I intend to do." I hoisted myself up and swayed toward the door. As I stepped outside, the bitter wind slapped my face and seawater crashed over the walkway, drenching my poncho.

The two men stood several feet apart, gazing out at the heaving sea, their hands tight on the rail. I stepped between them and said brightly, "Some ride, isn't it, gentlemen?"

Thatcher looked green. "I should have stayed on shore."

Cam kept his face tipped to the wind and rain. "Really, Dr. Thatcher, didn't you come because you knew I'd be here?"

Thatcher shot back, "Don't flatter yourself, Ellis."

I gripped my stomach and swallowed hard, musing with an agonizing irony, *I'm the crazy fool on watch! I should've stayed on land!*

Forty minutes later, our motor cruiser slowed as we approached St. Lazaria Island, a national wildlife refuge. The sheer rock island created a natural rookery for gulls, eagles, and sea birds. Its rocky coastline provided a watery playground for frisky sea lions, seals, and sea otters.

While the *Baranof Queen* bobbed in the rolling breakers, we transferred to an inflated motorized raft. My face was chapped and my hands numb with cold as David and I squeezed in behind the Thatchers and Ellises. I was grateful for the momentary warmth of closely packed, thickly padded bodies.

Our young seaman piloted us slowly into a huge, natural rock cavern where the rough sea turned to a gentle calm. I gazed around in wonderment and delight. The cavern walls, exposed by receding tides, were richly encrusted with starfish, sea urchins, soft corals, and barnacles—as if an artist had painted the chamber with variegated shades of purple and red, pink and orange and yellow. Kelp floated in the water beside a reef dotted with colonies of anemone, orange puff ball sponges, and Sea Strawberries with bright red lobes and white polyps.

Shortly, our raft cruised out of the cave and forged back into the thrashing, wind-driven waves. We circled the entire island, hitting the foamy crests head-on with crashing force. "Hold on," shouted our ebullient seaman. "We don't want to lose anyone!"

"Uh, have you ever lost anyone yet?" I squeaked nervously.

"Yeah, a young fellow went under just last week!"

"From—from this raft?" Noreen stammered.

"Naw, he was a kid from Sitka—hadn't handled a raft before."

"And they couldn't rescue him?" asked Jason.

"No, he got caught in the current and thrown against the rocks."

As our raft dipped precariously and slammed against another billowing swell, I fought horrifying visions of us capsizing, drowning. "If our motor went dead, would we just drift?" I asked timorously.

"Yeah, straight into those rocky cliffs," snapped Cam.

Minutes later, I sighed in relief as we stepped gingerly back on the *Baranof Queen*. As the sturdy craft propelled us back to Sitka's picturesque fishing harbor, David and I nestled together at the bow, windblown and water-sprayed, our faces tilted against the blustery, rainswept gusts. I reflected ironically that I was a queasy, bone-weary Sherlock with wobbly sea legs, my mystery still unsolved.

CHAPTER
TWENTY

That night I dreamed about Silas Winters. I saw him toppling over the rail and plunging in slow motion to the dark, swirling waters below. In my dream he never hit the sea. He just kept falling, his shriek echoing around me and through me. But I couldn't help him. I stood frozen to the spot, watching in horror, and the horror wouldn't end. His body just kept spiraling downward while his raw, anguished scream pulsated in my head and bristled my skin until I was screaming too. Then, through our reverberating cries I heard a man's voice say, "You killed my son. You killed my only son!" And finally, as the phantom waves broke with a symphony crash around Silas's body, I sat bolt-upright in bed and said starkly, "It's Cam!"

Suddenly I felt strong arms shaking me, and a deep voice called, "Michelle! Michelle!" I blinked my eyes against the darkness as David gathered me into his arms and said soothingly, "What's wrong, darling? Wake up. You were screaming."

"It was Silas. He was falling again. I kept seeing him—"

"But you shouted Cam's name. You said, 'It's Cam.' "

I drew back and brushed my hair from my eyes. "It's nothing, David. My dream—it was all jumbled—Silas, Cam, Jason—"

David massaged the back of my neck. "Go back to sleep, hon."

"I'll try," I said unconvincingly. I lay back on my pillow, my body taut, my mind racing. Why hadn't I put the pieces together before? Just before Silas went overboard, I had heard Cam's bitter accusation as he quarreled with Jason, but the shock of seeing Silas fall had temporarily erased the memory. I was convinced that, somehow, in the irrational, inexplicable ways of grief, Cam was transferring his bitterness against his son's doctor to Jason Thatcher, an innocent man.

I got up in the dark and dressed quietly. I couldn't sleep any longer, knowing the truth, knowing that Cam in his imbalanced state might still strike out with deadly force against Jason.

For a long while I sat staring out the window, weighing my options. At last, as the mauve shadows turned to ripe amber rays of dawn, I decided that the only thing I could do was confront Cam Ellis with the truth and make him realize how irrational he was being to take out his anger on Jason.

I waited until just before breakfast, while David was out jogging, to telephone the Ellises. "I know it's awfully early, Stephanie," I said, "but is Cam there?"

Stephanie's voice throbbed with apprehension. "No, he's gone. He paced all night, Michelle, more agitated than I've ever seen him."

"Where did he go, Stephanie?"

"He didn't say. But before he left he telephoned Dr. Thatcher."

"Were they going to meet somewhere?"

"I don't know, Michelle. Cam just promised he'd meet me later in the Sky Room for devotions."

"Then maybe everything's all right, Stephanie."

There was a long pause. I could hear Stephanie's short, labored breathing. Then she said timidly, "I'm worried, Michelle."

"Worried? What's wrong?"

"Cam's revolver—it's not in the drawer."

"He has a gun?" I asked in alarm.

"Yes, he always keeps it handy. It's the hunter in him."

My heart began to hammer wildly. "Are you saying—?"

Stephanie said despairingly, "I think he took the gun with him."

I drew in a sharp breath. "Stephanie, you've got to notify the captain."

"I can't, Michelle."

"Then if you won't, I will."

"Please, Michelle, I don't want him to get into trouble. I'm sure Cam won't hurt anyone. He's just so despondent. If we could find him, I'm sure we could reason with him. Will you come with me?"

I sighed. It was against my better judgment, but I said, "All right, Stephanie. You go check the pub and Lido Deck. I'll check the sun deck and Sky Room."

I scribbled a quick note to David: "I'm skipping breakfast, looking for Cam Ellis. Meet you in the Sky Room for devotions."

When I didn't find Cam on the sun deck, I hurried through the wide double doors to the Sky Room. The sprawling room was empty, but through the large eight-paneled front windows I spotted Thatcher and Ellis talking on the open deck by the railing. I darted through the side door and approached quietly. Jason looked apologetic, but Cam stood scowling, his hands shoved in the pockets of his windbreaker.

"Excuse me, Cam, Jason. May I speak with you?"

"What is it, Michelle?" Thatcher asked nervously.

"I need to talk to Cam. I think I can help you both."

"This is a private matter, Michelle," Thatcher insisted.

"But when you two were arguing on the fantail—just before Silas went overboard—I heard Cam say, 'You killed my son.' "

"Stay out of this," Cam told me. "It's none of your business."

"I want to help, Cam. Please let me talk to you—"

"How can you help, Michelle?" he countered, his voice erupting with a raw anguish. "Dr. Thatcher has already killed my son!"

When Jason didn't reply, I cried, "You're wrong, Cam! Think about it. How can you blame Jason for what happened to your son under another doctor's care?"

Cold perspiration dotted Cam's face as he shouted, "Because the doctor who treated Rodney—the surgeon who let my son die—this incompetent man was Hopewell's own esteemed Dr. Jason Thatcher!"

I stared at Jason. "You—you were Rodney Ellis's doctor?"

"I was his surgical consultant," Jason admitted. "The boy thought he had a lung tumor. He didn't. Normally I would have walked out of his room and never seen young Ellis again."

"Then why didn't you walk out, Doctor?" challenged Cam.

"When Rodney found out I went to Hopewell, he begged me to stay on as his physician. He said, 'Doc Thatcher, you're my only chance.' I became his friend. I tried to help him. God knows I tried."

"Tried? How hard did you try, Doctor? My son is dead."

"Look, man," said Jason, "if we could just sit down and talk—"

Something in Jason's placating voice struck fury in Cam. His face went livid. "Talk?" he screamed, whipping his revolver from his jacket. "Enough talking! I've planned my revenge!"

Thatcher stepped forward tentatively. "Put the gun away, Cam."

Cam aimed his weapon at Jason.

Instinctively I lunged toward Cam. He turned, springing back with the stealth of a cougar. "Get away, Michelle; don't interfere!"

I stepped closer, holding out my hand for the gun. "Please, Cam, be rational. Don't do something you'll regret."

Cam thrust forward and grabbed my arm. When I tried to wrench away, he tightened his grip. I looked around in desperation. Several people were already filtering into the Sky Room, several glancing curiously out the window. But would any realize the enormity of what was happening? Would they notice Cam's gun?

"Let Michelle go, Cam," said Jason. "This is just between you and me." He glanced back. "Look, Cam, people are arriving for the Hopewell devotions. Put your gun away. Let's go inside."

"No chance, Thatcher. I've waited too long for this moment." He waved his revolver over the waters. "Silas Winters can't come to your rescue this time, Doctor. I made a promise I'm going to keep. 'Just beyond the windswept sea, cold, cruel death awaits for *thee*.'"

I stared up in astonishment at Cam. "Then the poems—all those terrible threats—were yours? You were the man in the library?"

"Yes, Michelle; Stephanie's not the only one who writes poetry."

"Why, Ellis? Why all the insane poems?" Jason demanded. "Why that taped message? The telephone threats? The shattered flower vase? Did you have to terrorize the entire Hopewell group? You wanted me—why didn't you come get me? What kind of madman are you?"

Cam's eyes glittered. "Madman?" he choked. "Insane? I've never been called a madman in my life, Thatcher. Not until I mingled with you people, you hallowed Hopewell Christians."

"Is that it, Cam?" I forced the tremor out of my voice. "You think Christians have let you down again? Hurt you? Maligned you?"

"That's what you Christians did to Rodney too. He tried to be one of you." His voice rang with desolation. "And now Stephanie—!" He paused, scanning the gathering crowd. A deck officer, waving people back, shouted Cam's name and told him to put down his gun. Cam ignored him. "My wife— my Stephanie—she believes like you people now. Are you satisfied? You've won! I've lost her too!"

Suddenly I spotted David breaking through the murmuring throng, striding our way. He stopped several feet from us and said in a surprisingly calm voice, "Let my wife go, Cam. Give me your gun."

"Stay back, Ballard!" Cam swung me around and crushed me against his muscular chest, his burly arm pinning me against him. I couldn't move, could hardly breathe.

Two crewmen approached, their eyes fastened on Cam, their hands poised to take him. Cam aimed his gun at them. "One step closer, gentlemen, and someone's going to get a bullet."

"Careful, Cam. No one needs to get hurt," David soothed.

"Hurt? What do you mean? My son is dead because of Thatcher."

"You're wrong, Cam," I cried breathlessly. "Dr. Thatcher told you—he befriended your son in the—the last hours of his life."

"You're lying," Cam shrilled. "He let my son die!"

"Tell him, Jason," I begged. "Tell Cam how his son really died."

"He died from pneumonia," Cam thundered. "And this honorable Hopewell surgeon, with all of modern medical science at his fingertips, couldn't even save him."

"No one could save your son, Cam," I cried. "He was very sick."

"Sick? Oh, yes, sick! But no one ever told me he was dying."

"He didn't want you to know," Jason managed finally.

"I don't believe you, Thatcher. Why wouldn't he want me to know? I loved my son more than anything on this earth."

"But, Cam," I blurted, "would you have loved him if you knew he had AIDS?"

Cam's face registered shock, then uncontrolled rage. "My son never had AIDS!" He clutched me tighter. I felt a sudden spasm in my stomach. The sea of frightened, staring faces blurred for a moment, then flashed mirror-sharp. I recognized Jackie and Stevie, a distraught Noreen Thatcher, and even Erma Moosenbocker in the crowd.

Suddenly, Stephanie Ellis stepped forward, her shoulders squared, her voice thin, strained. "Yes, he did, Cam. Yes, our son had AIDS. And he was afraid to turn to us. Afraid we'd reject him."

Cam swayed momentarily. I thought he might topple us both. "Tell me, Thatcher. Tell me it's not true," he pleaded.

Jason's ashen face was grim. "It's true, Ellis."

"But the death certificate—"

"I know. I put down only a partial diagnosis."

"What kind of medical ethics do you practice?" Cam shrilled.

"I made a promise to your son, Ellis. I promised him I wouldn't tell you how he died. He wanted to spare you."

"But you lied!"

"Not exactly. Your son died of pneumonia, secondary to the acquired immune deficiency syndrome."

"Was he on drugs? Is that how he contracted the disease?"

"No. Your son didn't do drugs."

"Then a blood transfusion while he was under your care?"

"No, Ellis. He already had the disease before he came to me."

"Don't tell me—you're not saying . . ."

"Our son was a homosexual, Cam." Stephanie uttered the words with a ragged edge of anguish and despair.

Cam's gaze riveted on his wife. "No, not my son! Never! He was a man! He even said he was a—a Christian. . . ."

"And we never supported him," sobbed Stephanie. "We scoffed. Belittled his faltering faith. We never encouraged him, Cam." Stephanie moved slowly toward her husband. "Let Michelle go, Cam. These people have nothing to do with our problems. Please let her—"

"Stop, Steph. This is my fight, my vengeance, my chance for retribution, but people are twisting it, telling me my son was gay—"

"Your son was straight during his last months," said Jason.

"How do you know, Thatcher?"

"Because Rodney told me and I believed him." Jason leaned wearily against the rail. "In case you're interested, Ellis, I prayed with your son before he died. We went back over that journey he began back at Hopewell. Whatever your son did was forgiven."

Cam flinched. "Are you telling me my son was a sinner?" He spat the words on the deck.

"A sinner? Yes. Your son. You. Me. Michelle," said David appeasingly, stealing nearer, ready to spring. "All of us— sinners— apart from the blood of Christ, the power of redemption."

"It doesn't matter what the sin was, Cam," I said weakly.

Stephanie held out her hands entreatingly to her husband. "Cam, I've discovered this redemption myself. Christ extends forgiveness to everyone who repents and seeks Him. Please, put away your gun—"

"Don't talk to me of redemption!" Cam bellowed, waving his revolver wildly in the air. Several people gasped and backed away.

David took another bold step toward Cam, his face twisted with restrained fury, his fists doubled. "Let my wife go, Ellis!"

Cam held my head tight against his shoulder and shoved his revolver under my chin. "Don't try anything, Ballard, or I'll shoot."

Dry, immobilizing fear clutched my throat as I realized, *I'm going to die. In an instant. At the whim of a madman. Oh, Lord, the terrible irony of it—the insanity!* Then, with sudden, heart-stopping comprehension, I thought of my unborn child. *Oh, God, don't let anything happen to my baby! I love him! Please let him live!*

Unexpectedly, little Stevie broke loose from Jackie and bolted across the deck, screaming, "Let go of my Aunt Michelle! Let go!"

"No, Stevie! Come back!" Jackie shouted, grabbing for her son.

But Stevie came racing toward us like a brave pint-size warrior.

Cam jerked back, agitated, and took aim. "No, Cam!" I screamed.

Suddenly everything happened at once. David vaulted toward Cam. Erma Moosenbocker burst from the crowd and barreled like a linebacker toward little Stevie. She scooped him up in her arms just as David slammed against Cam, knocking the gun from his hand. I fell against the rail as Cam's weapon clattered onto the deck. Jason sprang forward and kicked the gun away. We heard it splash into the ocean below.

David sprinted over to the rail and caught me in his arms as Stephanie ran to Cam and embraced him. He crumpled against her, tears coursing down his bearded face. "Oh, Steph, I'm sorry. I didn't mean to—it's just—our son—he needed us and we never knew!"

They clung to each other for a long moment, then Stephanie turned to Jason, her face tear-streaked, and said, "Forgive me, Dr. Thatcher. I should have seen what was happening to Cam. I should have told him the truth about Rodney. Instead, I let him blame you." Her voice cracked with emotion. "And he—he almost killed you!"

Jason shook his head despairingly. "It's not entirely your husband's fault, Mrs. Ellis." He clutched the rail unsteadily. Noreen went to him, slipping her arm around his waist. Jason coughed—a deep, rasping sound—then continued hoarsely, "Once I realized Cam was Rodney's father, I knew he was after me. I egged him on. I deliberately used him—his hatred—for my own purposes."

Stephanie shook her head, baffled. "I don't understand—"

"It's really quite simple. I wanted your husband to kill me."

No one moved. We stood stone-still, speechless, staring silently, incredulously at one another. Cam Ellis's face was contorted, grief and disbelief etched in his troubled charcoal eyes.

"I—I took out a large insurance policy," Jason went on dispassionately. "You see, I had it planned—my, uh, death. I was going to jump overboard. Ironic, isn't it? Cam could have saved himself the trouble if he'd known. But no one knew—"

"Jason, what are you saying?" Noreen cried.

He rubbed her arm comfortingly. "I planned to commit suicide."

She clasped Jason's neck. "No, in the name of heaven—!"

"But I was afraid the authorities would discover that it was suicide and not pay the insurance money. I was counting on that money to provide for you, Noreen, and to see our girls through college. Then, when I realized Cam had murder in mind, I figured I'd let him do the dirty work, and there'd be no question about the insurance paying."

Noreen was weeping now, shaking her head in dismay.

"You played me for a sucker, Thatcher!" shouted Cam. "You were going to let me be a murderer!" He yanked free from Stephanie, stumbled blindly to the guardrail and leaned over, retching. David went to him and gripped his shoulders.

Noreen trembled as she pulled back and stared at her husband. "Why, Jason?" she demanded through her tears. "Why on earth would you want to—to commit suicide? Haven't I—?" Her lips moved, but the words wouldn't come. Finally, she sobbed, "Haven't I been a good wife, Jason? Haven't the girls and I made you happy?"

Jason gazed at Noreen, contrition written on his thin, waxen face. "Oh, my darling, you and the girls have made me happier than any man deserves to be. That day when Cam and I struggled on the fantail—just before Silas Winters went overboard—I knew suddenly that I wanted to live. Great heavens, how I wanted to live! I wanted to spend every minute I could with you and the girls. But before I could even cry out for forgiveness, Winters went over."

Jason paused, then lifted his hand toward Cam at the rail. "Ellis, forgive me . . . as I forgive you. My sin was the greater, for I had God's Spirit to guide me but I chose to forfeit His power."

Cam glared at Jason, then uttered an oath under his breath as three seamen approached. They escorted Cam and a weeping Stephanie back through the Sky Room as the crowd parted, whispering noisily.

David returned to my side and squeezed me tight. "Are you all right, Michelle?"

I clung to him, trembling. "Oh, David, I was so scared!"

"My foolish little darling. Why did you go after Cam alone?"

"I—I wanted to help. I thought I could reason with him—"

"Michelle, Michelle, I could have lost you!"

"Oh, David, hold me. Don't let me go."

"It's okay, sweetheart," he soothed. "It's over now."

"Thank God," I whispered.

After a moment, I looked over at Jason and noticed a trickle of blood dripping from his nostril, down over his blanched lips. "Jason, are you okay?" I asked.

Noreen looked up in alarm at her husband. "Jason, you're hurt. Ellis has injured you!"

"No, Noreen. Cam didn't hit me. It's—it's what I've been trying to tell you. I'm sick, Noreen. I'm dying."

There was a shattering shard of silence, then Noreen shrieked, "No, no, no! You're not dying! I won't let you die!"

Jason was rocking her now, standing on the deck cradling Noreen much as he would a wounded child. He leaned down and put his cheek against her head as drops of his blood streaked her blonde hair. "I didn't want you to know, Noreen, not yet. I didn't want the girls to know. That's why I sent them to Europe this summer. I wanted the two of us to have this last time together."

Noreen shook with convulsive sobs.

"I've been angry with God, my darling," Jason continued unevenly. "You know how I hate death, the process of dying. I didn't want to waste away in front of you—to be helpless."

Noreen's words were muffled against Jason's chest. "But I love you, Jason. You should have known I'd walk with you always, through anything. . . ."

"I don't have very long. God forgive me, that's why I wanted to take my life—to protect us both from what lies ahead." The blood trickled from both nostrils now.

Suddenly, my sister Pam pushed through the crowd with a wheelchair and touched Jason's shoulder. "Please, Dr. Thatcher, we've got to stop that bleeding. I've sent for Dr. Becker."

Jason nodded mechanically as Pam helped him into the wheelchair. Noreen knelt down beside him, patting his cheek, squeezing his hand. "Why didn't you tell me, Jason? Why did you carry this burden alone?"

Jason's words were nasal-twanged as Pam pressed beneath the bridge of his nose. "Noreen, I never wanted to leave you. I didn't want to be absent from this body, not now, not yet. I couldn't face my own mortality. I wanted to go on forever—"

"You will, Jason," she whispered soothingly. "In heaven—"

His eyes glinted with emotion. "For months I've been terrified of the specter of death—the slow, terrible agony."

"I'll be with you, Jason, every moment, every day," Noreen promised. "Death is only a shadow. You've told me that, Jason. You've taught it in your Bible studies. Only a shadow before glory."

As the crowd dispersed and Pam wheeled Jason Thatcher to the infirmary, David caressed me, kissing my face and hair. "Oh, Michelle," he murmured against my cheek, "When I saw Cam holding that gun on you, something inside me clicked. I thought, *Oh, God, don't take her from me.* I realized in that moment how terribly important you are to me. You—just as you are. No one else could take your place. I'm so grateful to God for you. I love you."

CHAPTER
TWENTY-ONE

For the next several hours, David and I sat in our stateroom with the Stoddards, the Thatchers, and Stephanie Ellis talking, crying, and praying together. We devoured 1 John again, as Stoddard pointed us to forgiveness, fellowship, Sonship. Our hearts ached for Stephanie as she sat stiffly in her chair, wringing her hands nervously. As he watched her, Jason broke into wrenching sobs and said, "I'm sorry, Stephanie. If I hadn't been bound by self-pity—if I could have faced my own dying—!"

Stephanie's fleeting smile was genuine. "Jason, please don't. We all have our own guilt to deal with. But, thank God, I'm learning about forgiveness. Now if only Cam—" Her words were lost in a sob.

We all knew as we parted at our stateroom door that Cam would have to face the consequences of his actions, perhaps even serve a prison term, but the Stoddards agreed to work with Stephanie and Cam in the days ahead, finding them appropriate psychological counseling and legal assistance through Hopewell.

That evening, David and I were subdued, pensive as we showered and dressed for our last dinner aboard the *Mendenhall*. I still had to find the right time and place to tell David about the baby. And the right words. But my ambivalence over my pregnancy was gone since this morning . . . since those terrifying moments when Cam had held his revolver on me, paralyzing me with fear for my baby's life.

Naturally, I would still feel moments of anxiety over pending motherhood—*Would I make a good mother? Would I still be able to maintain my writing career?*—but there was no more question about whether I wanted my baby. He—or she—

was a priceless gift, and I felt blessed already by this tiny, unseen person inhabiting my body. In my writer's notebook I wrote, "I am a neophyte explorer traversing uncharted terrain. I marvel over these strange new feelings of awe and delight."

But how to tell David? I decided to make a "date" with him for after dinner this evening in our stateroom. I would order our favorite exotic fruit drink and wear my shimmering peach negligee.

I approached David cautiously, not wanting the lilt in my voice or the gleam in my eyes to betray my secret. "Darling, there's something special I want to tell you. Can we talk after dinner?"

"We always do," he said with a flicker of amusement.

"I mean alone."

His smile broadened. "Sounds better already. What do you want to tell me—that you love me?"

"You already know that."

He gave me a big bear hug. "I know, but I like to hear it again and again." His eyes glinted merrily as he gazed down at me. "Now what is it you want to tell me?"

"After dinner, David," I said coyly. "Back in our stateroom."

His roguish brows arched expectantly. "We could skip dinner."

"No way. It's the captain's farewell dinner, and for the first time we don't have to worry about ominous notes and veiled threats."

David was silent for a moment.

"Well, David, is it a date?"

He grinned mischievously. "After dinner then, my sweet."

"David," I scolded, "why are you grinning at me like that?"

He winked seductively. "I'm hoping you've decided we can start a family tonight."

I gave him my most alluring "come hither" look, then turned away before he could catch me laughing.

Since we had a half hour before dinner, we decided to take one last stroll on the promenade deck. When we reached the starboard side, we found Seth Mueller sitting alone on the open deck, his expression as dark as the gray nimbus clouds blanketing the sky. As we sat down beside him, he looked up in surprise and said, "David, Michelle, I've been wondering about you two. Tell me, are you okay after all the excitement this morning?"

"I'm beginning to recover," I said with a faint smile. "At least my knees have finally stopped knocking."

"Well, the whole ship's talking about your ordeal. Imagine—Ellis going off the deep end like that. Who would have thought it?"

David shook his head somberly. "At least we can breathe a sigh of relief that the truth is out about those mysterious threats."

The three of us talked for several minutes about Cam and Jason—about the twists and turns that had brought them together and created such havoc for the Hopewell alumni throughout our cruise.

"How's Silas Winters?" Seth asked at last.

"He's okay. Just got out of the infirmary this afternoon."

"Did he explain how he fell overboard? Was he pushed—?"

"He says it happened so quickly, he's not quite sure himself," said David. "He got caught in the brawl, the momentum of the struggle, and suddenly he was over the rail, falling. He can't swear he was pushed, so he's chalking it up to an accident."

"He's a lucky man," said Seth. "Bet he's grateful to be alive."

I started to say, *He's relieved the cocaine syndicate wasn't involved*, but I caught myself and said instead, "He is relieved . . . to be out of the hospital."

"An experience like that makes a man take stock of his life," said Seth. "I guess we've all had lessons to learn lately. . . ."

I studied Seth curiously. The usual brassy, egotistical Seth Mueller was surprisingly melancholy, introspective; his cockiness was gone. "What lessons have you learned, Seth?" I ventured.

He stroked his mustache. "That it's God's job, and not mine, to provide the funds I need for my projects. Sometimes I depend too much on Seth Mueller, not enough on the Lord. And maybe not enough on good friends, either."

"Friends? You mean, friends like Abigail Chadwick?"

He smiled slyly. "Could be, Michelle. Could be."

Since we were on the subject of Abigail, I tried a bold tactic. "Seth, don't you have some time before you go overseas again?"

"Two weeks, maybe three. I have some speaking engagements—fund-raisers, actually. Tedious obligations, most of them."

"Will you be in Illinois?" I asked.

"Illinois?" He frowned. "Why?"

"I thought you might have time to take a course at Hopewell."

David gave me his little *stop meddling* glare, but I ignored him.

"A refresher course?" quizzed Seth knowingly. "What subject?"

I stifled a guilty chuckle. "Abigail's English lit class."

Seth threw back his head and laughed uproariously. "Michelle, Michelle, Michelle, you don't give up, do you! I must say, your motives are delightfully transparent."

David shook his head bemusedly. "That's Michelle's subtle way of saying you should spend more time with Abigail Chadwick."

"I confess," I said. "I want to get you two together."

Seth's expression was once again troubled. "It's too late, Michelle. But if I ever chose a wife, it would be someone like Abigail. I said that when I left college years ago. I've thought it a thousand times on this cruise."

"Then why—?"

"Why *not*, you mean?" He stood abruptly and ambled over to the ship's rail, staring out at the mist-cloaked horizon.

I went over and touched his arm. "I'm sorry, Seth. I have a way of running ahead of the game."

"Forever playing the romantic," mused David from his chair.

Seth gazed down somberly at the vast, trackless sea. "Frankly, I've missed the love of a good woman. Children." His voice was hoarse. "When I left Hopewell, I didn't have room in my life for anyone else. Seth Mueller was going to take the world in his iron grip, call all the shots." He struck his palm with a doubled fist.

From the corner of my eye I spotted Abigail Chadwick walking up quietly behind us. She stopped a short distance away, her expression tender, her gaze fondly on Seth.

"Tennis was my whole life," Seth went on. "I lived for those Grand Slams, the admiration and applause. Oh, God was always there in the background, but I wanted fame and I got it. . . ."

"Like the man Robert Service described in 'The Spell of the Yukon'?" Abigail asked softly.

Seth whirled around, his eyes riveting on Abigail. I stepped back quietly as Seth said, "Yeah, like the gold-thirsty man in Alaska. 'I wanted the gold and I sought it . . . I hurled my youth into a grave . . .' "

Abigail smiled knowingly. "Yet it wasn't the gold you were wanting 'so much as just finding the gold . . .' "

Seth nodded. "For me, the gold was the gold cup . . . fame."

"You earned your fame, Seth."

"At great cost. I was so self-centered. I wouldn't let you go, Abigail. In those early years I held on to you through letters."

"I wanted you to write."

"And I knew if I didn't, someone else would come along and you'd fall in love with him. I didn't want that to happen."

"Why, Seth?" she asked breathlessly.

"Because I didn't want to lose you."

"It's all right, Seth. I knew that the friendship we had could never be anything more. I stopped asking God for more a long time ago. I just wanted you to be happy."

Seth's facial muscles twitched involuntarily. His mustache bobbed as he said, "Years ago—after I won the Grand Slam at Wimbledon, I went back to my quarters and tossed my gold trophy into a suitcase. I thought, *Is this all there is?* I was miserable."

"You never wrote me after that."

"I tried to, but I was afraid I'd ask you to marry me. I didn't want to ruin your life, take you from your teaching at Hopewell."

Abigail's voice was tremulous. "I knew that I could never have you, Seth. We were so different. You couldn't be cooped up in a little college town. But I do wish you hadn't stopped writing."

"I did write," he said. "Day after day. But I threw all my letters away. I knew some things just weren't meant to be."

She touched his hand. "I'm glad you came on this cruise, Seth."

He smiled. "I wasn't going to. Me—an honored alumni? I hadn't done anything. Not like Michelle here, a bestselling author. Or Thatcher, a famous surgeon. Or Seaton, that space-happy astronaut." He leaned hard against the railing as the fog-rippled mists swept over the rising ocean swells.

"We'd better go inside," she suggested. "Before we catch cold."

"No, wait," he urged. "You need to know something."

She pulled her coat tighter around her. He reached out and fastened the top button for her. "I'd already written 'no go' to this cruise until Stoddard wrote and told me you submitted my name."

"Why, Seth?" Her voice wafted on the wind. "You've done wonderful work in feeding the hungry for over ten years. You're a visionary—a man with a purpose; you've accomplished great things."

"But people are still starving."

"But you love them, Seth. Doesn't that count for something?"

"I've loved you too, Abigail. But that hasn't counted either."

She blinked back blissful tears. "It does count, Seth. I've waited 25 years for you to say those words."

"But they don't change anything."

"I know. You still have to say good-bye. You have your work."

He reached out ardently and crushed her against his chest. As they kissed, David slipped over quietly and took my hand. "Time for dinner, Michelle," he whispered. We stole away without a word, leaving Abigail Chadwick and Seth Mueller alone on the fog-drenched deck clinging to each other, mellowing their 25 lonely years with a few cherished moments of tenderness and love.

* * *

The Sea Breeze Dining Room was decked out for a party, with colorful streamers and bright balloons crisscrossing the ceiling. The air was electric with excitement and frivolity; even the waiters seemed less formal, more prone to joke and laugh.

My sister Pam and Silas Winters arrived and greeted us, their words brief and subdued as they sat down beside Jackie and young Stevie. I shouldn't have been surprised by Silas's pale, drawn appearance, but I was. He had always seemed so strappingly healthy, so invincible. Now he looked vulnerable, dispirited.

Seth and Abigail, hand in hand, took their seats at our table just as the waiters were serving the salads. "Sorry we're late," said Seth, pulling back Abigail's chair. When they had sat down, he looked impishly at me. "I decided against auditing a course at Hopewell, Michelle, but I'm doing the next best thing."

I glanced from him to Abigail. "What do you mean?"

"I have a few weeks before classes start in September," said Abigail. The flickering candlelight caught the glow on her face. "So I invited myself for a trip to Thailand."

"I told her she was crazy," said Seth, squeezing her hand.

"And I agreed," said Abigail. "But I also insisted on going. I've always had a fascination for the Orient."

"I tried to warn her what a refugee camp is like. It's not exactly a tour. She'll be expected to help. To pass out food and wash wounds and hold kids that are dying." He glanced at me. "Maybe she'll even take the writing assignment I offered you, Michelle."

I nodded, swallowing my disappointment. "I'm sure Abigail would do a wonderful job for you, Seth, if you can persuade her to stay."

"Oh, he hasn't quite managed that yet," Abigail laughed.

David spoke up. "Seth, Michelle and I have decided we'd like to help out, contribute something from my investments, her royalties."

"I—I don't know what to say. Thank you. I'm overwhelmed."

"Our donation's in the name of my buddy, Rob Thornton, the Vietnam POW," said David. "Along with Rob, we have a special interest in the refugee camps in Thailand. Rob is consumed with going back to find Liana, the Hmong woman who saved his life."

"Those camps change so rapidly," said Seth. "People die, get lost in the crowd, go on to other countries, new homelands."

"Do you think there's any chance of finding Liana?" I asked.

Seth shook his head. "It's virtually impossible."

Abigail's slender fingers curled around Seth's broad hand. "They're not asking for the impossible, Seth. Just that you try—"

"I can't make any promises," said Seth. He looked at David. "This buddy of yours, Rob Thornton—is he well, able-bodied? I could use some manpower on my trips. Perhaps he could go with Abigail and me. If the girl's there, he'd recognize her. . . ."

"Oh, David," I cried, "it would be a dream come true for Rob!"

Pam and Silas had sat in moody silence through the meal, picking at their food, hardly aware of the rest of us. Had they had words? Was Silas not feeling up to par? Perhaps the doctor had discharged him too soon. Or was Pam simply feeling depressed over their impending separation? After a moment, Pam looked over at Seth and asked, "Do you just need manpower? Or would a nurse be useful?"

Seth brightened. "We sure could use another nurse on the team!"

Silas Winters tossed his napkin on the table. "Excuse me," he said, pushing back his chair. "I don't think I want to hear this. In fact, I know I don't." He stood, leaned down, and blew a kiss across the top of Pam's head. "I've got a feeling that God is winning out again," he declared, his tone clipped, wounded.

With tear-brimmed eyes, Pam reached out her hand to Silas. Their fingers locked for a moment, then only their fingertips touched as they gazed sadly at each other. Finally, without another word, Silas turned and walked out. Pam's words were choked as she said huskily, "What about it, Seth Mueller? May I join your team?"

"Are you sure that's what you want?" asked Seth kindly.

"Yes, I'm sure." Pam's voice trembled. "God called me to the mission field when I was a kid. It just took me a while to say yes."

"We're not affiliated with a mission organization, Pam, although we work with several. I never felt qualified for that high calling."

"Sounds like a mission to me, as long as God's in it," said Pam.

"You do talk to those refugees about the Savior," said Abigail.

"Well, yes, of course, but—"

Pam tossed her head back decisively. "Well, it looks like I'm heading for Thailand!"

"Oh, David," I exclaimed. "Everybody's going to Thailand!"

"Not everybody," David said emphatically.

An impish smile flickered across Pam's face. "Don't worry, David. We don't need anybody on the team heavy with child."

For an instant no one spoke. David's eyes darted to mine, mine darted to Pam's. Pam clasped her mouth guiltily.

"Heavy with child?" David echoed incredulously. "You're—pregnant, Michelle?"

My glare sent daggers Pam's way. "How could you, Pam?"

Pam looked chagrined. "Oh, Michelle, I'm sorry. I thought—"

"Michelle, does Pam know what she's talking about?" David implored.

I gazed around the table, helplessly embarrassed. Every eye was on me. I nodded, my face warm. "I tried to tell you, David—"

"Then you weren't seasick? You're actually going to have a baby?" His voice rose dramatically. People from the surrounding tables were glancing our way, looking curious, amused. "How could you not tell me I'm going to be a father, Michelle?"

"I did tell you the other night, but you were asleep."

"Good night, Michelle, I would've awakened for news like that!"

"Then, so much was happening, with Silas overboard and all—"

David's expression sparked with pride and anticipation as the idea of a baby began to sink in. Then, in the loudest shout of joy I've ever heard from David, he leaped to his feet, pulled me up beside him and shouted to the entire dining room, "Hopewell, did you hear that? Michelle and I are going to have a baby!"

CHAPTER TWENTY-TWO

As we left the dining room with Jackie and Stevie, everyone gathered around us, congratulating David on his pending fatherhood. He was exuberant, beaming, already strutting like a proud papa. When we paused to say good-bye to the Seatons, Brett grabbed David's hand and said, "Having kids makes a big difference. You'll love it."

"I'm expecting a son," David told him confidently.

"Who knows?" Candy teased. "You might have twins."

David swallowed hard. "Uh, let's not get too carried away!"

We all laughed, then with a final farewell, the Seatons were off ahead of us, hand in hand. As we started up the stairwell, David swung little Stevie up on his shoulders and said, "Next time we meet, Tiger, I'll have a playmate for you."

Stevie latched his arms around David's neck. "Like my baby sister Becky?" he chirped. "She's no fun, Uncle David. She just sleeps and throws up. She can't even play with my trucks."

David stretched his chin against Stevie's stranglehold. "Well, my kid will be playing football with you before his first birthday."

I laughed and told Jackie confidentially, "And instead of blocks, he'll be playing with computers, if David has his way."

Jackie smiled knowingly. "Steve was the same way. He bought Stevie his own soapbox racer when he was two." As David and Stevie lumbered on ahead, Jackie touched my arm gently. "Do you think we'll see each other again, Michelle?" she asked wistfully. "Ever?"

We linked arms. "Sure, Jackie. Our paths just have to cross. Best friends are like that. Besides, we'll see you in the morning when we dock in Vancouver—maybe catch the same taxi to the airport."

When we reached Jackie's cabin, David took her key and opened the door. Stevie ducked his head as they entered. David tossed Stevie on the bed and tickled him. They roughhoused awhile, then David said, "Get a good night's sleep, Tiger. See you tomorrow."

Stevie bounced up from the bed and wrapped his arms around David's neck again. "Go home with me, Uncle David."

David's eyes misted. "Not this time, Tiger. Maybe someday."

I winced, wondering if David and I could ever keep his promise. We weren't even allowed to have an address for the Marshalls. David strode to the door, slipped his arm around my waist, and said, "Come on, Mommy. We've got some packing to do before we turn in."

"I'm not 'mommy' yet, darling," I said in my sugar-sweet voice. I turned to Jackie. "I'm going to miss you. You've always been so special. Good night—I'll see you in the morning."

Jackie hugged me impulsively. "Yes, Michelle, until tomorrow."

* * *

The *Mendenhall* docked in Vancouver at 7:00 A.M. the next morning—a cloudless, sun-washed Saturday. After breakfast, David and I met Pam on the sun deck as she stood at the rail looking down at the bustling, noisy dock. "How are you, Pam?" I asked.

"I just wanted to see Silas once more, but I only caught sight of him from a distance. He was already leaving the ship."

"How? We haven't even gone through immigration."

"Silas met the authorities when they boarded."

An alarm sounded inside me. "What about Jackie? Stevie?"

"They left with Silas. He still feels so responsible for their safety. He had them cleared the moment immigration boarded." She looked blindly toward the dock. "He left a note under my door to say good-bye and to tell me he was taking Jackie and Stevie to the airport for an earlier flight."

"Will you ever see Silas again?" I asked gently.

"Not likely," Pam sighed. "We're going in different directions. I was fooling myself to think we could have a life together."

David squeezed Pam's shoulder. "Surely those terrifying moments in the icy water made Silas think of dying . . . of eternity."

"He did say it made him do some serious thinking. I'll never stop praying for him, Michelle. Maybe someday—"

Before Pam could finish, Stephanie Ellis approached and touched my arm. She looked frazzled. Urgently, she said, "I had to see you before we left. The authorities are ready to take Cam off the ship."

I clasped her hand. "Are you going to be okay?"

"I think so." She drew me off to one side. "Michelle, pray that it will work out for us—that Cam won't have to go on trial—to prison. He can't stop crying since he found out about Rodney. It's tearing him apart. But he needed to cry—he hadn't since Rodney's death. He keeps saying, 'I loved my son. Didn't he know that?' "

"If there's ever anything David and I can do to help . . ."

"Well, there is one thing." She handed me a slip of paper with a name and address. "Would you write to Rodney's friend for me? The last time I saw Kent I wanted to slap him hard, hurt him. But he needs forgiveness too. I don't feel right about getting in touch with him myself. Cam would never understand. But I want Kent to know about Jesus."

"I'll be glad to write him," I said. I hugged Stephanie goodbye. "Maybe someday David and I can contact Kent personally for you."

"Thank you, Michelle. You really are a good friend!"

Stephanie turned away tearfully and was gone as quickly as she had appeared. When I turned back to Pam, she was alone. She smiled and said, "David left. He wants you to meet him on the promenade deck in five minutes. That handsome hunk has a surprise for you."

"That's what I love about David. He's full of surprises."

When I arrived on the promenade deck, David was already there, a briefcase in hand. "Really, David, our vacation's not even over, and you look like you're ready for business," I teased.

"I'm always ready for *monkey* business," he quipped, "but this briefcase is for *your* business."

"What are you talking about?"

"My gift of love to you, Michelle," he said gallantly, handing me the exquisite leather briefcase with a flourish. "Your name's etched in gold just as your love is etched upon my heart forever."

"David, I don't understand. What's this for?"

"For my favorite author. For your promotional tour. To show my faith in you and my support of your career."

"But when did you have a chance to buy it?"

"In Juneau while you were at the flower shop. They delivered it to the ship that evening before we sailed."

"But I—I thought you didn't want me to mix babies and books."

He patted my tummy. "It looks like that's exactly what we'll be doing."

"And you don't mind me mixing a writing career with motherhood?"

He took me in his arms and nuzzled my neck. "I know you can never be a stay-at-home wife and mother, Michelle. It's hard for me to admit, but you need to be in the mainstream of things, sometimes poking your nose where it doesn't belong, writing, traveling, maybe even with the baby strapped on your back. You're a free spirit, my darling. You've got to write, capture life the way you see it."

I searched his eyes. "Can you live with that, David?"

"I'll try, Michelle. I may need a little reminding from time to time, but we'll work it out. I'm committed to you and our marriage."

I touched my fingertips to his warm lips. "I love you, David. Need you. And I love our baby. I'll always be there for you both."

David and I sealed our promises with a lingering kiss, as the S.S. *Mendenhall* lay anchored in the safe harbor of Vancouver, far beyond the roiling, windswept sea.